Everything Will Be Fine

Twenty-One

February 14th

"Happy Birthday to my sweetest granddaughter!" My grandmother glides toward me in her smooth, gentle way. I still call her grandmother even though she raised me and was so much more than what you would consider a traditional grandmother. For all intents and purposes, she is my mother.

"I'm your only granddaughter," I reply with an obvious eye roll. She had one daughter who also only had one daughter.

"Doesn't change that you're the sweetest," she says as she pulls me in for a hug. I chuckle as she gives me a kiss on the cheek. I know her red lipstick will leave a stain on my face, but I ignore it and savor her embrace.

"Thanks for doing all this," I say as I pull away and move my eyes around the room. She secured the Chairman Suite at the Venetian in Las Vegas for a week. It's 9,000 square feet and more room than my friends and I could possibly need. She insisted, though, on going all out for my big twenty-first birthday. She, of course, is staying on the sixth floor in a standard room.

My grandmother started creating her own colors of nail polish back in the 70s. There wasn't much to choose from back then, all pinks and reds. She broke the mold and started mixing other colors, trying different consistencies and textures, and experimenting as much as she could. Fast forward more than 50 years and she owns the company with the longest lasting nail polish sold in stores. She is a millionaire many times over, but if you met her on a random

—

day in a random place, you would never know it. Grandma Mae is as humble as they come.

My four closest friends and I arrived on a private jet this morning. After a stretch limo brought us to The Venetian, my lovely grandmother met us in the lobby and escorted us up to the massive suite. We spent a day enjoying the in-suite luxuries. We got massages followed by a half hour in the steam room. After showering off the oil and sweat, we moved into the salon and received hair and makeup treatment from the in-house glam squad. We are now fully coiffed, dressed to the nines, and starting the night at the private bar inside our suite. With our own private bartender. Times are tough, eh?

"You ladies heading out soon?" she asks as she reaches for a piece of birthday cake.

"Soon enough. The night is young," I reply. I wink at my grandmother and move a portion of her white hair behind her left ear. I know that my friends are desperate to leave the gorgeous suite and hit the town, but I want to spend a few minutes more with the angel that spent a ton of time and money to give me such a wonderful birthday.

I'm the last of my friends to turn twenty-one so this night has been much anticipated. We can finally go to every bar, casino, male burlesque show - you name it, we can all attend. Not that my friends aren't grateful for this ridiculous suite and the Dom they are currently sipping, but they want to take this show on the road. While I don't blame them, I also don't care. We will stay with my grandmother as long as it takes for her to feel appreciated and content. Just looking in her direction causes a smile to cross my face and a calm to wash over me.

"You're the best grandma in the world. Has anyone ever told you that?" I ask her, getting a little misty in the eyes.

"You have, only about a million times." She sips from her champagne flute, yes my grandma knows how to party, elderly style. "Now go on, get out of here." She makes a shooing motion with her hands.

        "No, I'd rather be with you," I confess, holding her tight and taking a large gulp of champagne. I flick my hand in dismissal of her attempt to move me out of the suite.

        "Who said I wasn't coming?" The room freezes. I look at my grandmother who now has a smirk on her face. My friends are frozen in place, waiting to see what happens next. No one ever expected that my grandmother would want to come out with us, myself most of all. No bodies move, but all eyes move from one face to another before all eyes land on me.

        "You're going to come out with us?" I ask, not even trying to hide the surprise in my voice. "But... but we have tickets to Thunder From Down Under."

        "I know," she says as she drains the rest of her champagne. "So do I. If we don't leave soon, we'll miss the whole thing."

        While the idea of sitting next to my dear, old grandmother as nearly naked men are hopping from table to table and dancing around us does not excite me, the idea of spending more time with her does. My friends clearly don't feel the trepidation that I do and are energized by the idea of Grandma Mae joining us. They all start screaming and screeching so loudly, I cannot hear my own response to her. I think I tell her I love her, but it is impossible to be sure since hearing anything over their noise is out of the question.

        Before I know what's happening, everyone is chanting "Grand-ma MAE!" and taking turns drinking from their flutes in a circle around my sweet granny. Champagne is being poured from what seems like invisible hands as we drink from our crystal flutes. If I hadn't seen it with my own eyes, I would have never believed it to be possible. Grandma has the biggest smile on her face and she appears to be actually enjoying herself!

        Once I join the circle that has formed around Grandma Mae, we all hold our glasses up to the center and scream "Cheers!" After everyone's glasses are empty, we grab our coats and head out to The Strip countless floors below.

The same stretch limo that picked us up from the airport is waiting outside the entrance to the casino. I know it's the same stretch because it's a BMW and it's turquoise. The combination is non-existent in real life. I cannot imagine the amount of money my grandmother dropped on this party.

As we pull up to The Excalibur, we leave our plastic champagne flutes behind in the limo and head inside. My grandmother tsks at our general admission tickets and presents her six VIP passes to the front row table. The area includes cushioned velour chairs, a long, sturdy table, and bottles of wine and liquor waiting for us on ice around the table. There is even a thick, velvet rope that separates us from the rest of the viewers. It's obvious with these seats we are begging the men to dance on our table and in front of our faces. I shoot my grandma a look from across the table, letting her know she went too far. She only shrugs in response and silently takes her seat.

To say that I was highly uncomfortable sitting near my grandmother when a gorgeous, muscular man walked up to me and put a sash that read "Birthday Girl" over my head while giving me a lapdance, would be the understatement of the century. It was, however, the most fun I'd had in quite some time.

"See Valentina, it was a good time. Was it not?" Grandma Mae asks after the show. She pulls me close as we leave The Excalibur.

"I had a good time," I agree. Luckily alcohol was flowing, otherwise I would not have been able to function with my grandmother so near male thongs and thighs.

"Well, now it's time for you young ladies to paint the town red!" Grandma Mae looks at me with a sparkle in her eye. She's so cute, I cannot bear to tell her how outdated her phrase is. I am excited she is not going to ask to share any further wild experiences with me tonight and I am eager to get her into her hotel room, safe and sound.

"Let's get in the limo, GM, and we'll get you back to the hotel."

February 15th

Knock, knock, knock.

I hear a faint pounding. I have no sense of direction nor can I even make a guess of where it is coming from. I don't care enough to even open my eyes. I am fairly certain I am not in my bedroom, but I cannot remember where I am or how I got here.

Knock, knock, knock.

There it is again. I gather all of my strength and force my right eye to open just enough to see where the hell I am. There is no one in bed next to me. So far, so good. I open my left eye as I roll over and see beautiful mountains out of my floor-to-ceiling windows.

"Valentina?" I hear a soft voice call my name and I immediately recognize it belongs to Grandma Mae. Vegas! Awareness slams into my brain. I'm in Las Vegas! My friends are here! My grandmother is here! Yesterday was my birthday!

Flashes of the night before flood my head. Dancing at a secret club inside The Cosmopolitan. Singing karaoke somewhere in Old Vegas. Seeing the World's Largest Elvis Impersonator. Shots, so many shots.

"In here Grandma," I say with a froggy voice. I look down to make sure I'm clothed. Luckily, I see I was at least able to put a t-shirt on before passing out.

"Hi sweetheart," she says as she enters the room and walks directly toward my bed. "Your friends are all still sleeping. I was hoping I could take you to brunch. Just us."

"Sure, I'd like that." I squeeze her hand and move toward the edge of the bed. I feel way too good for the amount of alcohol I had and all the shenanigans we took part in.

"I'll wait for you in the living room," she says and she leaves me in private to get dressed. I stumble to the closet where I dropped my bag after our arrival. Since we are staying the rest of the week, I will need to unpack and hang up most of my clothing after brunch.

After throwing on a slightly wrinkled sundress, I brush my teeth, clean my face, and head out of the master suite. Grandma Mae and I move down to the lobby in silence. She waits until we are sitting at a table in Bouchon before she drops the hammer I have been anticipating since we arrived in Las Vegas.

"Darling, I hope you are having a wonderful birthday so far," Grandma Mae opens.

"I am, GM, thanks so much for all of this! You have really gone above and beyond." My sincerity is real, I do appreciate her and everything she has done for me.

"I'm so glad to hear that, sweetheart. I want you to enjoy this week as much as possible."

"I will, Grandma," I say. I know there is more coming.

Luckily we are interrupted by the server taking our orders and her flow has been interrupted. She doesn't say anything for a few beats after he has left the table.

"Thank you, again. The suite is unbelievable," I offer. I am fully hoping this offer of gratitude will end this portion of our conversation.

"You're very welcome, my dear." She pauses and dabs her mouth with her cloth napkin even though she hasn't eaten anything yet. "When you return to New York next week, I expect that you will give MaeDay your full attention and dedication."

There it is. She's leaving Vegas today to head back to work and she couldn't return home without a promise of my future with her company. I knew it was coming, I fully expected this, but I'm still a little sad. Is that what this entire week was? A bribe to enter the full-time workforce with MaeDay? That leaves a bad taste in my mouth and I have a hard time believing my beloved grandmother would do something so conniving. She obviously has good business sense, but there's no way she would do this to her only grandchild. I know what I am feeling is written all over my face.

"No, dear, this is not a bribe. You enjoy your birthday in Sin City with your closest friends. That is happening no matter what you decide for the future. I just want to make my wishes known, so there will be no confusion with us."

I sit back in my seat. This should be good. "Wishes?" I prompt her.

"Yes, my wishes," she replies more sternly than before. "My first wish is to dote on you for graduating early. That is a huge accomplishment and you should be celebrated." Ok, she took me by surprise with that one. "It's amazing that you took so many extra college credits in high school and that afforded you the opportunity to graduate with your Bachelor's degree a year ahead of schedule. You should be very proud of yourself. Now, if you choose, you can go on to get your MBA at a record pace. I'm very impressed with your intelligence and capabilities."

I'm shocked. I thought this brunch was all about forcing me to take the company over from her and run it until I pass it on to my daughter or granddaughter. This has taken a turn that I wasn't expecting. I thought it was just assumed I would do everything I could to get as many letters after my name as possible so I could keep the company thriving. Little did I know that people were actually cheering me on.

"I appreciate that, GM. Thank you for noticing all my hard work," I tell her with emotion in my voice. I don't know what else to say.

She reaches over and pats my hand that is resting on the table. She leans back in her seat again and folds her arms over her chest, almost in a defensive position. Oh boy, here comes the heavy stuff.

"My next wish is for you to start working directly with me on a full-time basis." She lets this settle. "Then I will groom you and teach you everything you need to know in order for me to retire and you to run the company."

"I was expecting that one," I say with a half smile. I take a sip of my water, glad that the conversation is over and it wasn't anything worse than I suspected. I take a deep breath and let my shoulders relax. I expect we'll discuss this 'grooming' next. I have some ideas of my own about how this should happen.

—

"I have one more wish." She is still sitting in her defensive position across the table. My eyes fly to hers and again in surprise. What more could there be? "My final wish for you, my darling child, is to find a partner in life."

"Grandmother, you know how I feel about that. I've never had a boyfriend and I'm not sure I want a man holding me back. I enjoy my freedom." I'm pouting now and I know it. I don't care though because I'm starving and working through a hangover, while my grandmother tells me she wants me to get married. I'm too young for this shit. "Not to mention, shouldn't I start working at the bottom of the company so I can understand every part of it? Sales, production, corporate relations, customer service, each division is just as important as the next."

My grandmother stares at me from across the table. She lets a small smile spread across her face. "I don't expect you to get married now, Valentina. I know where your focus lies currently and I'm glad it's on your education and business future. I'm going to give you until you turn 35 to get married. I do not care if you have a husband or a wife, or some other type of lifelong partner that I don't even know about yet. But I want you to find someone to share your life with. I want that for you. You will not be fulfilled otherwise. You will live a smaller, sadder life if you don't and everyone in the company will suffer. We have thousands of employees depending on you and we cannot allow a lonely, mean version of my wonderful granddaughter to be their ruler. So, if you are married by the time you are 35, I will retire fully and leave the entire company to you."

The server has impeccable timing because he shows up then to bring our plates. It requires us to be quiet for a moment and allows me just a second to digest what she has said. Her desire for me to have a partner is ridiculous and antiquated but I appreciate her love for me and the company. I also somewhat understand her reasoning, however, I absolutely refuse to start *looking* for a partner and I most definitely will not marry someone just to get the company. I'm certain of both these ideas. But, am I open to marrying the right person if he comes along? I'd like to think so.

Once the server leaves, my grandmother leans forward like she's going to tell me a secret. I lean forward on instinct.

"As for starting at the ground level of the company, I couldn't agree more. That's exactly how I know you're the right woman for the job." She picks up her fork and her eyes flick to me. "Let's eat."

I feel lost after the brunch with Grandma and her departure. My mind is going in a million different directions as I walk back to the suite. All of my friends are awake when I return and are sitting in the lounge area, drinking coffee.

"Hey!" Robin greets me with wide-eyed enthusiasm. Robin is my oldest and closest friend. She has this amazing ability to be brutally honest and curious at the same time. It doesn't matter what she says to you, or what crazy question she asks you - you will still love her. It's impossible not to. "Where have you been?"

"I had brunch with GM before she left," I say, still a little shaken. I sit on the couch in between Robin and Amy, another friend I've had since elementary school. I lean my head back against the back of the couch and close my eyes. I'd been preparing to take over the company since I started junior high, but is it truly what I want to do with my life? Or just what I've been groomed to do? Do I want to marry someone? Do I want a partner? Someone who will keep me on a leash? Someone who will take away all the freedom I currently thrive on?

"Helllloooo?" I hear Robin say. I feel her shaking my leg before I open my eyes. "Did you hear Nisha?"

"Hm? I'm sorry, what did you say?" I look across the room to my sweet friend. "I'm sorry, Nisha."

"It's fine," she says and waves her hand in a dismissive gesture. "I just wanted to know what you want to do today?"

That's a great question. What do I want to do? I know what I do *not* want to do, and that is to dwell on the future for the next five days. I want to have fun and enjoy my youth while I still have it. I want to celebrate this milestone birthday with my closest friends, in this wild city, having the time of my life. If I do ever get married, I want this week to live forever in my memory as a time of fun and freedom that I had when I was young and fun!

"Hike. Shop. Casino." I tick the answers off on my fingers. I'm so grateful to see a room full of smiles at my response.

I know in my bones that I do want to take over MaeDay. I want to follow in my grandmother's footsteps and make her proud. I want her legacy to live on. I want her legacy to become *my* legacy. Not only can I do this, but I want to. I love everything my grandmother has created. I love that we can experiment with color and formula, but there is also a branding side that I love. It's fun to think of new ways to make the nail polish exciting and different. I love the people we work with in each department and how different they are. I love it all. I want it all.

My plans for the next year are… ambitious. But, *I* am ambitious and I know I can handle it all. I am ready to focus on finishing up my undergraduate education and graduating with the best GPA possible.

First, I will graduate. This is a no-brainer. All I have to do is finish my coursework and continue my current path. I can do this with my eyes closed. Finishing school feels more natural to me than breathing. I am prepared. I am ready. I will accomplish this goal.

Second, I will start working for MaeDay. This is where things get tricky. I won't do it in the way my grandmother sees as the path to success, which is, needless to say, following her around all day. I cannot imagine a worse way to learn about the company and be a successful leader. My grandmother did not start at the top and neither will I. I want to learn every aspect of the company. I want to see how every employee functions in their position. I want to see the importance of every role. My grandmother has experienced all of this, because at one point she was every position. She didn't have investors or partners. She grew this company, on her own, from the bottom to the top. She learned and adapted along the way. As the likes of Instagram and TikTok emerged, she created a social media team. She now has influencers on the payroll and celebrities wearing her polish and telling people about it. It's remarkable what she's done and I know I cannot absorb it all simply by following her around.

I've lived with my grandmother since I was seven years old, so I have some general company knowledge and knowhow. I do not, however, know the ins and outs of the industry. I do not know how to manage employees or land corporate accounts. I need a lot of training that my dear old granny cannot provide. I need to see it all in real time, with real people. That is what I intend to do. I want to learn firsthand how to do these tasks and then use that information to make an even bigger and better MaeDay.

My last goal will be by far the easiest. It is to not even look at a man. I know my grandmother wants me to find my soulmate, but that shit just does not happen when you are twenty-one. If and when I find my soulmate, it will be much later in life. I will drop my blinders to men as I become settled in my career and successful. I will not allow a love interest to steer me in the wrong direction. I want to continue thriving without a man demanding my time or attention. Once I have learned more about my future career, I can begin to think about my future companion. That time is not now.

Twenty-Two

February 13th

As it turns out, things did not go as planned for my twenty-first year. Sure, I graduated as I expected I would, but it was not as easy as anticipated. I had to retake one of my econ finals due to a cheating allegation. Apparently, the person who sat next to me during the test said I reached in my bag and looked up an answer in the textbook. This was absurd. I did no such thing. I did reach into the front pocket of my bag for a tissue when I had a huge sneeze that rocketed entirely too much green mucus out of my nose and onto my sleeve. Excuse me for finding out three days too late that I had Flu A.

As annoying and ridiculous as the accusation was, I retook the test in front of the professor and she watched my every move for those ninety minutes. She saw with her own eyes that I did not cheat and that I knew the material. I smiled as I handed in the exam. She probably thought I was irritating or overconfident. I didn't care. I knew the information and I was relieved to have her watch me take the test. Nothing further could be said and I graduated, as I had planned.

Starting at the bottom was also more difficult than imagined. Turns out, if you are semi-famous within the industry and your grandmother owns the company, no one tells you what they actually do on a day-to-day basis. They all inflate their job responsibilities. They want you to think they are more powerful and important than they really are. They tell you tall tales and half-truths.

I had almost given up the notion of growing with the company on the same trajectory as you grow and navigate life. I thought I could begin as an infant and grow into a wise and knowledgeable woman. Then I met the marketing team. It was the last department I was scheduled to visit before my twenty-second birthday. They were different and wild. They didn't work like any other division I had seen up to that point. They were fun and unconventional, creative and collaborative. After wading through sales, research and development, and human resources, I had finally jumped in head first with a department I could jive with.

I loved the energy and the vibes in the marketing department. I often found the department employees throwing balls against a wall while lying under their desks with their feet propped on the windowsill. It was not uncommon to find the department having a "meeting" in the conference room with not a single person sitting in a chair. Lying on the conference table, sitting on the floor, bringing your own bean bag chair were all considered acceptable forms of meeting attendance. People laughed constantly and yelled over one another. I felt myself looking around wide-eyed on the eleventh floor on a daily basis. Every other floor was tragically filled with silence while marketing felt crowded with sound and life.

No one *ever* had a bad idea. Even if it seemed like the worst idea since electrified water, no one would dismiss it. Every spoken word was seen as a jumping off point, and the team would always build a bigger, better idea from it. Some of these ideas would continue to evolve into full blown campaigns and marketing strategies while others would flop and eventually die off. Regardless, every thought was viewed as beneficial and valued. I saw this as a safe space to express the little bit of creativity I possessed. It was a reprieve from the pressure to excel that I constantly felt. I could say anything, literally anything at all, and the team would come together to "snowball" that idea into something spectacular. The support and fun I experienced while working with the marketing team was the breath of fresh air I needed.

For the first time since Las Vegas, I was excited to celebrate my birthday.

"Happy Birthday, Valentina!" Robin yells, even though she has her arm wrapped around my shoulders. I lean away and lift my shoulder in a ridiculous attempt to save my eardrum.

"Yes! Cheers to our fearless leader!" Stuart says from the back of the room as he raises his glass in my direction. Stuart is the only person from Marketing that I despise. He is a shrill, unhappy man and I cannot stand him. The way he insists on referring to me as the leader, princess, and even sometimes *heir* - makes my animosity toward him multiply. I want him to see me as a co-worker, someone he can trust and have a genuine conversation with. There will be a time for me to be his boss, but that time is not now. I honestly wish he would shut the hell up most of the time. My birthday happy hour is one of those times.

To be completely accurate, my twenty-second birthday is not until tomorrow. My grandmother has another big party planned, however, tonight I am out with nearly everyone from the marketing department and my four closest friends: Robin, Amy, Nisha, and Ansley. Mae demands every employee take their birthday off, paid of course, so tomorrow I will not have to move from my bed before noon. This knowledge is fueling my desire to have an amazing night with some new, and old, friends. That is, if Stuart doesn't ruin it all.

Just as Robin lets go of me, *Sweet Caroline* comes over the speaker and she grabs someone from the bar to dance with her. I see Amy approach me with a smile. She has her arm wrapped around her new girlfriend, Mackie. Amy has never seemed to fall hard for anyone, always keeping herself at arm's length from anyone she could possibly develop feelings for. Mackie brings out an entirely different side of Amy. Mackie is quiet and reserved, but completely confident and sure of herself. She has a way of commanding Amy, our friends, even the entire room without a single word. She is powerful in a silent, content manner. We all adore her and hope that one day Amy will allow herself to fall in love with Mackie. Mackie is good for her. Mackie is good for everyone.

"Valentina, I am so happy to celebrate with you today!" Amy lets go of Mackie to pull me in for a real, legitimate hug. I allow myself to sink into her embrace and enjoy the comfort only a close friend can provide.

"Thanks, girl," I reply from over her shoulder, eyes closed and still locked in the hug. I pull back and leave my hands on her shoulders so I can look her in the eyes. "You and Mackie are coming to GM's party tomorrow, right?" The unsettled look Amy gives me makes my stomach flip. "I know it's Valentine's Day, so I understand if you can't. I don't want to tear you away from anything…"

I know my birthday happening to land on the most romantic day of the year is problematic. I fully expect that my friends and family will eventually meet partners and get married and fall in love. On Valentine's Day, they will spend the evening with their lover and certainly not with their oldest friend. I know this. I accept this, for my future. I just thought that we were still young enough to party together as a group of close, loving friends for a few more years. I guess I just hadn't realized any of the five of us had reached the point of celebrating the holiday separately, as part of a couple. I feel surprisingly sad.

"Don't make that face, Lenni," Amy chokes out as she wipes at my nonexistent, but about to fall, tears. "Of course we're coming."

"But?..." I can feel the 'but' in my bones.

"But… we're going to dinner first. So, we'll be a little late." Amy immediately brings her thumbnail to her mouth and begins chewing, her telltale nervous twitch.

I pull her thumb from her mouth with care. I feel my shoulders fall and my body deflate a little. She is still going to come, but just be late. I lean in and kiss her on the cheek. I give her a really good smile to telepathically let her know there is nothing to worry about. Everything will be fine.

"Everything will be fine," Amy says, mirroring my thoughts exactly.

Isn't it funny how family and friends have that ability? That weird, unnamed ability to read your exact thoughts. Sometimes it seems impossible that I know what my grandmother is going to say during a speech or meeting, but I'm never wrong. My friends and I joke about our FRESP (friend extrasensory perception) and here it is, on full display.

As I smile at Amy, I catch sight of my second least favorite person in marketing, Colt Arden. I'm nearly positive his real name isn't 'Colt' but I don't currently have any proof of that theory. If I had known him before my stint in HR, I might have been able to dig a little deeper. As for now, I have to go with the notion that no one in their right mind would name their son Horse, or I guess more accurately, Colt.

"Valentina," he opens. He is one of the few people, in any department, to consistently only call me by my first name or my nickname, Lenni. Everyone else calls me Miss Cooper most of the time, sometimes timidly sneaking in my first name. Not Colt. From the beginning he has called me 'Valentina' and his unwillingness to be intimidated by the CEO and Founder's granddaughter is what has him ranked above Stuart.

"Hello, Mr. Arden," I reply. It seems to unsteady Colt when I call him by his last name, so I do it as often as possible.

He clears his throat with a soft rumble. His hands are in his pockets and he rocks back on his heels, just a bit. "Are you enjoying the night?"

I smile and take a sip of my favorite cocktail, a Paloma, before responding. "Very much so, thank you."

I have no idea why we are being so formal. Colt is older than I am, but not by much. We're not at the office. We've spent every day together for the past two months. There is not one reason for us to be speaking to each other in such a way. It's almost as if our conversation is a final exam for finishing school.

"I'm glad to hear it," he says and takes a step closer to me. I'm instantly uncomfortable and shift my weight. Did I mention that Colt is gorgeous? Not the aftermarket, 'spent an hour getting ready' type of handsome. He is just naturally beautiful. He has dark wavy hair, but it has some natural highlights that are sprinkled within his hair. There is no rhyme or reason to the lighter, blonde strands that shine through at the most inopportune times. Like right now. I can see one glimmering just over his right eye and I'll be damned if it doesn't have my full attention. Which is an impressive feat. His face is a chiseled fucking masterpiece. He has perfect light blue eyes and a nose that is large enough to look great, but not so large it looks out of place. His lips are perfectly proportionate and always the best color of pink. If I'm being entirely honest, I spend way too many hours of my day wondering what those lips taste like. But all of this means nothing, because I haven't even gotten to his jawline. His jaw is the best part of his face. It is definitive and strong. I can read his every emotion by looking at the corner of his jaw. Is it ticking from annoyance? Is it soft while he's deep in thought? Is it tight from his lips pulling back from his decadent white teeth into a killer smile?

Alright, let's refocus. He is unbelievably good-looking but that is something I will never, ever admit to anyone out loud. Those thoughts exist only in my head. He is speaking to me right now and I need to stop staring at his jawline and look him in the eyes. Where are those again? Oh right, there they are. Blue as the sky.

"I hope you're having a good time," I say to him as I take a step back. He takes another step toward me. I retreat again, only this time he gets the hint and does not move any closer.

"I am," he agrees. He folds his arms over his chest, staring at me. His jacket from work is long gone and his shirt sleeves are rolled up. Remember how I said his jaw is the best part of his face? Well, his forearms are the best part of his body. Not that I've seen a lot of his body. Of the little bit I have been privy to, his forearms are my favorite. They are fucking delightful.

"Good," I respond. I don't know what else to say to him and I'm having a hard time tearing my eyes away from his forearms. I congratulate myself for not staring at his lips, but I need to move my eyes elsewhere.

"So, are you done in the marketing department?"

"Done?" This seems like an odd question to me. I will never be 'done' in any department. I will own and run the company and will always be part of every aspect of the company.

"Yeah, are you moving on to another division next week?" He uncrosses his arms from his chest and moves them to his hips. I hate him for this motion because it forces me to notice how trim his hips actually are. I know I said he is naturally beautiful, but his body is unnatural. Again, I've not seen much of it, but even through clothes I can tell he is up to his elbows in gym memberships. His shoulders are broad, his waist is lean, his legs are toned. It's all just absurd.

"Yes… yes, I guess you could say that." I pause and shake my glass a little bit. "You'll never be rid of me though." I instantly hate how that sounded. It seemed like I was coming on to him and I was not, at all. I was letting him know that even if I'm not physically on the eleventh floor, I am still a part of the company. A *huge* part of the company at that.

His eyebrows lift in surprise and a bit of panic flits across his face. "No! I wasn't saying that. I was just wondering if you were going to move floors next week or if we would still be seeing you on a regular basis."

His lips press together as if he is trying to stop himself from talking. His left hand moves down his face and stops to do an extra scratch on his jaw. Once his hand drops, he looks around as if he's lost something.

"You alright?" I ask before taking a dainty sip of my drink, looking up at him through my lashes. I'm enjoying his discomfort entirely too much.

"Yes." Pause. "I'm fine." Pause. "I'm just going to go find the table I left my drink on." And with no further ceremony or notice of departure, he walks away. I watch him go, marveling at the outline of him.

February 14th

I wake up remembering why Colt annoys me so much. He does not say a lot, but what he does say is perfect. Remember all those good ideas the marketing team has? Well, whenever Colt has an idea, everyone stops. The basketballs flying through the air, the rubix cubes being twisted, the pens scratching aimlessly across the paper - all stop. Everything ceases to move. Not only the people in the room, but all the inanimate objects also freeze. Everyone and everything waits with bated breath to hear what Colt is going to say. It will undoubtedly be genius. It's almost as if everyone thinks if they are the most silent, they can hear his idea first and share some sort of ownership of it.

It's equally annoying that he doesn't do any of the usual 'creative tricks.' He doesn't throw any balls or sit on the table. He stands. Or he walks. His hands are usually in his pockets and he rarely acts in any sort of unexpected way. He is a tall, solid stallion that always stands strong and occasionally makes noise by communicating a brilliant idea. Infuriating.

I roll over in bed, set on forgetting about Colt. Even though this morning is starting much later than my usual mornings, I am determined to do my morning workout. I am equally resolved to remove Colt from my mind entirely. I will not let him have a monopoly on my thoughts any longer.

Moving on, I plan my exercise for the day. I did weights and strength yesterday, so I decide that if I can just get a good jog in today, I am allowed to call it quits once I'm done. It's the perfect day for a jog, too. It's not brutally cold today like it usually is in February. There's no snow on the ground and I won't get frostbite while I run. I put on a sweatshirt and running shorts. I absolutely hate running in pants. After saying good morning to my favorite doorman, Gene, I step out onto the chilly streets of New York City. I stop just a few moments to stretch my legs before taking off in a light jog.

As I move among the people on the busy streets, I let my mind wander to the upcoming birthday festivities. As is the custom, I will have a meal alone with my grandmother before moving on to more… energetic portions of the evening.

This particular party is going to be at my grandmother's house in the Hamptons. I know, we're so very cliché. Her Hamptons house, however, is unbelievable. Not only does it have a private beach (that we won't be able to use in the cold), it also has a pool (we won't be able to use this either), a huge deck that wraps around the entire house (there will be heaters outside so we can use this), a wine cellar (we will absolutely use this), a bar that looks like an actual bar in the basement (we'll use this too), six bedrooms (we will use most of these), and a special room that is set up just to drink your morning coffee in (definitely using this). Is there anything better than your first cup of coffee in the morning? I agree, there is not.

Grandma Mae and all her friends, some of our family friends, and my friends will attend the party. As the night continues and the 'kids', as my grandmother calls us, continue when she wants to sleep, my grandmother will head back to her best friend's house.

Mae's best friend is Annie Pathie. Annie has known my grandmother since childhood and is the only person, other than me, in the world that Mae trusts. They are both widowed, both lost a child, and both know depths of despair greater than most people can fathom. Their bond is unbreakable and they have never gone longer than a couple of hours without speaking to one another. Even if one is mad at the other, she will call her friend just to gripe and yell about whatever the other one did to piss her off. Then they hash it out and everyone moves on.

There was one dark day many, many years ago when they did not talk for an entire twenty-four hours. No one talks about that day. We all act as if it never happened. If you ask Mae about it, she will tell you it was a leap year so that day doesn't really count anyway.

I'm grateful my grandma has such an amazing friend to rely on, but I also love Annie and I am excited to see her tonight. I let my mind flutter through some fond memories of Annie while I run my second mile of the day.

To keep my mind occupied for the third mile, I think about my guest list. My favorite four ladies will be there, some later than others, but that's alright. I also invited an old neighbor, Milo. He used to live down the street from Mae's Hamptons house and I would see him occasionally at events or getting takeout from our favorite cheap Mexican restaurant in Sag Harbor.

Milo was always friendly but distant. At a young age, when boys and girls still played together and long before romance was a thought in anyone's mind, I would try to get Milo to be my friend. I would always invite him to play with me and Robin in the ocean or at the pool. He was notorious for his rejections. For some reason, it just made us that much more interested in finding an activity that he wouldn't turn down. We began asking him to accompany us everywhere. Bowling, dinner, taking walks, and getting ice cream were all rebuffed. As time progressed, Robin and I started to feel petty and bitter about his refusal to be anywhere near us. We did what any normal prepubescent girl would do when feeling scorned, we ignored him. We thought this master plan was foolproof and would bring him running up to us, begging, *pleading* to be part of our friend circle. When this genius plan didn't work, the avoidance simply turned into indifference.

Milo's mother hated the craziness of the city so his family lived in The Hamptons full time. Robin and I went to school back in the city, so we mainly saw Milo during the summer months. One summer, a couple summers after our own bodies had started changing, Milo walked up to us on the beach and we didn't recognize him. He had to convince us that he was, in fact, the Milo that lived down the street for the past ten years. Robin and I were floored. How had the gangly, awkward creature from our youth grown into this Adonis? He had easily grown six inches in height since the previous summer and had put on more muscle than I would have ever imagined to be possible. His voice was unrecognizably deep and he had a five o'clock shadow. His blond hair was long and wild from the salt water. His skin was already sunkissed even though summer had just begun. That was the first summer Robin and I swooned over Milo.

From that point on, if he ran into us in Sag Harbor or on the beach, he would stay and chat. He would be friendly and joke with us, always bordering on the edge of flirting without ever taking the leap. We stopped inviting him everywhere, but would watch him from afar. Each summer he became increasingly more confident and his motions were smoother and more self-assured. We'd occasionally see him with girls or driving around town in his Jeep, but it has easily been three years since I've set eyes on him.

I texted him about the party, mostly because it seemed rude not to. He wouldn't be able to miss the noise and lights coming from my grandmother's giant house, especially in February when most Hamptons summer homes are closed up and empty for the winter. That is, if he still lives with his parents down the road. There is a small part of me that wonders what he looks like now and what he is doing. Is he in college? Does he have a job? Does he still live year round in Sag Harbor? He'd only replied to my text with a thumbs up emoji, so I am unsure if he will be attending or not. I hope so, if only to learn about what he is up to these days.

My thoughts of my friends and Milo keep my mind busy as I round the street corner to head back to my building. I pick up my pace so I can sprint the last block before reaching home and I feel the adrenaline push me forward. I'm dodging people walking on the sidewalk but I'm feeling great. I cannot wait to check my watch for my time. This could possibly be the best pace I've ever kept during a run. Excitement rushes through me as I see the gold door of my building. I move my legs even faster and pump my arms as quickly as they will go. I dip around a mom with a stroller, seeing the home stretch in front of her.

Instead, it's not the home stretch, it's a brick wall. Or at least it feels like a brick wall. All my momentum goes into that wall and it doesn't move. But I do. I go flying backward, arms waving, feet in the air. I am helpless to stop the fall. I land on my butt. Hard. Thankfully, my head hits the mom's diaper bag on the way down instead of the ground and I am able to keep my skull from colliding with the concrete. My butt and legs are not so lucky. I can already feel the road rash and scratches up the back of my lower body. My hands are bleeding from the scrapes and the effort of keeping myself upright.

"Holy shit, Valentina!" I look up when I hear my name. Fuck me. It's Colt. Not a brick wall at all, but Colt. Where did he come from? "Are you alright?"

Colt bends down, still holding his coffee. What the hell? How did he not also fall from the collision? Or at least drop his coffee? I was running full speed when I ran into him. I am now doubly angry; first, that he ruined my personal record and second, that he wasn't affected at all by the impact.

"I'm fine," I grumble. I look at my hands briefly to confirm they are in fact bleeding. Indeed they are. I put them back on the ground behind my butt so I can push myself to stand up.

"Fuck, you're bleeding," Colt says as his eyes roam all over me. "Don't stand up! Did you hit your head? Do you have a concussion?"

"No," I reply, trying for a second time to stand and get into my building. He is leaning over me and I won't be able to stand while he is in this position. He finally sets his coffee cup on the ground. "Please move and let me stand."

"I don't think that's a good idea," he says, shaking his head. I look at his jaw and I can see that he's concerned. His eyes are drawn in and it looks like he is clenching his teeth together.

"Colt, I'm fine. If you'd let me stand, I could show you." I lean back on my left hand, fuck that burns. I shoo him away with my right. He moves back only a few inches, barely giving me enough room to stand. Leaving his coffee on the ground, he puts his hands under my arms and helps lift me to a standing position. Honestly, he does more than help. He

---

basically lifts me to a standing position. Without wanting to, I am immediately self-conscious. I am sweating profusely from my run and I can only imagine how bad I smell. He should probably go wash his hands.

He doesn't take his hands off of me, afraid I will fall over. I move to wipe off my behind and legs while he watches me with such intensity, I can actually feel each spot his eyes touch.

"Let me help you get cleaned up. Do you live around here?"

"Yes, I do, but I can handle it." I look up at him, his expression still concerned. "What are you doing over here anyway?" I ask.

His eyes flick from the street to the building behind me. He's clearly confused by the question. "Oh, I, uh, had a doctor's appointment down the street."

Gene comes rushing up to us at this point. "Miss Cooper! I saw you fall, are you alright?"

"Hi Gene, yes, I'm fine. Thank you," I say politely with a smile.

Gene takes it upon himself to put his arms around the right side of my body without touching me, as if he is going to block any further danger from coming my way. On the right side of me, anyway. Colt is less cautious and puts his hand on my back and begins guiding me in the direction that Gene came from. He figures out which building is mine, thanks to sweet Gene, and leads me into the lobby.

"Thanks for accompanying me back to my building," I say to Colt with a nod. I turn away from him and toward the elevator. I would normally take the stairs but my ass is on fire from the fall. After pressing the call button for the elevator, I know without looking that Colt is behind me. "Go back to work, Colt."

"I'm going to help you," he declares.

"Miss Cooper," Gene says from behind both of us. We turn to look at him. His eyes travel between us. "Do you want me to escort him outside?"

I feel horrible for Gene at this moment. He is a small, older, gray-haired man with arthritic fingers and a slight frame. Colt towers over him and is probably double the size of Gene. The thought of Gene escorting Colt outside is comical. I would never want Gene to put himself in that position for me. My resolve softens.

"No thanks, Gene. It's fine," I say with another smile. As soon as Gene walks back to his post, I glare at Colt. He is looking ahead at the elevator doors, a smile tugging on the corners of his mouth. I send him telepathic bolts of annoyance. He doesn't seem to receive the message.

The elevator dings, announcing its arrival, and Colt nods his head toward the elevator, telling me to enter first. I roll my eyes and walk in before him and press the button for my floor. I cross my arms over my chest to show him my irritation but it hurts my scratched hands to fold them that way. Wincing, I uncross them and put them at my sides, watching the doors close.

Colt watches my every move. When I wince, he moves his leg like he is going to step toward me. As if he can help my already scratched hands somehow. He stops moving when my eyes fly to his face with a cutting glower. He stops in his tracks and puts his hands in his pockets.

"I'm not sure why you're so mad at me," he says while staring ahead at the elevator doors. They ding and open, and again Colt waits for me to leave before following behind me.

"Are you serious?" I reach to the secret pocket in my running shorts to get my key. It hurts my hands like hell to maneuver my shorts and unzip the pocket, but I refuse to let my face show any pain. I don't want Colt to move toward me again. When I look at him, he is watching me. He is specifically watching the outside of my shorts ride up my leg while I am yanking on the material trying to get to the pocket. I stop moving and he realizes I am watching him watching me. He clears his throat and looks to my door.

I open it after freeing my key and leave it open since he is clearly going to follow me everywhere I go today. I hear him shut it with a quiet click.

"This is your apartment?" He looks around in astonishment. His eyes are wide and his mouth is open a little. His eyes move from the kitchen to the living room before stopping on the closed door that leads to my bedroom.

"Yes, this is my apartment." I double check there isn't anything embarrassing lying around. I send a silent thanks into the universe for the clean apartment and look back to Colt. "Why do you say it like that?"

He is still looking around. He finally cuts his eyes to mine and pauses for a moment. "I don't know. I guess I was expecting something else."

"Something else?" I question him.

"Yeah, something…bigger, maybe? Flashier?"

"Ohh, I see now." He's thinking he was going to walk into a huge, multi-bedroom apartment fit for a queen. Something fit for Grandma Mae. He had no idea he was going to walk into a 600 square foot minimalist space. "You thought you were going to find me in some sort of palace that was given to me by my rich grandmother. Something I did not earn or pay for myself."

"Well, you've only been working at the company for a few months. I guess I just assumed your grandmother would buy you whatever you wanted."

I walk to the kitchen and get the first aid kit out of the pantry. I begin wetting paper towels and blotting them with soap to wash out the scratches on my legs and hands. He follows me, of course.

"Well, you thought wrong. I bought this apartment when I turned eighteen, without my grandmother's money," I say as I reach behind myself, trying to clean the backs of my thighs. I'm struggling to see what I'm doing and if I'm reaching all the bleeding spots. Colt squats down behind me and takes the towel out of my hand. He begins gently wiping my legs with the soapy towel.

"How did you do that so young and without her money?" he asks as he continues wiping my legs. I can feel his breath on my skin and I am suddenly hyper aware that his face is mere inches from my butt. I turn my head and look down the sink to focus on something else.

"With the money from my parents' life insurance policies."

That catches him off guard. He stops cleaning my legs and I can no longer feel his breath, so I'm guessing he's not breathing either. I look down to make sure he's still conscious.

"I'm so sorry, I didn't know." He wipes the lower portion of my legs, the half I could easily reach. I let him. "No one knows anything about your parents," he whispers.

"Yeah, well, they died when I was little. Now you know." I'm fussy. I hate talking about my parents and I'm still pissed about the rundown that happened on the sidewalk. I take the paper towel out of his hand and toss it in the trash can. I turn on the water to wash my hands in the sink.

"So why is it you're so angry with me, again?" Now he's beside me. I want to tell him to back up, but I am so happy he changed the subject, I decide to let his nearness slide.

"I would think it should be obvious, but do you not see my injuries? I went flying through the air!" I toss my wet hands in the air to emphasize my point. He swipes at a drop of water that landed on his cheek. He lets a soft chuckle escape.

"That's not my fault," he says, pointing at his own chest. "*You* ran into *me*."

"Yes, but you didn't move! It was like running into cement," I reply, annoyed again. I flick my wet hand in the direction of his chest. This makes him fully smile. I can see so many of his teeth with this smile. How does he get them so white?

"Again, not my fault." He hands me the dish towel that is hanging over the oven handle, silently encouraging me to dry my hands. I snatch it out of his hand while shooting daggers at him. "I don't understand how it would have been any better for you if I had fallen down, too?"

He has a point. "It's ridiculous and annoying that you didn't even move when I ran into you. I was *sprinting*." I say, like that explains it all.

"I stumbled a bit," he tells me. His eyes are sparkling and I hate how much he is enjoying this.

"I stumbled a lot," I utter. "That reminds me, do you want to wash your hands?"

His face draws into its center, confusion written all over it. "Why would I need to wash my hands?" he asks, cocking his head to the side.

"Well, outside, you touched me." He just looks at me, waiting for more. "I'm sweating. I was sweating a ton when I was running," I explain while I motion to my sweaty shirt.

He looks down at his hands. He is staring at them like he forgot for a minute that they were still attached to his wrists. He looks back up to me and puts his hands in his pockets again.

"Nah, I'm good," he says casually. He turns his back to me and walks toward the front door. I stare after him, surprised. How is he not going to wash his hands after touching my sweat? What kind of freak is this guy? He reaches the front door and turns the handle. He looks at me over his shoulder and smiles. "Oh, and Valentina? Happy Birthday."

February 15th

I am not happy about my twenty-second birthday. I had to really hustle after collision-gate with Colt. I was dangerously close to not making it to The Hamptons on time for my dinner with Grandma Mae. After a quick shower, I threw some clothes in a bag and got in the car she sent for me. I was able to get ready in the backseat while the driver, Hank, did his best to keep the car moving smoothly for me. Did I mention that I love Hank?

Grandma Mae and I were able to have a lovely dinner together. She only mentioned my future life partner one time and only in passing. She praised me for my work in MaeDay's different divisions and told me how excited she was for me to continue to grow within the company.

The party was a total bust. Amy and Mackie never made it. Nisha got in a fender bender just outside the city and got diverted for so long, it was basically useless for her to come. Robin showed up, on time, but she very quickly met the son of one of GM's Sag Harbor friends and took off back to his place.

Ansley and I were the only ones left at the party come 9:00. We cleaned up a little bit and then headed to the master suite for a little sleepover. We watched a romantic comedy and ate popcorn. I loved this bonding time with Ansley, especially because it rarely happens. When you think of Ansley, think of Doogie Houser, but for science. She is a very important scientist and works in a think tank type of lab. The lab is incredibly secretive and she is not allowed to talk about their current projects. None of us know precisely what she does or even what *type* of projects her team works on. All we know is that she loves it, she runs a team of many people, and she makes a buttload of money.

We met Ansley through Robin's sister, Jo. Jo and Ansley were friends growing up but one day Jo got sick while we were all out to dinner and went home. Ansley stayed out with us and the rest is history. Jo and Ansley still see each other, of course, but Ansley is definitely part of our inner circle and she completes our group in the best way.

Ansley is always quiet and thoughtful. She is about five years older than I am and is definitely the mother figure of the group. She always gives the most insightful advice and if you are ever in a real jam, or a serious moral dilemma, you go to Ansley. Not only will she listen intently, she will know exactly how to handle the situation. Even her energy is calming.

I heard Ansley's phone buzzing in the middle of the night and when I woke up the morning after my birthday, Ansley was gone. She left a lovely note about the joy she experienced spending the night together and getting to celebrate my birthday with me but something came up at the lab and she had to get back to the city. And just like that, I am alone in the house.

I go to the kitchen and make myself a cup of coffee. Once it's ready, I take it into the special coffee room that has oversized furniture and overlooks the ocean. My favorite blanket in the world resides in this room. First, it is huge. It is big enough that I can wrap it around my body, twice. It is impossibly soft. It's made to look like it has pelts and is so soft and white, we call it the Snowshoe Hare blanket. I tuck my legs up under me on the ginormous chair that is directly in front of the bay window. I wrap the blanket all around me, only allowing my hands to stick out and hold my coffee mug. I sip my coffee and watch the ocean while I plan my twenty-second year of life.

First on the list, continue working in all departments at MaeDay. I want to resume learning every single thing I possibly can about MaeDay, the nail polish industry, and the employees that make our company function.

Next, I am going to go on at least one date. Looking back at my life, I have never gone on one single date. This should be something that you'd think I'd have realized by now, but it just seems to be glaringly obvious at this moment. It took the coffee room to make me realize that I am a bit lonely. I'm not a completely unfortunate looking person, but I'm also not what I would call 'beautiful.' I don't think it will be too difficult to go on just one date, but just the idea of the whole process causes anxiety to bubble up inside of me. I do my best to ignore it and decide to focus on finding one single person who would like to romantically share a meal with me. I can do this.

I would also like to do something for Grandma Mae. I want to show her my appreciation for everything she does for me. I will need to put some more thought into this, but it will need to be something sentimental. Money and fancy material things mean nothing to Mae, she needs something to show her how much I love her.

Lastly, given that Milo did not show up to the party and his absence piqued my curiosity about his life, I would like to try to reconnect with him. For some reason, I need to know what is happening in his life.

———

34

After setting my intentions for the year ahead, I look out to the ocean. I watch the waves roll in and then slide back out. It's quiet enough in the house that I can even hear the waves. The sound and the visual of the massive ocean soothes me. My mind settles, my body calms, and I fall into a deep state of contentment.

I finish my coffee but cannot bring myself to leave the ocean. I stare out at the water, wondering what the depths hold. I am perplexed by the creatures living in that water and how the sea moves. When I wake up in the chair, hours later, I know exactly what I need to do.

Twenty-Three

February 13th

Well, twenty-two was alright. Let me catch you up with some bullet points: I went on two dates, I gave Grandma Mae a gift, I have now visited every department in MaeDay, and I spoke with Milo, sort of. Technically, I texted with Milo, but we'll get to that.

Let's start with the least eventful topic: work. Mae built an amazing company. The culture she created and the work she puts in to make the company successful is all mind blowing. She is the best leader any company could ever hope to have and I am now positive I will never live up to the standard she has set.

I speak to her about this often and she always reassures me that I will learn so much in the coming years that taking over the company will seem natural. I try to explain to her that it's not the knowledge I'm worried about, but the way she leads. She is just so dynamic, caring, and gritty. I'm none of those things. Again, she tells me these characteristics come with time and experience. I guess we'll see.

The gift I gave her was a painting done by an unknown, but amazing, artist. It is a painting of the two of us sitting on the front steps of MaeDay headquarters. It is of our backs, with our arms interlaced, our heads leaned into one another, and us overlooking the city. When the artist showed it to me, I cried. When I gave it to Mae, she cried. Cried is not the correct word for what happened to Mae when she saw it, sobbed is closer, but still not perfect. It's now hanging behind her desk where we can both see it every day. This was my greatest success of the year.

I'm also placing the two dates in the success column. The first date, Lucas, was a setup. Robin has what seems like an endless amount of friends. She knew a single guy, not surprising whatsoever, that she deemed would be perfect for me. We met up for a drink one night and I felt nothing. He was cute and sweet, but he did not have whatever it is I find attractive. Figuring that out needs to be a goal for my twenty-third year because I still feel lost about my "type" of guy.

The second date, Rich, was a man I met at a coffee shop. I thought it was a match made in Heaven, since we all know about my love for coffee. We both take our coffee black, in huge mugs, and extra hot. Could there be a better pair? Turns out, yes. When we left the coffee shop and went to dinner he was incredibly rude to the person seating us, and then even more rude to the server. Oh, and don't forget about the people waiting in line for the bathroom. They may have gotten the worst of his rudeness. Clearly, I refused his request for a second date. Rudeness is never attractive.

Like I said, I still see these as successes. I've learned about dating, a little about vetting the person you're going to go on a date with, and popped my own dating cherry. Speaking of popping cherries, I feel it is important to state that I am not a virgin. I know, I know, I said I've never been on a date. And that is true. High schoolers do not require dates to have sex. Coincidentally, neither do college students. Everyone I've slept with up to this point, though, is someone from my friend groups or maybe a friend of a friend. I'm realizing now that I didn't necessarily find them attractive. They came on to me, I played hard to get for a while, and then would eventually give in to the ones who continued to pursue me. I didn't want anything long term and neither did they. Easy peasy. It should be evident that I have a lot to work on.

Moving on to Milo, oh Milo. I found out this year that Milo loves to only use emojis. I sent him a text (with words) asking if he wanted to meet up to connect again and catch

up. His only response was the coffee mug emoji. I assumed
this meant he wanted to meet up for coffee. I asked him
where and when he wanted to meet (again, with words) and
his response was the shrugging with hands in the air emoji.
Confused as ever, I left it alone and didn't respond. About a
week later he actually texted me the word "Coffee?" I agreed
and asked where he wanted to meet. Sadly, he was in Sag
Harbor and I was in Manhattan so that didn't work out. I
texted him that I would let him know the next time I was in
The Hamptons and he responded with a thumbs up.

So there we have it. My twenty-second year all
summed up. I am enjoying a nice evening alone at home,
reflecting on my past year while uncharacteristically drinking
tea. I bought myself a smaller version of the Snowshoe Hare
blanket to keep at my apartment. I am snuggled with that, in
my living room, drinking tea, and reading a book when the
buzzer blares. I head to the door and pick up the phone that
connects me with Gene down in the lobby.

"Good evening, Miss Cooper. I'm sorry to disturb you,
but there is someone down here asking for you." The girls
and Mae are all on the list to visit whenever they want so I
am at a loss as to who it could be.

"You don't know who it is?" I ask.

"No, miss. I've never seen this gentleman before."

"Did he give you a name?"

"Rich." Rich? Who the hell is Rich? Could it possibly
be horribly rude Rich?

"Please do not let him up, I'll come down," I instruct
Gene.

"Yes, miss."

Unsure what is waiting for me in the lobby, I put on
actual shoes and a coat. I head down on the stairs, not
wanting Rich to see what floor I came from. When I open the
lobby door and walk toward Gene's desk, my fear is
confirmed. It's Rude Rich. What the hell is he doing here and
how does he know where I live?

"Hi Rich, what are you doing here?" I ask as I
approach him, carefully.

"Valentina! It's good to see you again!" When I say nothing in response he continues. "You never agreed to a second date, so I thought I'd swing by and see if I could change your mind." He turns his right hand into a gun and pretends to shoot me with one eye closed. It is abundantly clear that he is drunk. His stench is starting to reach me and his speech is slurred. My eyes flick to Gene and I am immensely grateful he is here to share this moment with me. He is already reaching for the phone.

"Rich, how do you know where I live?" I pull my coat tighter around myself.

"What the hell are you talking about?" he spits at me. "I walked you home after our date!" He stumbles forward a step, but thankfully does not fall over.

"You most certainly did *not* walk me home." I use the strongest voice I can muster through my fear. This situation is escalating and Rich is twice the size of both me and Gene. "You need to leave, now." I point to the door.

"Why are you acting like this?" Rich is trying to sound smooth, but I am furious. How dare he show up at my apartment drunk and yell at me. Who does this idiot think he is?

"Rich, you are not welcome here. You will never be welcome here. Get the fuck out and never come back," I demand. When he makes no movement toward the door, I gather my courage and put my hands on his shoulders to turn him around and usher him out. Gene is already at the door, holding it open.

Rich shakes my hands off. "Fine! Be a bitch," he mumbles as he stumbles through the doorway. Gene looks as though he is thinking about saying something to Rich as he leaves, but I shake my head to discourage him. Gene closes his halfway open mouth and gives me a nod.

"If he returns, Miss Cooper, I will not call you. I will call the police," Gene promises.

"Thanks, Gene." I sigh. I give him a little wave and head to the elevator. I opt out of the stairs because I want to be safe in my bed the fastest way possible.

February 14th

All of the coffee in New York would not be able to perk me up. Sleep evaded me all night. Once I did finally fall asleep, any small noise or horn honk would have my eyes flying open. I blocked Rich's number and all his profiles on every social media platform we are connected on. Even though Gene promised to call the police if he returned, I still feel unsafe. I need to get an alarm system installed in my apartment immediately.

I am scheduled to meet Grandma Mae for lunch at noon. The thought of leaving my apartment to exercise nearly paralyzes me, so I give myself the morning off. It is my birthday, after all.

I lock myself in the bathroom and take a very steamy shower. I take my time getting ready, but I'm still an hour ahead of schedule. I sit on my couch and try to read a book, but my mind keeps wandering. I keep thinking of better ways I could have handled the situation. I also keep thinking of possible future scenarios and what I will do if each happens. It is easing my anxiety about Rich, but the next time I look at the clock, I see I'm late.

I grab my coat and run out the door, checking twice to make sure it is locked. When I was in middle school, we took a student trip to Washington D.C. The school hired security to roam the halls during the night, but as an extra layer of preventative measures, the teachers put a piece of tape across our doors with their signature on it. If the tape was broken or moved, they would know we'd opened the door. I remembered that while sitting on my couch this morning and brought out a little piece of tape to do this trick on my own door. I put it low enough to not be completely obvious and left for my lunch with Mae.

"Happy Birthday, my sweetest granddaughter!" Mae holds her champagne flute over the center of the table, waiting for me to clink my glass to hers. I had originally turned down the offer of a champagne lunch but I quickly reconsidered when I thought it might make me sleepy enough to take a nap this afternoon. I tap my glass to Mae's and instead of making a birthday wish, I hope for sleep.

"Thanks for lunch today, Grandmother," I coo. "Twenty-two was a good year." I take a little sip and feel the bubbles slide down my throat.

"It was, my darling. I am so proud of you and the progress you've made this year!"

"Thanks, GM, I've been working very hard to get to know everyone and everything about the company." Another sip.

"No, not about that," Mae says and waves her hand in a dismissive manner. "I mean, I am proud of you for going on dates! You'll meet your soulmate in no time!"

I can't help but roll my eyes. "Gran, both dates were horrible. I can't imagine Mr. Perfect is just around the corner." I opt not to tell her about Rich's visit last night. She will insist I move in with her. Or hire personal security.

"You never know…"

"I guess that's true," I agree. Anything for Mae.

Another sip, the champagne is going down easier than expected so early in the day. Mae is smiling at me over her glass.

"Don't be surprised if he makes an appearance very soon," Mae insists.

Mae also insists on taking me shopping around the city as a birthday gift. She declares nothing is off the table and the sky's the limit for this shopping spree. Normally, this offer would excite me, but the champagne has done its job. I am sleepy and want to go home and lie down for the rest of my birthday. I am also desperate to know if the tape is still in the same spot I left it earlier.

I try to tell Mae that I appreciate the offer but I need to go home for a nap. She is having none of it and buys me a shot of espresso from a Starbucks on the corner. It does wake me up quite a bit and while in Prada, she again insists we have more champagne. The second glass is no competition for the espresso and I power on. We visit store after store and she buys anything she believes looks good

---

on me or would look good in my apartment. By the middle of the afternoon, I have given up on any hope of actually getting a nap.

Mae's last insistence is that we have one final glass of champagne together. She ushers me to this new sleek and modern bar a couple blocks from my apartment. She instructs Hank to drop the bags off with the doorman at my apartment building and take the night off. He opens the door for us to exit the car, thanking Mae and promising to get the bags to my apartment. Mae takes my hand and leads me to the bar.

"SURPRISE!" I am bombarded the moment I open the door. There are dozens of people inside. Most of them I recognize from MaeDay, along with a few friends spattered about. I see my four favorites in the back corner of the bar. Mackie is there with Amy; yes, they are still together! Jo is also there with the group. I wave to them and after waving back they point to the bar. Mae finds Annie and the two walk to the bar. Mae hands me champagne and says food will be out soon and the bar tab is on her. She stays for just one drink before heading out with Annie.

"Thanks for coming, Amy and Mackie. I know it's Valentine's Day, so don't feel like you have to stay," I assure them. After taking the champagne from Mae and making sure her and Annie were alright to leave, I joined my friends in the back corner.

"It's fine, we celebrated together earlier today," Amy tells me with a huge smile on her face.

"Quite a few times, actually," Mackie mutters before taking a swig of her drink. Amy swats at her and Amy's face turns as red as a tomato. I hide my laughter behind a swallow of champagne.

"We're yours for the night," Amy promises me.

"You're the best!" I pull Amy and Mackie in for a hug and kiss them both on the cheek.

"So, the bartender's name is Rocco. How hot is that?" Robin yells over the music.

"Pretty hot," Nisha agrees. We all nod.

"I'm gonna get him to start karaoke," Robin announces.

"How the hell are you going to do that?" I laugh. "This isn't a karaoke bar!"

"We just need a microphone and some music. Be right back." Six sets of eyes watch her walk back to the bar and pull Rocco closer to her over the bartop.

"Just let her do her thing," Jo says. "It'll be easier that way." We all nod in agreement.

I turn to say something to Amy, but she is sitting in a booth, making out with Mackie. It doesn't look as if they will be coming up for air anytime soon. I grab another glass of champagne from the bar before Rocco leaves to gather the karaoke materials.

It takes approximately six minutes for Robin to have Rocco find a microphone and a minute after that, both are standing on the bar singing along to Bon Jovi. I clap along while I sip my drink. I head back to the group to see that Amy and Mackie are long gone and Ansley is on the phone. I know what is about to come from Ansley before she says it. She gives me a sad wave and heads out the door.

I stand next to Nisha, hoping to hop into her conversation with Jo. The only problem is they are discussing aliens. Not just the general possibility of their existence or the probability thereof, but real facts. They are using very large words and talking about mathematical certainties. I don't have the mental bandwidth to participate in this conversation and the exhaustion is catching up with me.

I stalk over and flop down on a barstool. I wonder, once again, if the tape is still in place on my door. Another glass of champagne magically appears in front of me as I am contemplating how much longer I have to stay. I look up to thank Rocco, but he is still singing with Robin. They have moved on to Madonna.

Colt is standing behind the bar. I hadn't noticed him all night and it's been months since I've seen him at the office. Did he get *more* muscular? His scruff is definitely scruffier.

"What are you doing back there?" I ask Colt, pointing behind the bar.

"Well, I used to bartend and this bartender isn't bartending, so I took over." He shrugs at his own explanation.

"Oh, ok. Thanks for the drink," I say as I slump down on the barstool.

"You ok?" He stops rinsing the glass he is holding and leans forward on the bar. Damn, I forgot about his forearms.

I drag my eyes from his forearms to his eyes and he is smiling. "You're drunk," he accuses.

"No, no, I'm not." I am. "I didn't sleep well last night and the champagne is a lot when you haven't slept… or eaten."

Without saying a word, Colt fills a glass with water and places it in front of me. Did he just wink at me? Things are a little fuzzy so it's completely possible that didn't just happen. But if it did, that was sort of sexy. He returns before I can think about it too much and puts a plate next to the water. It is full of cheeses and crackers, chips and salsa, and some sort of meat inside a croissant.

"Why don't you eat a little bit to soak up all that champagne and then I'll walk you home."

I slowly look up at him, the blurry version of him anyway. "Ok."

I chug the water and eat all the crackers and the meat croissant before I declare it is time to leave. I text the girls group chat that I'm drunk and heading home while Colt gets our coats. We walk out into the freezing air and instead of it sobering me up, I stumble. The cold air is a shock and I turn to go back into the toasty warm bar. Colt chuckles and leads me away from the door instead.

I look around and try to read the street sign, but it's useless. "Are we going the right way?" I ask Colt.

"Yes," he says through his smile.

"Are you sure? You don't know where I live."

"Yes, I do."

I stop walking and look at him. How is this happening to me two days in a row? "How the hell do you know where I live?"

He looks almost offended at my question. "Valentina, it was one year ago today that I was at your apartment."

I search the far corners of my brain for this memory. When I try to picture Colt sitting on my couch, the memory of him cleaning my legs in my kitchen floods my mind. How could I forget that? It's hysterical that I forgot that! So hysterical, that I am now laughing uncontrollably. Colt is doing his best to keep me on my feet, but I'm not making it easy on him. He's holding me around the waist and eventually he begins laughing, too.

"How could I ever, *ever* forget that?"

"I don't know, Valentina." He gets me righted and turns me toward my apartment and we're walking again.

"Oh, shit, that was funny." I'm still suffering from laughter aftershocks. I'm wiping the tears that are falling down my cheeks.

"Yeah, it was," Colt agrees. He's supporting a majority of my weight. How is he walking and holding me up? I need to get a better look at his muscles.

"Colt? Mr. Arden?"

A smile. "Yes, Valentina?"

"Will you do me a favor?"

"Possibly." A suspicious look. "What is it?"

"Show me your arms." It's not a question, I say it like a demand.

"What?" He's laughing with discomfort.

"I don't understand how you are able to walk, hold me up, and help me walk all at the same time. Your arms must be monsters. I want to see their teeth." That made more sense in my head.

"I have no idea what you're talking about," he says and doesn't look in my direction.

"Are you mad at me now?" I glance at his jaw, trying to read his emotions. "Now that I want to see your arms?"

"No, I'm not mad." He lets out a long sigh. "You weigh almost nothing, this isn't difficult. You don't need to see my arms."

I look at his face. "I don't think I believe you. But I've had too much champagne to know for sure."

He laughs and looks down at me. This is the first time I noticed we're not moving. I look around the snowy street.

"We're at my building!"

Colt chuckles at my surprise. "Yes."

"Let's go see if the tape is there," I whisper to him and start tiptoeing inside. I'm still on my toes as I walk through the lobby and to the stairs.

"What tape?" he asks from behind me. I open the stairwell door, but he redirects me to the elevator. I guess that's probably for the best.

"Come on, I'll show you." I'm still whispering. I don't have a clue why, the tape can't hear me, certainly not in the lobby.

I lean against Colt in the elevator. He's so warm and so strong. I could lean against him until I fall asleep. When I open my eyes he is smiling down at me.

"Oh no!" I yell too loudly. I startle myself and jump a little, drawing my body to a standing position. My hands fly to Colt's chest, reaching for help. I think.

Colt is immediately on the defensive. "What? What's wrong?" His eyes dart around the elevator.

"I forgot to say hello to Gene," I whine, fighting tears.

Colt's shoulders relax. "It's ok. He wasn't there."

I also relax and move my hand across my forehead in a very exaggerated 'whew' motion. Colt likes this and his eyes are sparkling again.

Once the elevator doors open, I hold my pointer finger to my lips as the universal sign of being quiet. I motion for Colt to come down the hall with me. I tiptoe again and he tries to be as silent as he can be, bless his heart.

When we get to my door, I kneel down and Colt quickly follows. I put my left hand on my door to brace myself and suck in a huge breath of air.

"What is it?" Colt asks.

"The tape's only on the door." I can only describe the look he gives me as 'befuddled.' "It's on the door, and not on the doorframe *and* the door. The door has been opened. Someone's inside," I explain. I am much more calm than I should be given the situation.

"You put tape on your door to see if someone is hiding in your apartment?" His tone is incredulous. I nod in response and stand.

I pull my key from my purse and take a small step to get closer to the lock. Colt takes the key from my hand and moves me away from the door. He leans me against the wall next to the doorframe. He puts the key in and opens the door quickly. He turns the light on and walks in slowly. I follow him even though he motions for me to go back. I ignore him and walk quicker into my apartment, my heels clicking on the floor, already taking my coat off.

"Go outside," he growls quietly at me. I don't move a muscle. "Please," he adds with a much gentler tone. I contemplate my next move for a few seconds. I hold my hands up in a gesture of innocence and turn to walk back out. I sit on the ground and wait.

He reappears in the hallway after a few minutes. "There's no one in there." I look at his face and give him a thumbs up. "But there are a shit ton of shopping bags on the couch."

"Ohhhh! It was *Hank*!" I smack my forehead. I try to stand as gracefully as I can, which isn't very, and push past Colt to get in my apartment.

"Valentina?"

"I need my Snowshoe Hare!" I stomp into my bedroom and wrap the blanket around me.

"Valentina?" Colt calls from the living room.

"Come in, I found it!" I kick off my shoes and lie down on my bed with my second most favorite blanket in the world.

I am rubbing my face against the furriness of the blanket when Colt walks in my room.

"Valentina, why did you tape your door?"

"There was a guy. It's fine," I mumble. My eyes are closed.

"A guy? Valentina?"

"Hmm?"

"Valentina, why is there tape on your door?"

But, I am already asleep.

February 15th

I wake up feeling much better than I deserve. I actually feel perfect, which is shocking. What is not shocking is that I slept for fifteen hours. Which, I guess, explains why I feel perfect. I put on workout clothes and head into the living room and I see a piece of folded paper on the kitchen counter.

It all comes back at once, fuck. Colt knows about the tape. How am I going to explain this to him? What if he tells Mae? She will make herself sick with worry! I have to get ahead of this. I have to find solutions to this problem. The first step is quieting Colt.

I walk into the kitchen and read his note.

V -

I took your key and locked the door. I slid it back under your door once I locked it. Go get it now. I made sure the night doorman knew NO ONE was to come up to your apartment. I would appreciate a text in the morning to let me know you're alive. My number is in your phone. Our conversation about the tape is not over.

-C

Why does Colt have to be so thoughtful, but yet still so annoying? I go and get the key from my floor near the door, bossy little bugger, and then go to find my phone. I need to call the home security company anyway. Sure as shit, his number is in my phone. Fine, I'll text him.

I'm alive.

Good morning to you, too.

Good morning, Colt. Thank you for walking me home.

You're welcome. Why was there tape on your door?

I explained last night.

You did not. You said there was "a guy". What guy? Is someone bothering you?

No, everything is fine.

Obviously not! You taped your door.

It's not really any of your concern.

His texts stop. I get a response about twenty minutes later, once I'm already stretching and getting ready for my run.

I suppose you're right. If you are ever in any trouble, you have my number. Use it.

During my five mile run, I set my intentions for the upcoming year.

The first is easy and obvious: figure out what I find attractive in a partner.

The second is a bit more difficult: find a partner that I find to be attractive.

The third goes without saying: continue to grow within the company.

The fourth: purchase a security system and feel comfortable enough to stop taping my door (I plan to do this every time I leave my apartment for the foreseeable future).

The fifth: Spend more time with my friends.

I've got this.

Twenty-Four

February 13th

After spending the entire day in Mae's office, I am ecstatic to return home to my apartment. I want to take off these killer heels, the work outfit, and remove my makeup. All that is standing in between me and pajamas is checking the tape on my door and turning off my home alarm. After climbing the stairs, I see the tape is intact, and I open the door to my apartment and enter the alarm code on the wall panel.

Yes, I had it installed and I have amped up all security measures. I still haven't told anyone about Rich's visit last year, especially not Grandma Mae. The security system was installed two weeks after my birthday and I settled into a nice routine with my tape and alarm. And then one day about four or five months ago, I had the feeling I was being followed. I couldn't shake it. It felt eerie, and I felt highly uncomfortable as I was enjoying the fall weather and walking on the streets of New York. It was unnerving to be surrounded by thousands of people, but to just know that someone was singling me out and watching me. I hated it. The next morning, I set up a car service. I explained to Mae that I would like to use the commute to be more productive. She never second-guessed my reasoning.

One day, not long after the car began picking me up every morning, I thought I saw Rich walking on the sidewalk on the other side of the street, across from my apartment building. I stepped around the towncar to get a better look before getting in, but whoever it was had disappeared. After that, I felt confident in my car service decision and did a better job of paying attention to my surroundings.

MaeDay has incredibly tight security. We have to swipe a badge to enter the lobby; the badge is also programmed to only allow you to go to certain floors and must be swiped for the elevator to move. A different badge has to be swiped to even enter the MaeDay headquarters, the hallway to the upper level offices is locked and requires a badge, and the door to each office has a fingerprint-enabled lock. Not to mention the security team that is in place, along with the three million dollar camera and emergency system that is wired around the company floors. I feel very safe while at work, oddly it's the time spent at home that I feel most exposed.

My own alarm system makes me feel much more safe while in my apartment though. It is rare that the alarm is not enabled. I turn it off once I enter through my door, but immediately re-engage it so that if someone opens my door, it will go off and the police will be notified if I don't disable it. After the possible Rich sighting, I also had a motion-activated camera installed outside my apartment door, just in case. So far, nothing has come up on the recordings, but it still makes me feel better.

My friends have been very curious about the uptick in security. I told them as I continue to grow in the company and become more recognizable, I need to be more careful. In my defense, this is partly true. I would need to amp up security at some point, I just left out the part about Rich showing up and that the experience forced me to come to terms with my own vulnerability. They are all very supportive and agree that I should be as safe as possible.

Amy and Mackie are engaged, and we are all blissfully happy about it. We are not only happy for Amy, but also elated for Mackie to join our group. Nisha is dating a doctor, but declares it's nothing serious. Ansley is continuing to climb the ladder of success at her mystery lab job, as we all knew she would. And Robin… is Robin. She is still as fun, lovely, and unpredictable as ever. She isn't dating anyone, but just got a new job on the marketing team for the New York Philharmonic. She loves it and we are excited for her.

Now that I have been through all of the divisions of the company and am very familiar with the staff, especially officers, upper-level management, and department heads, I am spending most of my time at MaeDay shadowing my grandmother. We work together and, under her tutelage, I am gaining knowledge at a breakneck pace.

Not only am I absorbing her leadership techniques like a sponge and doing my best to keep all of the facts and figures about the nail polish and beauty industry stored in my brain, I am also contributing. Over the past year I have felt comfortable enough to share some of the techniques and knowledge I learned while at Columbia. After two years, I am really feeling like I am part of the team. It's nothing short of amazing.

There is only one downside at work. At the turn of the new year, about six weeks ago, Colt was promoted to Head of Marketing. I was shocked given his age, I learned he is currently thirty-one, but in Mae's words "that is the one department that needs to be kept young." She says it's the younger crowd that needs to take the lead and figure out the best ways and places to promote. There are older members of the marketing team, of course, she just wants the young people who are "in the know" to lead the team. She orders me, daily, to trust her. I am trying.

I don't see Colt every day, but I see him *way* more often than I used to. This will be especially true now since Mae announced last week that managing the department chairs will be my responsibility. She is going to gradually move things off of her plate and on to mine. She believes checking in with the managers of each department and assisting them however they need is something I can currently handle. I agree, and I believe it will only help me learn more about each department. This means I will be having regular one-on-ones with Colt. Awesome.

On the partner front, I did my best to figure out what is attractive to me. As it turns out, I don't have a "type." I like many different looks. Their features, their shape, their height make no difference on their level of attractiveness. I couldn't care less what color their hair is or if they have washboard

---

abs. All I have found to allure or deter me is their smile. You can tell a lot about a person by their smile. Some are warm, wide, and toothy, those are good people. Some are tight-lipped and look almost painful, those people are hiding something. Some smiles look like work, they look completely fake, and those are the people that I avoid. Nothing makes me weak in the knees like a good, genuine, sparkling, crinkling-eyed smile. Those are the best.

I put my smile theory to the test and went on some dates. Ok, a lot of dates. Men of all shapes and sizes, but only with good smiles. This research was amazing, I've been having a blast! These are almost all good guys who just want to enjoy my company. Sometimes the smile is *too* good and I had to learn this lesson the hard way. These men, with too good of a smile, are after something else entirely. They want access to my grandmother and her company. It's disgusting, but it's true. I can now spot these smiles a mile away.

I'm getting really good at first dates. I used to be nervous and worried about saying the wrong thing, but after a lot of practice I have calmed down. I am able to take a deep breath, settle my nerves, and speak like a normal human. Who cares if they don't like me? I'm not looking for anything serious. Yet.

February 14th

I wake up thankful I didn't have another run-in with Rich the night before my birthday like last year. I slept well, I feel rested, and I am excited for my day. Things are going to be a little different this year because Mae is out of town. I won't be able to have a meal with her on my twenty-fourth birthday, which is a total bummer, but I understand that sometimes work has to come first. She is touring production centers in different Asian countries. The trip will take three weeks and it simply could not be put off because I wanted to have dinner with my grandmother on my birthday.

We are in wildly different time zones as well, so we probably won't Facetime or speak to one another either. This makes me a little sad, but I understand, again. I know she loves me and would be here with me if she could.

After my morning workout at the gym, I am bundled up and walking home in the snow when I think I see Rich outside my building. I squint, trying to get a better look, but it's the big, heavy snowflakes that are falling. Visibility is nearly impossible and the closer I get to my door, the more I think my mind is playing tricks on me. I can barely see the facial features of the person standing next to me, how could I recognize Rich from a block and a half away?

"Hello Miss Cooper," Gene greets me as I blow into the building, bringing at least an inch of snow with me.

"Hi, Gene! How are you? How's Mary Jo?" His wife is just as sweet as he is.

"She's great! Thanks for asking." He smiles warmly at me. "Two things, Miss Cooper. The first is I want to wish you a happy birthday. Second, you have a package." He hands me a small box, wrapped in Tiffany blue paper with a big, white ribbon tied into a bow on the top of the box.

"Thank you for the birthday wishes!" I take the box from his hands and hold it up. "And thank you for this!"

"Of course, Miss! Can I call the elevator for you? Or will you be taking the stairs?"

"I'll take the stairs, but thanks anyway, Gene. See you later!"

I bound up the stairs, excited to open my birthday gift. After checking the door tape and turning the alarm off, and then back on again, I sit on my couch and very carefully pull the ribbon off. Once the wrapping paper is off, I see a tiny little piece of brown paper that reads

> To my sweetest granddaughter -
> I hope you love this as much as I love you!
> Happy Birthday!
> GM

I open the box to see a beautiful, silver locket outlined in diamonds. I open the locket to see a photo inside of my grandmother holding me on one side and a photo of my parents on their wedding day on the other. It's the most gorgeous piece of jewelry I have ever seen. I burst into tears. Not sweet, dainty tears that travel slowly down my cheek. No, ridiculous sobs wrack my body, snot is coming out of my nose, and my sleeves are soaked from using them to sop up all my fluids. This is the best gift I have ever received.

I latch the locket around my neck and take a photo of myself all splotchy and with bloodshot eyes and send it to my grandmother. I don't even know how to thank her for such a gift. I know she'll see my tear-stained cheeks and immediately know how much it means to me.

Knock, knock, knock.

I nearly jump out of my skin at the shock of someone knocking at my door. I pull up the camera app on my phone to see that it is my four favorites standing there waving at the camera. Robin is holding champagne, Ansley is holding flowers, Nisha is holding a cake, and Amy is holding a suitcase. I disarm the alarm system and open the door.

"What is all this?" I ask as they push past me. I close the door once they're all in and turn the alarm on again.

"Well, we know Mae's out of town, so we are going to spend the day with you," Nisha explains, an excited gleam in her eye.

"Aw, that's so sweet, what about your new boyfriend?" I ask her. "What about Mackie?" I direct to Amy.

"Mackie will be here later," Amy tells me, taking a seat on the couch.

"Max and I are NOT ready to spend Valentine's Day together yet," Nisha says. She waves her hands back and forth in front of her as if to say "no way."

"OK, if you say so." I smile at my friends and point to the suitcase. "What's with that?"

"That's the best part!" Robin unzips it and pulls out matching flannel pajama sets. They are baby blue and with a white trim. They look incredibly comfortable and warm. I cannot wait to put those on.

"Does this mean you're staying the night?" I ask.

"Sure does," replies Ansley.

"Wow, you are the best friends a girl could ask for!" I wrap my arm around Robin who is standing next to me. "This is going to be a great birthday!"

"Fucking right," Robin says before kissing my cheek.

We hang out at my apartment all afternoon and leisurely drink the two bottles of champagne that Robin brought, followed by another one I have in my wine fridge. We chat, play a few card games, watch a romantic movie, and then we feel a little cooped up. Luckily, the girls planned ahead and made a dinner reservation at a new restaurant called *One Type*. It is supposed to be nothing but guiltless pleasures because everything on the menu is low carb, all natural, and no sugar added. I am very excited to try it and the girls and I scope out the menu as we walk there.

Walking there is a decently difficult affair given the amount of snow that has already fallen, and is continuing to fall. Our outfits and shoe choices aren't helping. We are sliding all over the sidewalk and hanging on to one another for dear life. We manage to make it to the restaurant without too many slips and zero falls. This is a big win for a snowy, winter birthday. These coincidentally are my favorite birthdays. I love to watch the snow fall. It's so peaceful and soothing. It amazes me how so much liquid can fall silently.

They seat us at a large, circular table in the middle of the restaurant, which is perfect for us. We can still enjoy the view of snow falling over the city outside, but we are deep enough in the restaurant that we feel the full ambiance and none of the cold. We order four appetizers and two bottles of Cabernet to get us started.

"It's time for your gift," Robin says to me, eyes dancing.

"My gift? Today is my gift. You all are my gift. This is such a wonderful surprise. I couldn't ask for anything more or a better birthday." I am shocked to hear they planned a birthday gift on top of everything else, it's too much. I'm still blown away from my grandmother's gift that is now resting around my neck.

"I agree, we are the *best* gift. That does not mean we are the *only* gift." Robin's hands are underneath the table, and I do not have one single guess what she is hiding under there.

She pulls out a mid-sized jewelry box. It's too small to hold a necklace but too big to hold a ring. I'm very intrigued. I take the box out of her hands, shooting glances at everyone around the table. They are all clearly excited. All four women are smiling and leaning forward, waiting for me to open the box.

I slowly open the velvet box and inside is a beautiful copper bracelet. It is thin and the color is beautiful. When I take it out of the box, I feel that it is not smooth. I bring it near my eyes so I can take a closer look. I see that the bracelet is stamped. All of our names are stamped around it. It's an adult friendship bracelet, and I melt inside at their thoughtfulness. My eyes begin to prick and I know the tears are coming.

"Girls, this is so - " I pull my eyes from the gift and up to the table. All of the women are holding out their own wrists to show me the same bracelet on each of their arms. We all have matching bracelets, with all of our names on them. Words cannot express how much I love this gift. I can't get it on my wrist fast enough. Once it's on, I hold it in the center of the table just as my best friends are doing. I swipe a tear away.

"I love it so much," I tell them.

"We do, too," Nisha replies.

After ordering our meals and drying our eyes, I head to the bathroom. I check my phone for a response text from my grandmother. I have nothing from her, but I do have a text from Colt.

Happy Birthday, Boss. No exclamation point. No emojis. Nothing.

Thank you. I respond with the same level of enthusiasm. I expect this to be the end of our conversation, so I put my phone away and head into the stall. I hear a ding before I'm finished. I leave the stall and wash my hands.

    How's your day? Anything special?

    My day is wonderful. I am spending it having a great time with my friends. We are at dinner right now.

    That's great. I'm glad to hear it. I apply more lipstick and decide not to respond. As I'm packing my purse, I hear another ding.

    Not having any trouble this year, are you?

    Of course not.

    Well, if you get home and the tape isn't right, call me. Don't go inside. Hm, that's interesting. Does he think I only tape the door on my birthday? I've been taping the door for the past 366 days.

    I think I've got it covered.

    Like I said, you have my number. Don't hesitate to use it.

February 15th

My friends and I all wake up in our matching pajamas with our matching bracelets and I could not feel any more elated. Mackie joined us later in the evening and she had matching pajamas waiting for her once she got to my apartment.

    I am awake first and sneak out of bed so I don't wake Robin and Ansley, who are also sleeping in my bed. Mackie and Amy are sleeping on the fold-out couch while Nisha made herself a bed on the floor with what appears to be about a thousand cushions. I tiptoe around all of them and begin making everyone breakfast.

    I try to stay quiet, but the noise from the kitchen wakes up Nisha first and she comes in the kitchen to help. She gets coffee going while I am mixing pancake batter. Once the pancakes are cooking, I mix up a bunch of eggs and pull turkey bacon out of my fridge. Once everything is sizzling on the stovetop, Mackie and Amy are up and sitting on the barstools at the counter. Everyone is sipping coffee while watching me work.

"Are we going to wake up Robin and Ansley or let them sleep?" Amy asks with sleepy eyes.

"Coffee. Now," Ansley says as she stumbles out of my bedroom. I chuckle and Nisha pours her a mug. The pleasure Ansley takes in her first sip of coffee makes all of us smile. She enjoys her coffee with such fervor, the rest of us can't help but watch her enjoy it.

By the time everything is off the stove and on serving plates, Robin makes an appearance and pours her own cup of coffee.

After a quiet, but great, breakfast together, everyone packs up to get back to their lives. Mackie and Amy are off to plan their wedding, Ansley is no doubt off to the lab, Nisha is probably off to see Max, but Robin stays behind.

"Hey lady, you doing ok?" Robin asks me. She is sitting on the barstools watching me clean up the kitchen from the breakfast mess.

"Yeah, of course. Why do you ask?" I look over my shoulder at her.

"It's just you've been doing a lot of first dates and not many second dates." She pauses and I stop cleaning to turn around and look at her. "I'm also a bit worried why you've got so many security measures happening." She waves her hands around.

"I'm fine with the dates. I am just figuring out what I like and don't like in a man. I can't figure out what makes a great partner until I've worked my way through some bad ones, right?" I hope talking about the men will distract her from the security question.

"I guess that's true. It's just never been your style."

"Well, you know GM wants me to find a life partner, and I'm just not in any hurry. I definitely don't want anything serious."

"What about Milo?" Robin asks.

"Milo?!"

"Yeah, Milo. You don't think you could get serious with Milo?"

"I haven't even seen Milo in years. I don't know what kind of adult he is. He might be terrible!"

"Yeah, he might be. But he could also be awesome." Robin takes a sip of her coffee and looks at me over the rim of her mug as she drinks.

"Good point," I admit. "I've reached out, we've just never been able to connect."

"Maybe you should remedy that?"

"Maybe."

Goals and intentions for twenty-five are not difficult.

The first is to master my role as the manager to the Department Chairs at work.

The second is to continue shadowing my grandmother and learning as much as possible from her. I know she can teach me so many things and I want to learn them all. This is nothing new.

The third is to find and purchase the most kickass wedding gift for Amy and Mackie.

My last goal is to make contact with Milo. I have not forgotten about him over the past couple years and I would truly like to meet up with him again and see the adult he turned into. Is he kind and generous? Is he cutthroat and domineering? Does he run his own business? Does he give beach tours all summer? I just need to know more about the childhood mystery that grew up alongside me.

Along with reconnecting with Milo as my last goal, I am going to add something. Spend more time at my grandmother's Hamptons house this summer. She travels there often, but I'm usually too busy with work or events in the city to go. I want to spend at least one weekend each month this summer in The Hamptons. I want to enjoy the sun, get away, and relax. It can only help, right?

Twenty-Five

February 13th

Well, I did spend more time in The Hamptons. I was able to sit with Mae in the coffee room and on the giant porch many times during the warmer weather. We spent a lot of time together and I would bring friends when they were available. Throughout all my visits, though, I only saw Milo once. And it was in passing. I was coming in from a swim in the ocean. I had to travel back to the city that afternoon after a quick shower, so I was in a hurry. Milo was heading out with his surfboard. We said hello and asked how one another was doing. He promised to attend the next birthday party of mine that he is invited to. That was it. I do feel inclined to say, however, that he has a great smile. It used to be timid and shy, but now it takes over his entire face and shows all of his teeth. It's a smile I am excited to see again. Looking at the rest of him… is also wonderful. He has the body, and six pack, of a surfer, with long, light wavy hair. His skin is tanned and freckled from the sun. He carries himself in a way that lets us all know he is comfortable in his body. I hope he holds true to his promise of coming to my birthday party.

Speaking of birthday parties. I am having a party in the city tomorrow night. It is at the same place where my grandmother threw me a surprise party two years ago. We had a good time and thought the location was great, so we are recreating the fun we had that night. But this time, not a surprise.

Before I can get to the party tomorrow, I have to get through a day of one-on-one meetings with all of the Department Chairs. I have worked very hard at excelling at

---

this position within the company. I think I have done well with it over the past year, but I know it is something that will take me years and years to perfect.

I have made it through most of the meetings and I only have one left. The last thing on my schedule for the day is a meeting with Colt. Awesome. He's amazing as Head of Marketing. Everyone loves him, his team loves him, his campaigns are all successful, and we are getting more followers on social media than ever before. It drives me crazy how effortlessly he is outstanding at every single thing he does. Most of us have to work and work hard to rise the corporate ladder, but all Colt does is show up and he's amazing. It's downright rude.

"Hello, Colt, please come in and have a seat," I say as I gesture toward the chair on the opposite side of my desk.

"Afternoon, Valentina." He strides into my office and has an uncharacteristically large smile spread across his face. "How are you doing today?" he asks as he sits down in the seat and crosses one leg over another.

"I'm fine, thank you. How are you?" I return the pleasantry.

"Great, great. Are you excited for your birthday party tomorrow?"

"I am, actually." I can't help but smile now.

"I hope it goes well and you have a great time." He's still smiling at me. I hate it. Well, hate is a strong word. I don't hate his smile, at all. I do hate how good it is though. It's a beautiful smile. He has great lips, with just a little stubble around them, and perfect, white teeth peeking through. I also hate how much I find his smile appealing. I need to get down to business.

"Ok, Colt, let's get focused here and look at the quarterly numbers," I instruct.

He drops his head to his notepad and stops smiling. We go over the current live campaigns, where the team stands with television, radio, and magazine ads. He has an equal number of team members that work solely for our online marketing strategies. He catches me up on the

---

websites and influencers we are using to market with, and then discusses what we are posting and ads on our social media platforms. I can't help but praise him for the amount of return we are seeing from his team's work, how current he is with his team's progress, and the connections he has made that we have been working toward. Fuck me if this isn't the most impressive and easiest meeting I've had today.

"So, Valentina," he says as we are finishing up. "How are you liking it here at MaeDay?"

"I love it here," I answer with complete honesty.

"That's good. Everyone was hoping you would." He uncrosses his legs and sits up just a bit taller.

"Everyone? What do you mean?" I am flustered at this change of topic.

"Everyone at MaeDay, we all wanted you to stay. We weren't sure if you'd want to try to explore a new industry, or maybe even start your own business. We knew you were very intelligent and had a great mind for business and we'd hoped you'd stay with us."

I am shocked. I had no idea anyone at all cared what I would decide to do, or that my decision would impact everyone. I especially had no idea that Colt cared what I did with my life.

"Oh, uh, I, uh, I am flattered." I pause, unsure how to continue. "I guess I thought everyone would think since I am so young, I don't deserve this or maybe that people would think Mae is just handing me the company." I cannot believe I just confessed something so personal to Colt. What am I thinking? I resist the urge to put my face in my hands and growl.

"No, not at all. We all love Mae. She's the best. We like that the company will stay in the family. It makes us happy, but it will also make Mae happy." He starts packing his things up. I am still recovering.

"Well, thanks again. I am happy the company will stay in the family, too. I hope to make her proud." I fold up my portfolio as well and start tidying my desk.

"You do." He stops and gazes at me longer than I feel is appropriate for a work meeting. "She loves you very

———

much, we can all see it. You are very lucky to have one another." The intensity with which he is making eye contact with me has my entire body in paralysis. I cannot move. I am frozen in my big, cushioned, work chair and I cannot tear my eyes away from his. Now I am the one staring for longer than is appropriate.

Luckily, he breaks the trance before I have to do something drastic. I shake my head, trying to clear away the memory of his blue eyes and stand to walk him to the door. When we reach it, he puts his hand on the doorknob and stops. He looks at me over his shoulder and opens his mouth to say something. He closes it again, but then opens it once more. He closes it a final time, turning his head away from me, and walking out of my office.

What was that?

I head home after I have cleaned up my desk and cleared out my inbox. After stopping to say hello to Gene, I walk up the stairs, check the tape, open my door, and immediately take off my work shoes. There is not enough room to leave them in the entryway, so I take them into my room and place them in my shoe holder. I put on my favorite flannel pajamas, the ones given to me last year by my friends, and snuggle up with my second favorite blanket.

I started doing something unexpected over the past year that provides me with a lot of comfort, something that sort of happened by accident one night and now I'm addicted.

I talk to my parents.

One very hot, summer night my air conditioning went out. I called the building maintenance man, but he was busy with a massive leak on the fifth floor. He wasn't sure if he'd be able to make it that day, or even the next day depending on the damage. The heat was unbearable and after spending the afternoon in a coffee shop, trying to stay cool, the time had come to head home. It was a Sunday afternoon and I hadn't had any luck getting ahold of anyone else to come fix it on short notice on a Sunday. The building maintenance man was still working on stopping and fixing the leak. He hadn't even gotten to repairing the damage caused by the leak. I got an old box fan out of the back of my closet and set it up to blow directly on me while I slept.

The fan worked for a while, but when I woke up drenched in sweat, with wet sheets in the middle of the night, I couldn't get back to sleep. Being seven stories up on a 90 degree day was just too much. I got up and messed with the thermostat, played around with my power switches, and then finally yelled in frustration.

"Come on, dad! Help me, please!"

I hadn't planned to say that. I didn't have a single thought in my head about speaking to either of my parents before the words left my mouth. In fact, when my dad was alive he wasn't even very handy. I would have never asked him for help fixing an appliance. I was surprised when I heard the words enter the atmosphere.

I was equally surprised to hear the hum of the air conditioner start back up. Less than five seconds after I'd spoken to my father, it kicked back on and started working again. After I'd begged for my father's help. I couldn't believe it. I was so overwhelmed, both with emotion and relief to be out of the heat, that I began crying. I leaned forward against the wall, put my head on my forearms, and let myself cry.

"Dad?" I lifted my head and asked the empty room. The air conditioning unit stopped blowing air and then started again. I smiled and laughed even though there were tears in my eyes.

I cannot put it into words, but it was clear to me at that moment that my dad helped me. I was more certain of that than my own name. In between sobs, I would thank my dad. Then I apologized to my parents for not talking to them sooner, for not realizing they were always with me. I apologized and thanked and weeped for so long, I fell asleep on the floor underneath the thermostat.

I woke up the next morning, eyes puffy and exhausted. I looked around the room and I said, "Are you here?"

Again, I cannot explain it, but I just *knew* that they were there with me. I've heard people say they can feel a presence, but it was more than that. Yes, I felt something, *someone* there in the room, but I was absolutely certain about *who* was there. Without a single shred of a doubt, I knew my parents were in that room with me.

"Have you always been here?" The lights flickered. I didn't know I had started crying again, but I had. Tears were flowing down my chapped cheeks, but this time I was smiling with the tears. My parents were there. They had always been there. This comforted me as much as curling into my mother's lap when I was little. She might as well have been stroking my hair and singing to me, just as she used to.

For the first time since I started at MaeDay, I called off work. I was terrified if I left my apartment that my parents might not be there when I returned. I didn't feel ready to leave our safe space, my tiny apartment. I wanted them to surround me and help me, I wanted to talk to them. So I did.

That day, I told them everything. I told them how amazing Grandma Mae had been my entire life, I told them I missed them so fiercely that sometimes I have to splash water on my face just to get myself breathing again, I told them all about MaeDay, and everything about my friends. I talked to them the entire day. I know you think I'm exaggerating, but I am not. I talked to them for about nine straight hours. I spoke to them as I put my laundry away, cleaned the bathroom, made food. I turned on a movie in the afternoon and talked to them about the movie during the movie. Once the movie ended, I made dinner and sat at the table and set place settings for them as well. Most people would probably think it's crazy that I did that, but it felt right. It felt rude to leave them out. For the first time in fourteen years, I felt like I could communicate with my parents and I was embracing the opportunity.

My voice was gone by 6:30 pm. It was scratchy and hoarse. My vocal cords were raw and I just couldn't say one more word. I smiled and knew they understood, I got in my bed, enjoying the chilly air conditioning and slept so soundly knowing my parents were supporting and helping me. Simply that they were just there.

That night I dreamt of my parents and me walking down the road. Then, my dream changed and they were in Grandma Mae's office at work, watching her work. Next, they were sitting in the towncar with me while I traveled home from work.

I woke up feeling reassured. They would be with me, always. No matter where I went, they would be with me. I was overjoyed. I got dressed for work, excited to tell Mae everything.

Mae, of course, had experienced many visitations from them over the years. She knew once I allowed it, I would as well. She was happy for me and was even happier I took time off to spend the day with them. We allowed ourselves a few moments to cry before getting to work.

The extraordinary attachment I had to my locket multiplied tenfold that day. I would find myself holding it and tracing its outline anytime I needed comfort. It had been so meaningful before the air conditioning incident, but it meant even more after. I loved having them near, I needed to have them near.

I continued to dream of them and they sent me messages every week. I loved when I would see something that reminded me of them. It felt as if a new chapter of my life had begun.

My new ritual at night began about a week after the air conditioning went out. I would eat dinner with my parents every night. I would always set empty plates out for them, and then I would tell them about my day. I would tell them about everything that happened and anything I thought they would find funny or would make them proud.

Tonight, the night before my twenty-fifth birthday, I sit down with my parents for dinner. I made myself my favorite chicken dish and poured myself a glass of wine to celebrate my birthday with my parents.

"So, work was long but good today. First, I had a meeting with Dayvonne, she leads product testing and consumer feedback, and she had some really interesting ideas." I tell my parents all about my meetings and how each department is doing. I finish my food quickly, but sit there for a while, letting myself leisurely sip my wine.

"I have my birthday party tomorrow, I hope you'll both come. It's at a bar just down the street. I'll understand if you need to visit someone else, but it should be fun and you'll get to see a lot of people. In fact, Milo might be there! Do you remember Milo? He used to live down the street from Grandma's Hamptons house. He was still small and scrawny when you knew him. He used to be so odd and awkward, but not anymore! Now he's gorgeous." I pause and take a sip of wine. "If we end up coming back here tomorrow night, I'm sorry but you'll have to go home with Grandma Mae because you will not be welcome!"

The light in my bedroom goes off and I chuckle. "Oh Dad, calm down. Everything will be fine."

February 14*th*

I wake up this morning exhilarated to start my day, my first birthday with my parents in more than a decade. I get ready and tell them how happy I am that they are able to be with me today. I go for a run and come back to get dressed to meet Grandma Mae for lunch. We plan to have a lovely lunch together, probably involving champagne knowing my wild grandmother, and then to go out and buy me a party dress for tonight. Sounds like the perfect day.

We are in Bergdorf's after enjoying a delicious lunch, which as expected did include champagne. I have tried on, easily, twenty dresses and outfits at this point. Nothing that I put on, though, has excited me or Grandma Mae. We take a break to have some more champagne.

"Thanks for all of this, GM, you're the best grandmother anyone has ever had!" I lean over and kiss her cheek. She reaches up and touches the spot I've kissed, like she is cherishing the touch.

"Of course! Only the best for my sweetest granddaughter," she says as she gives me a gentle shove

---

with her shoulder. I give her my standard eye roll at this response.

"I'm excited for tonight,I think it's going to be really fun," I tell her. "I hope my parents come."

"Even if they don't, you can always tell them about it tomorrow." She pats the top of my thigh and then lets her hand rest there.

"I have selected a few more items I think will look stunning on you," the Bergdorf stylist announces. Our glances snap to her face and we follow her back into the personal fitting room.

I walk in and see the different dresses hanging up, and one catches my eye immediately. It is black with white stars outlined all over it; they are overlapping and look almost as if they are neon lights. The left side is a full sleeve and a puffed shoulder and the right side is sleeveless. It cinches at the waist with a belt made of the same material and lands about mid-thigh. I put it on and it fits perfectly. It's form-fitting, but not too tight. It accentuates all my fabulous parts while hiding all of my not so fantastic areas. No dress has ever felt this perfectly made for me in my entire life.

I walk out knowing I am buying this dress, no matter the price. As soon as I step out of the fitting room and see Grandma Mae's face, I know she feels the same way.

"That's it. That's the one," Mae says with glistening eyes.

"I agree!"

The Bergdorf glam squad freshens us up and we get fitted into our new dresses (yes, Mae got one, too). Mae had also insisted on buying us new shoes. She bought me a pair of chrome heels that are to die for. She bought herself some black kitten heels, and, as always, she is adorable yet stylish. We are feeling extra spectacular as Hank drives us to the bar for the party. Grandma Mae tells me on the way over that she has already pre-ordered many off-the-menu catering items and once again, there is an open bar.

We walk in the door arm-in-arm and I am surprised by the number of people there. There is applause and cheering so loud, I cover my ears. Once I see my friends, I start screaming as well and we all hug one another with Mae in tow. She leaves us once she sees Annie and we all head to the bar to order drinks. It is packed and difficult to move, so it takes us a minute to make our way up to the bar.

I don't recognize more than a handful of people as we travel as a group toward the two bartenders that have been hired for my party. It takes us more time than it should to work our way through the crowd. We are ducking around people and asking everyone to excuse us as we push past them. How many people did Grandma Mae invite?!

After we finally have drinks in our hands and we are moving to the back corner, a less crowded corner of the bar, I feel a hand on my elbow.

"Valentina, happy birthday!" It's Colt.

"Hi Colt, thank you. Thank you for coming." I'm not quite sure what to say. Niceties seem to be appropriate.

"Of course." He pauses and does not take his eyes off of my face. "I must tell you… when I saw you walk in, I had to come find you. You look unbelievable" His eyes quickly find the floor and he scratches the back of his neck. "I mean, you look really beautiful."

I feel Robin elbow me in the ribs. "Oh, uh, thank you, Colt." I'm a little surprised by his compliment, but just buzzed enough to fight through it.

"Well," he seems unsure of what to say next. "Well, have a good night. I'll see you around." He mimes tipping his hat at me and walks away quickly, the girls and I erupt in giggles.

"So, we've been meaning to thank you for our honeymoon," Mackie says to me. "The upgrades, first class, the hotel, everything was spectacular. We don't know how to thank you."

"Mackie, you gave one of my very best friends the happiness we all can only dream of. You don't need to thank me for anything. Your happiness is thanks enough."

"It feels too generous…"

"It shouldn't. It's what I can afford and what I want to give you."

"OK, well thanks all the same." I can tell Mackie is highly uncomfortable at this point. I give her a hug and a kiss on the cheek and walk away, giving her time to recover.

And that's when I see him. Skin still tanned, even though it is February, with hair bleached from the sun, and a body built to stop traffic. It's Milo. He's standing across the bar, wearing a black suit with a white shirt underneath, unbuttoned of course. He's holding a tumbler of brown liquor and looking at me. Damn, he's sexy. Before I can register what's happening, he's gliding toward me. It's as if he's moving across clouds, he's so smooth.

"Lenni," he opens.

"Hi Milo. I'm so happy you could make it."

"I promised you I would." He takes a swig of his liquor. I take a dainty sip of my wine in return. I know I am touching my hair and shifting my weight, but I can't help it. Milo makes me too aware of everything.

"Thanks for coming." I blink my false lashes too many times. "How long are you in the city?"

"Hm, what's that?" He seems distracted. "Oh, not too long. I'm staying with a friend. He's meeting me here in a bit, I hope you don't mind."

I'm not sure what to make of this. "No, not at all. That's fine!" I know my voice is too loud and overly enthusiastic. I need to calm myself.

"Cool."

"So, Milo, I've been wondering what you've been up to? What do you do for a living? Where are you living?"

"Oh, uh, yeah, I'm about to finish law school and I'm going to take the bar in Connecticut and New York."

"Wow, that's incredible! Very impressive! Congratulations!"

"Yeah… I don't know if it's that serious." He is clearly uncomfortable and begins looking around the room.

"I'm sorry, I just think it's great you're finishing law school. Not everyone can achieve that." Silence. "So what university are you at?"

"Yale." More looking around.

"Wow, Yale." I try to keep my excitement to a minimum since he is clearly unhappy with any sort of attention.

"Yup. So, hey, I'm gonna step out and call my buddy. I'll see ya," Milo says as he walks out of the bar and slides his glass across the nearest table. What just happened? The conversation ended so abruptly, I might have whiplash. Why did he run away from me? Am I so horrible he can't stand to even talk to me?

I try to let the conversation with Milo go, but I think back to it all night long. We all dance and drink and have a great time together. My friends leave one by one, and before I know it, I am left alone in the bar with the two bartenders, Jake and Josh. They offer to call me a cab or walk me home, but since I only live two blocks away, I sweetly decline. I thank them too much for their kind offers, ensure my grandmother has left a generous tip, put on my coat, and leave.

I walk home in the freezing air, watching my breath blow out in a white puff and then disappear. Watching my breath against the dark sky, I realize I am sad for two reasons. One because I know my parents are not with me. I haven't felt them since I had the conversation with Mackie about their honeymoon. I'm guessing they anticipated something with Milo and bolted. Which brings me to the second reason I'm sad: Milo. What is it about me that he hates so much? Am I too annoying? Too ugly? Too dumb?

I arrive at my building, a little sad yet again that Gene isn't there. I know he works the day shift but I would love to see him right now. I shrug off the emptiness of the lobby and begin my climb up the stairs. I know I've had too much wine because I stumble over a step or two and immediately laugh at myself. It is my birthday after all.

Relieved to finally be on my floor, I stop halfway down the hall to take off my shoes. The chrome heels are amazing, but I cannot wear them one more moment. I walk up to my front door and wave to myself on the camera. A moment after I wave, my phone dings with a notification that motion has been censored by the camera. I chuckle that I notified myself of my own arrival and pull out my apartment key. I glance down to check my tape and stop.

For the first time in two years, the tape is not in place. It's on the door, but not on the door jam. I know someone has been through this door and I panic. I run to the elevator and push the button at least ten times. I am too afraid to be in the stairwell by myself and I need the elevator to carry me to safety NOW.

It dings, announcing its arrival and I jump in. I push the button telling the elevator doors to close until they do. To be clear, there is no one in the hallway or the elevator. I am just so terrified of the tape being disturbed that I am losing all control.

When the elevator arrives on the ground floor, I am unsure if I should leave my building in case there is someone, namely Rich, here in the building. Or is it more dangerous to go out into the dark streets of the city alone? What if Rich is waiting outside my building? What if he was in my apartment and will come out looking for me? I'm scaring myself with all of the options that could potentially put me in harm's way or keep me safe. I decide to check the camera app before going anywhere.

I pull it up and there are no motion notifications outside of my own. I watch back for hours looking at the hallway and other than seeing my neighbors walk to their doors, there is nothing of interest on the camera. I don't know what to do. I know I cannot go into my apartment at this moment, but I also don't want to leave the building. If I call one of my friends or Grandma Mae, this will turn into a much larger issue than I want.

I decide to bite the bullet and call the most unexpected person.

"Valentina?"

"Hi, yes, it's me. I'm sorry to call so late." I'm nervous and breathing too quickly.

"Hey, what's up?" He's clearly been sleeping, his voice is scratchy and he sounds groggy.

"Oh, um, you know how you told me I have your number and I can use it?"

"What's wrong?" Colt's voice is much more alert. I can almost hear him sitting up in bed.

"Um, well, it's maybe nothing…"

"Where are you?" I can hear him rustling around.

"I'm at my apartment building, and I really don't know if anything is actually wrong. I just came home and for the first time the tape isn't right. I mean, you were there for the first time the tape wasn't right, so I guess this is the second time…" I'm nervous and tipsy and sputtering words out as they come into my mind.

"Did you go in?" More rustling.

"No, but I was thinking maybe you could just stay on the phone with me while I go in? That way you could just call the police if you hear a scream or something? I checked my camera app and no one came in through the front door so I don't think there's someone in there. Maybe the wind blew the tape off, I mean there's no actual wind in the hallway, but you know. I was just thinking of someone being around for backup. There's no doorman on duty or I'd have him do it, I just thought if you're willing to talk to me while I walk in - "

"Valentina!" I hear a large slam.

"Yeah?"

"Where are you in your apartment building?"

"I'm in the lobby."

"Do. Not. Move." His voice is so deep and scary, I cannot respond for a moment. "I fucking mean it, do not move from the lobby. *Fuck*. Unless someone comes in and scares you, then run out into the middle of the sidewalk screaming. Do you hear me?"

"Yes, I hear you, but no one is around - "

"Great. Stay there, I am in a cab around the corner. Don't move."

"Ok, but you didn't need to come. I can just go in while speaking to you on the phone."

"Absolutely not! Do not enter your apartment without me!"

"Ohmygod, chill. I already told you that I'm in the lobby."

"Valentina, I cannot *chill*. You just told me your tape isn't right."

"Ugh, I should have never told you about my tape."

"It was the smartest decision you've ever made. I'm pulling up now." The line cuts.

I zip my phone inside my purse and as I look up, Colt is walking in. He's wearing a long, black winter coat over a white hoodie sweatshirt and gray sweatpants. There is no reason for this outfit to look good on anyone, but on Colt it is fucking sexy. His hair is a mess from sleep and he has major scruff on his stellar jaw, which by the way, is ticking like crazy right now.

"Hey Colt, thanks for coming, but you didn't need to do that! We could have just stayed on the phone with each other!"

Colt's eyes are snapping all over the lobby. They eventually find their way back to me. They search my face before he gently pushes me down into a chair in the lobby.

"Stay here."

"No."

"Yes." He stomps toward the stairs.

"Colt!" I scream. My desperation is clear in my voice and I do not care. Colt has known about my tape for two years and he hasn't told anyone. I know I can trust him.

"Don't leave me!" He stops and turns to me in one quick motion. I run to him. "Colt, please, don't leave me!"

His expression softens. "Valentina…"

"Colt, I'm sorry, I know I had no right to call you and maybe I shouldn't have. But I'm scared, terrified might be a better word. I'm terrified and I don't want you to leave me alone down here in this lobby where anyone can come in. Rich can come in!" My words are coming out too fast and my voice sounds strange, even to me. My hands are shaking and I am tapping his chest uncontrollably.

"Rich? Is he the guy you were talking to at your party tonight?" His face is *angry*.

It takes me a moment to understand that he is referring to Milo. "No! No, not at all. That was Milo. I grew up with him. Rich is… Rich is no one."

"Then why are you afraid of him? *Terrified* of him?"

I blow out a frustrated breath. "I went on one date with him and then refused a second. He showed up here at my apartment months later even though he didn't pick me up here or walk me home."

"He came here? Just the one time?" His face is still angry. His jaw muscle is still ticking.

"Um, yeah…"

"I don't believe you."

"I think I saw him another time outside my building one morning when I went to work. But I wasn't absolutely sure."

"Fuck, does your security team know about him?" His hands are running through his hair in unease.

"I'm my security team, so yes."

He runs his hand down his face and growls in frustration. "Valentina, tell me this moment that you have personal security."

"I installed an alarm system and a motion activated camera outside my apartment. That's all I need!" The way he looks at me, with such disappointment, I cannot stand it. "Don't forget about my tape system!"

"Let me get this all straight. First, you are your own personal security team?"

"Right." I pause. I hold up a finger to emphasize my point. "And doing a marvelous job, might I add."

This earns me a side eye. "Second, you haven't told anyone, other than me, about your need for security or your *tape system*."

"Correct."

"Third, you failed to mention to anyone, including myself," he points to his own chest, "that there is a man currently stalking you."

"Wrong!" He looks affronted at this outburst of mine.

"You've told someone about it?" He backs up a step. "Who? Milo?"

I shake my head in confusion. What is he talking about? "No, no I haven't told anyone about anything. When I

76

said you were wrong, I meant that you were wrong about the stalking. No one is stalking me."

"Valentina." He says my name barely above a whisper. "Open your eyes. Many, many things are going to change tomorrow."

"Colt, everything is fine!"

"Lenni."

"Don't 'Lenni' me!"

"Come on, let's go check out your apartment." He turns away from me and I am angry. This is exactly the reason I do not want a boyfriend. They order you around and take away your freedoms. I don't need Colt telling me what to do in my own apartment building.

"I don't need you! I will go alone, you can go home! I should have never called you!" I'm irrationally furious now. I know Colt is trying to help, and he told me to use his number, but he is also being incredibly annoying in the process. If he tells everyone about this, Mae could have a heart attack. My friends will be relentless. Everyone will want me to move. I can't move, I finally have my parents back!

"Valentina, I can go home, but if that happens - you are coming with me." His voice is calm, yet firm. He is staring at me with such intensity, I have to shift my weight. He grabs my hand as if asking the question of where we are spending the night. I sigh. I don't have the energy to argue with him. He's won.

"That's not necessary. Let's go." I motion toward the elevator doors.

Once we're on my floor, Colt stops about halfway down. He turns, still holding my hand, and looks at me. "Thank you for calling me."

"Um, you're welcome?"

"If you are ever in trouble, or need help with anything, you call me."

Not only am I too tired to fight, but now that we're near my door, I am so happy to have him here. I nod in agreement. "Ok."

Without another word, we walk down the hallway. Colt bends down to inspect my broken tape. He holds his hand out for the key and scoots me behind him. We enter and when he hears the alarm beeping and asking for the code he looks at me. I start entering it and he looks away, giving me privacy.

Once the alarm is off and the front door is shut. Colt holds a finger up to his lips, telling me to be quiet. He points to the ground, silently telling me to stay there. Then he points to the alarm panel. He's telling me to use it if I need to. I nod.

He slowly walks into my apartment, entering the kitchen first. When he sees no one in there, he takes a large knife out of the butcher block before going into my bedroom and bathroom. He reappears a minute later, alone.

"There's no one here," Colt announces. He sighs and lays the knife on the kitchen counter. He scrubs his hand down his face again and sighs deeply. He seems to be relieved.

"I'm so sorry, I'm so embarrassed that I called you," I confess. I'm having so many emotions about the night that I feel my eyes fill with tears. My throat constricts and I put my face in my hands.

"Valentina, don't be embarrassed," Colt says. I feel him touch my shoulder.

I'm so desperate for human comfort that I spin around and fall into Colt's embrace. I let him hug me and hold me close. I let a long sigh release while he embraces me. For the first time in a very long time, I feel safe.

I eventually pull away and look at Colt's face. For a fleeting moment, I think about kissing him. I was not prepared for him to show up all sexy and sleepy. I've never seen him in something so casual before, and he looks just as good in sweats as he does in a suit. I am taken aback at how his toughness and protection are such turn ons. I've always thought I am a strong independent woman who doesn't need anyone. I guess that is technically true, but it is so nice having Colt here with me. Having him help and comfort me while I'm petrified and alone is making me want a boyfriend. Well, it's making me want one more than I have ever wanted one before. I've been so worried about losing my freedom to a man, I never saw the amazing benefits a man could offer. One look at Colt, and I know kissing me is on his mind as well. He is staring at my lips and leaning toward me. I am so thrown by this change of events and suddenly thinking about the terror of kissing an employee that I shake my head to get myself out of the moment. Something catches my eye.

"Valentina?" He notices my attention has shifted.

I pause. "What is that?" I point to the wall next to the refrigerator. There is a piece of paper taped to the wall. I pull away from Colt and stomp over to rip it off the wall.

Dearest Valentina,

I'm sorry I missed wishing you happy birthday in person. I couldn't wait any longer. I will be back though, don't worry.

All my love

Colt yanks it from my hands before I can finish reading it. I don't need to, I know what it says.

"The fuck he isn't stalking you!" Colt's eyes are wide and glaring at me. His eyes travel all over my body. I'm sure they see me shaking and scared, which is exactly what I am. "Come on, let's get you ready for bed."

He puts a gentle hand on my back and leads me into my bedroom. We walk into my closet and I pick out pajamas. Colt leaves the closet and closes the door behind him while I get dressed. I open the door and walk back into my bedroom and he is standing outside my closet, his arms crossed over his chest, his legs spread wide, and his back to the closet door.

He watches me brush my teeth and wash my face. He tucks me into bed and promises he will stay the night. I am so comforted by his presence and his promises, I don't fight it. I let him take care of me.

I wake up in a fog. My eyes feel dry, my head feels too heavy. I blink a few times until all the memories of the night before rush back to me like a river rushing toward a waterfall. My body fills with the regret of telling Colt, and well… everything. I am dreading going out into my living room. Since Colt promised to stay the night, I'm sure he did and is in just outside my bedroom door.

I would rather eat only lima beans for three days straight than go out there and face Colt. What is he going to say? Who is he going to tell? I want to make sure I am in charge of my own life. I cannot allow him to try to control anything about me.

I am simultaneously trying to forget how safe I felt with him and how dangerously close I came to kissing him last night. I wanted to, in a big, bad way. I try not to let myself think about how closely he leaned in or how I could feel his breath on my lips because he was as into the moment as I was. I will not think about how great it felt to have someone protect me. I've never allowed that before and now I'm not sure why not.

"Mom, please help me get out of this bed and go face that man," I whisper toward the ceiling. My mother wastes no time. A moment later, my foot is tingling. It's tingling in that terrible, annoying way that only means one thing. It has fallen asleep. I move my toes and twist my ankle to no avail. If anything, the tingles are getting worse. I am going to have to stand up and walk on my foot to get this horrible feeling to stop. Touché, mom.

I stand up and start moving around my room. Immediately, the crazy feeling in my foot stops. I get a robe out of my closet and wrap it around myself. I go to the window and peek outside for just a moment. It's snowing and that brings a smile to my face. As one last act of stalling, I go to my bed and take the small Snowshoe Hare blanket. I wrap it around myself for one extra layer of protection.

The instant I open the door, I smell coffee. If Colt thought that serving me coffee first would improve my mood, well, then he thought right.

"Morning," I say to Colt, who is sitting on my couch watching the TV on silent.

"Hey, how'd you sleep?"

"Actually, really well." I take a sip of the coffee I just poured and it tastes like heaven. "I'm sorry that you're still here. Did you sleep at all?" I'm so embarrassed about him spending the night in my apartment, I still haven't looked at him.

"Yeah, a little on the couch."

I stay hidden behind the barrier of my kitchen counter as long as he lets me. Which isn't long. About one minute to be exact.

"Can we talk?" He turns the television off.

"Uh, sure." I'm nervous and there is a flicker of anxiety in my chest. "What do you want to talk about?"

He holds up his hand and starts ticking his list off of his fingers. "All of it. Rich. The tape. Lack of a security team. *The note*. Where would you like to begin?"

I can tell he is not going to drop any of this, so it's time to face the music. I take my mug and go sit on the coffee table in front of the couch so we are facing one another. I'm taking control of the situation.

"Let's start at the beginning. I went on a date with Rich ages ago. He was horrible to everyone at the restaurant. My friends and I ended up calling him Rude Rich because he was such a jerk. Then one night, months later, Gene buzzed me. He told me that there was someone in the lobby asking for me. So I went down and he was clearly super drunk. I kicked him out. The next day I started taping my door."

"How did he know where you lived?"

"I have no idea. We met at the restaurant and I didn't let him walk me home. He must have followed me," I explain. "Quickly after he showed up here, I had an alarm system installed. Then months after that, I felt like I was being followed so I started taking a car service to and from work

---

81

and had the motion-activated camera installed outside my apartment."

"We need to watch that," he says, his jaw ticking once again.

"I watched it before I called you and there is nothing on it. It doesn't make sense."

"Well, we need to watch it again then."

"Ok, whatever," I say and sit up taller. I cross my legs and rest my coffee on my knee.

"Why haven't you told anyone about this?" His tone is calm but stern. I can tell he is trying to keep his cool so he doesn't scare me.

"Because if Mae finds out, I'm afraid she'll have a heart attack or give herself an ulcer. She is too old to deal with stuff like this."

"OK, what about your friends? Or hiring a security detail?" He is speaking slowly, as if I am a child that he is trying to explain a hard math problem to.

I shrug. "They'll bother me to move."

"That was my next point." He sits up and leans toward me. He lifts his coffee mug in my direction. "You need to move."

"No. I don't." I use a firm tone to let him know this topic is not open for discussion.

"Yes. You do." He did not get the memo.

"I won't." There, take that.

"You won't move?" He's suspicious now. This doesn't make sense to him. "Why not?"

I decide to give him the truth, just not the whole truth. "This apartment is the last connection I have to my parents and I will not sell it. I love it here."

His face muscles relax a bit and he does the very slight nod that usually accompanies an epiphany. He might as well be saying "Ohhhhh."

"Since you bought this place with your parents' money, you want to stay here." Sure, let's go with that. He's not asking a question, so I have nothing to confirm or deny. To my credit, that was the exact reason that I did not want to sell, until about six months ago.

"Well, if you want me to keep your secret," he opens.

"I do."

"Then I have some conditions." I grit my teeth to keep from rolling my eyes at him. "First, you have to hire personal security."

Even though I knew it was coming, I wasn't expecting such a big dog to be let out of the cage first. "Seriously?"

"If you have a problem with that one, you're definitely not going to like the rest. You should just tell everyone and then you won't have to deal with my conditions." He knows he has me. Damnit.

"Go on..." I say through my gritted teeth.

"Two, I want access to your exterior camera."

"FOR WHAT?" My screeching tone surprises even me. But what the hell? That seems ridiculous.

"To make sure he doesn't come back, obviously." He leans all the way back on the couch and puts one ankle on top of his opposite knee.

"Wouldn't that be what the security team is for?"

"Ideally, your security would be with you. This way I can keep an eye on the hive to make sure it's safe for the Queen to return."

"No, nuh uh, this seems like a total invasion of my privacy. I will not give up my freedom." I might as well stomp my feet and hold my breath.

He lifts his shoulders and lets them drop as if he doesn't have a care in the world. "Those are my terms. Do you want to hear the third one or should we just call Mae now?"

"There's *more*?!"

"Just one. Want to hear it?"

I wave my hand in a 'get it over with' gesture.

"I will be making unannounced visits and occasionally walking you home. I already know you're going to ask why." He's right, I was. "And the answer is simple, I want him to see you with another man. That's the best technique to scare him away."

"This is fucking blackmail, you know."

"It's not. Those are my conditions for keeping your secret. I *want* to tell everyone. I'm pretty sure that blackmail usually involves money, which I want none. Also, the conditions don't benefit me in any way. They are for your well-being. " Fuck if he doesn't have a point.

"What if I get a boyfriend?" That question puts a look on his face that I've never seen. Shock is in his expression, maybe mixed with confusion, and possibly a little bit of hurt? His face makes me want to retract my question, but I don't. I wait to hear what his response will be.

"Well, in that case, I would still require camera access so I can watch your door when you're not home, but I would stop visiting or walking you home." He doesn't make eye contact with me while he speaks and now I'm the one feeling a little hurt.

"Ok, deal." I hold out my hand to him. He looks at my hand, then at my face, then back to my hand before he takes it in his and shakes it. Neither of us let go and we continue to shake hands for far too long. Finally, he stops the shaking motion. He holds my hand for a couple extra seconds, and then lets go.

He stands up and grabs his coat that is along the back of the couch. "I am going to go home and get some sleep. I'll send you names of some security companies this afternoon."

"Hey, can't I make you breakfast before you go? As a thank you for helping me last night," I offer. I keep my voice light and friendly.

He puts his coat on and walks toward the door. He stops and turns around. "My help doesn't come with a payment plan. Just keep yourself safe and share the camera app with me. I expect to have it before I get home. And I don't live far."

This time, I allow myself to roll my eyes. "Yessir." I give him a salute.

He turns and walks to the door. "Goodbye, Valentina."

"Goodbye, Colt."

I send him the app thirty minutes later just to rebel against his demands. I am sure he was home long before I shared access with him. Everything that happened last night and this morning leaves me with only one goal for the upcoming year: get Colt out of my personal life.

Twenty-Six

February 13th

I had many ideas of different strategies to get Colt out of my personal life. My initial thought was to be so annoying, he would actively find ways to avoid me. I immediately enacted this plan to my fullest capability. This blew up in my face, also pretty immediately. No matter my level of rudeness, pettiness, bossiness - Colt never faltered. He carried on as if I was acting like a normal human. He still watched my camera (I know this because I could see every time he logged on - I made sure of this before sharing access with him). He would still randomly decide to walk me home or ride home with me some days (I am almost positive these "random" trips coincided with the days I was most annoying. It was as if Colt knew that it was a punishment and forced me to be closer to him on the days I wanted to the least). He would still drop by whenever he wanted (in the beginning this occurred way more than I anticipated). As a result, I gave up on this tactic decently early. It was exhausting being a terrible person.

My next idea was to be compliant. Or at least lead him to believe I was being complaint. True to his word, Colt sent me the contacts for three different personal security teams after he left my apartment almost a year ago. He told me I had to choose one or he would choose one for me. Not wanting him to control any further aspect of my life, I called all three and made a quick decision. It ended up being the perfect decision and I absolutely love my team. They are with me *a lot*, way more than I feel is necessary, but they are both silent. Therefore, I love them. One is a sleek looking

---

woman who never, and I mean *never*, smiles. Her name is Gina. The man is named Rob, and he seems a bit more carefree, but that's not saying much. He's built like a brick shithouse, is bald, and only wears black. There's only ever one person with me at a time, but both are very quiet and inconspicuous. Not to mention, they make me feel very safe. Given that is their sole job duty, they are definitely excelling.

I had high hopes that having security would give Colt a reason to back off, but again no dice. Whenever he sees Gina or Rob in the lobby at work or on the street by my apartment, he smiles. Not just a nice, pleasant grin - a full blown smile. It's weird the amount of joy these two people, who never smile or appear to be happy themselves, bring Colt.

My last idea to rid myself of Colt's oversight, was the best idea. It would undoubtedly work. Unfortunately, this plan is much easier to fantasize about than to actually accomplish. I needed to get a boyfriend.

Originally, a week or so after my birthday, I thought of all the ways I could get a man to fall in love with me and push away Colt. After all, isn't that what he said would be the best way to scare off Rich? But then, during my plotting, I had a wave of guilt hit me. It took my breath away, just as if someone had thrown a cup of cold water on me in the middle of a hot shower. It felt like I was tricking or duping a person to love someone who didn't actually exist. And that felt awful. How could I ever play with someone's emotions like that? I would never be able to keep up such a façade, and would definitely end up crying, or vomiting, or fainting from the wrongfulness of it all. No, there was no way I could inorganically have a relationship with someone.

For a brief period of time, I considered paying someone to be my boyfriend. Hire a man who knew he was simply there to pretend to like me, sleep on my couch, go out to dinner with me only to drive away another man. Short of authentically dating someone, this was the only other boyfriend scenario I could fathom.

One day, just as spring was starting to make its first appearance, I realized that the boyfriend plan had to die. All I

---

was doing was trading one man's control for another's. I wasn't even interested in having a serious boyfriend, and there I was scheming how to make someone fall in love with me, or worse, *pay* someone to pretend they liked me. I took the blooming flowers and the green trees as a sign that I, too, needed a fresh start.

I had a long hard talk with myself, and my parents, about my future and my safety. I knew what I had to do. It took me almost three months to accept it, but it was obvious I needed help with my safety. I had hired help. Great! I could easily let them do their jobs and we all get along harmoniously. I had digital help. These were amazing technological accomplishments, that I could also allow to do their jobs. Cameras are made to record, alarms are meant to sound. Easy enough.

It's the last bit of help that I had been fighting. Colt. He was just an extra set of eyes and ears that were constantly looking out for me. I loathed this, because it was not his job personally or professionally. He had no intimate attachment to me so he should not care about my safety on such a familiar level. It was also not his concern to have any sort of care about my wellbeing. Hell, the man worked in marketing for a nail polish company! Why was he acting like the damn Terminator?

Regardless, and whatever his reasoning, Colt had accepted this duty that no one appointed him to. He was spearheading this movement, and I just had to accept it. Fighting him and pushing back was getting me nowhere.

During the summer months, I decided to be more open about the need for security. Grandma Mae hadn't given me too much of an inquisition about it, but when it continued and then increased over the months after my birthday, she started to worry. I eventually told her that I wasn't always feeling completely safe and comfortable around my apartment. She didn't press too much more, but she did ask a few follow-up questions that I was able to generalize my way out of.

All of that led us here. In my grandmother's office, the day before my twenty-sixth birthday. Gina will be here soon.

Due to the high security measures at the office, we all (by 'all' I mean myself, Gina, Rob, and of course Colt) agree it is not necessary for anyone to accompany me at work. Mae and I have been going over the upcoming summer and autumn colors for hours. I'm feeling unusually drained today. I just want to put my head down on Mae's desk. It's hard to resist doing just that, especially since the ability to focus has completely vacated my body.

"My darling, why don't you go home?" Mae suggests. She rubs my back and looks down at me with a worried expression.

"Hm? Oh, I'm fine, Grandma," I reassure her.

"You're clearly run down! You've been working too much. Go home." She has given up all pretenses of kindness and crossed over to passing out demands. She isn't wrong, though. I *have* been working a lot of hours.

Leaving work early, though, doesn't exactly excite me. Amy and Mackie are deep into the longest honeymoon phase of all time. Nisha is getting more and more serious with Max, they are basically living at his place. Ansley is so fixated on her work, I think I see her less than Nisha or Amy. My friends are always busy and having a bodyguard watch me all night doesn't necessarily add up to me wanting to be home. I'd rather stay late and work than head home and do nothing alone. I am fully aware how desperately I need a hobby.

The exhaustion feels like too much, though. I can barely hold my head up and keep my eyes open. Both of those seem strenuous, which is just ludicrous.

"OK, thanks GM. I'll see you tomorrow for brunch." I stand up and leave her office. As I enter my own, I send Gina a text saying I am leaving work early. She texts back and says she'll be here in twenty minutes and asks me to wait. I sigh and weigh my options. Do I leave without her, piss her off, and possibly put myself in danger? I am leaning toward this option, because it gets me to my bed sooner than the other option. The other option is to wait. Neither is entirely appealing. I decide to clean up my desk and check my emails one last time. If she's not here by then, I will tell

—

her to just meet me at my apartment and she'll have to deal with it.

I finish my tasks in about five minutes and decide to leave. I'm too tired to wait. I pack up, turn off my office light, and double check that my office door is locked. I turn around and walk directly into someone.

"Whoa, hey, you alright?" I should have known it was Colt since it felt like I walked into a statue.

"Yeah, fine, just going home." I barely acknowledge him. I walk past and try to get to the elevator as quickly as I can.

"Hang on. Valentina!" I hear him call my name, but I keep walking. His footsteps are getting closer. "You don't look fine."

"I'm just overworked, I need to go to bed." I walk toward the elevators again.

"I'll walk with you," he offers.

"I'm fine, go back to work." I wave my arm toward his office.

"I'll walk down to the lobby with you." I roll my eyes. There is no use fighting him.

We ride down to the bottom floor together in silence. I've gotten to the point with Colt that I don't feel the need to fill any silence between us. He seems just as comfortable in the quiet. I appreciate that because I don't have enough energy to participate in small talk or fake interest with him. He isn't forcing me to do either and I am relieved. I can just be my tired, grumpy self with him in this elevator and he doesn't expect anything more.

The door opens and he waits for me to exit first. He follows me all the way out the front doors and I look for the Uber that I called while we were in the elevator. My car service isn't expecting to pick me up for another couple hours and I am too tired to walk. I think I see it, a block away and sitting at a stoplight.

"Wait, where's Gina or Rob?" Colt is holding his hand up to his forehead, blocking the sun and helping him to see better.

"Gina didn't plan on me leaving early so she is just going to meet me at my apartment," I explain.

"You can't be serious?" His jaw is ticking.

"I am." I hope mine is ticking, too. I am not in the mood for a lecture.

"Valentina, this is unacceptable. This isn't safe!" He throws his hands in the air, disgusted with me.

I've reached the point of exhaustion and weariness that I can feel my throat choking up and the tears gathering behind my eyes. I shake my head and look him in the eyes. "Colt, I can't do this."

All of the air leaves his body and he completely deflates. He can see I am on the verge of tears and that I am too tired to argue with him. "Ok… ok." He simply nods his head in agreement.

"Hey! Valentina?!" A voice draws our attention. My Uber driver is yelling at me from a lowered passenger window. We both look at him. Colt looks at me and nods again. He walks over and opens the backdoor for me. I know before it happens that he is going to get in behind me. He does.

We drive back to my apartment, again in silence. I can barely keep my eyes open but I occupy myself by texting Gina that Colt is with me and to meet us back at my apartment. I also cancel my car for the afternoon trip home.

"Hey, it looks like there is an accident up ahead. Might be faster to walk," the grouchy driver announces.

I look up ahead and sure enough, there is traffic stopped as far as I can see. I check the cross streets and realize we are only three blocks away from my apartment. It feels like my body is running on empty, but I can handle three blocks.

"Thanks," I say and nod to Colt to get out of the car. He scoots across and gets out, holding the door open for me to follow him. Once we are out of the car and on the sidewalk, Colt wraps his arm around me to help support my weight as we walk. Ever since the moment we almost kissed, he never touches me. It's obvious how much he actually avoids touching me. For so much of his body to be touching so much of my body, then he can clearly see how run down I am. I am grateful, for the first time, that he offered to help me get home.

We haven't walked more than fifty steps when I see him. He's walking toward us, half a block away. He hasn't seen me yet and is looking down at his phone. Colt's grip tightens on me just enough for me to wonder if he recognizes Milo from my birthday party. It wouldn't be difficult for anyone to remember him, he's memorably gorgeous.

Milo looks up when he's just ten or so feet in front of us. Recognition lights up his face. After the excitement of seeing someone you know on a crowded street leaves his expression, he's clearly taken aback by another man with his arms around me. He rearranges his features quickly to hide his surprise. Colt makes a low noise, close to a growl, next to me. I feel it rumble in his chest more than I hear it.

"Valley Girl! Hi! How are you?" Milo is looking directly at me. He does not acknowledge Colt in any way.

"Hi, Milo. I'm fine, thank you. I'm sure you remember Colt from my birthday party." I motion toward Colt's chest. "How are you?"

"You're not fine," Colt interjects. He is looking down at me, still with his arm around me. He looks up to Milo. "I'm afraid she's overworked and exhausted. She needs to get home."

Milo doesn't get the hint and I am furious and mortified that Colt thought he could speak for me. My mouth hangs open for a moment while Milo responds. "I'm sorry to hear that. I would have thought working for your grandmother, you wouldn't..." his eyes flick between us, "have such demanding hours."

"Well, you thought wrong." I am full blown pissed off. "I work very hard for the company because I want to do my best and do what is right for the company I love. I am not 'overworked' as Colt puts it. I am simply tired. I have been working more hours than normal lately, but that is my doing and no one else's."

I try to move out of Colt's grasp. He holds on tighter. Milo watches it all.

"Wait, I'm confused," Milo says, his brow dipping and confusion crossing his face.

"About what?" I inquire, still squirming. Colt is holding me tighter than ever.

"How you have a boyfriend?"

"Hey, now," Colt does growl this time. He takes a step toward Milo, but doesn't let go of me.

Milo holds up his hands. "No, no, not like that. I just meant that I'm confused that you were fangirling all over me at your birthday party and all the while you had a boyfriend?"

Colt lets out a snort.

"What the hell are you talking about? I wasn't *fangirling* you!" All fatigue has left my body now. I am trying to get out of Colt's arms now because I want to rip Milo's throat out.

"You were going on and on about me being a lawyer," he says. He looks shocked that I am denying being a fangirl for him.

"Wow, I was congratulating you on your accomplishments. I was just being polite and supportive. I was cheering you on!" My hands are flailing about as I try to explain that I was simply being nice to him. I had no idea his ego was so large.

"Or as some might call that, *fangirling*," Milo repeats.

"You have some nerve! I was simply being nice!"

"Ha!" Milo barks out a laugh. "Nice? I had tried blowing you off for months, you practically had your hands in my pants!"

I feel like I am about to explode, but I refuse to fight with Milo, in the middle of the street, about whether or not I was trying to get into his pants. I mean, I sort of was, but he certainly doesn't need to know that.

"Wow, Milo, you have it all wrong." My voice is calm and steady. "I was just an old friend trying to reconnect and see what you were up to. I am not now, nor have I ever been, a fangirl of yours. You have now achieved your goal, though, I will never contact you again. Consider me 'blown off'." I start walking away but Colt hasn't moved, which is making it impossible for me to move. When I tug again and he doesn't move, I glance at his face for the first time in a few minutes. His face is red, his jaw is ticking, his muscles are clenched. It looks as if his rage is barely being contained.

"You're a real dick, you know that?" Colt's tone actually scares me. It is deep and raspy. "You were lucky enough to have someone as amazing as Valentina contact you and here you are, treating her like this. You don't deserve her. Any man would be fucking lucky to have her in the same room as them, let alone speaking to them." Colt starts walking and there is nothing I can do to stop him. We are moving much faster than we were before and within minutes we are inside my apartment building. Colt stomps us to the elevator, gets us up to my floor, and in front of my door.

While I am unlocking my door, I hear both of our phones alert us to the motion from the camera app. My phone lets off a decently pleasant bell sound. Colt's phone alerts him with a horrible, horrible noise. It sounds like the most annoying fire alarm in history. And it is *loud*.

"That noise seems a little over the top," I say as we walk into my apartment. He ignores me and walks me to my bedroom. He waits until I sit on the bed before walking into my living room. I close the door to change my clothes. I can hear him pacing in the living room.

I reappear in the doorway moments later. He crosses his arms over his chest.. "Ok, well, I need to get back to the office and you need to get into bed. You are clearly getting sick and need all the rest you can get."

"Whoa, whoa, whoa!" I put up my hand to stop him as he uncrosses his arms and approaches me. "I'm not getting sick, I've just been working too hard."

His eyes search my face. "You're exhausted, pale, and your body feels like it's on fire." Without telling my hand to do so, it reaches up and touches my forehead. It does feel a little warm.

"Those could all be signs of working too many hours," I push back.

His eyes hop from one of mine to the other. "Yup, absolutely." He puts his hand on my back and leads me to my bedroom. "Either way, you need rest. Is there anything I can get you?"

"No, no thanks." I allow him to march me directly to my bed and to tuck me in. I don't think I've even rolled over before I am asleep.

February 14th

I wake up and immediately know I am ill. I am sweating, yet freezing. I feel like I cannot open my eyes. My entire body hurts. Everything feels wrong. I. Am. Miserable.

I hear people in my living room, moving around and talking, but I can't even entertain the thought of going out there to see who's here and what's happening. My head is pounding and my body feels like I have added weights to all my muscles.

"I am aware of that, Rob," I can make out Colt's voice.

"Bro, I've got it," Rob responds. I think it's Rob, anyway. I've only heard his voice maybe twice in my life.

"Yeah...yeah. I'll head out." Lots of shuffling noises.

"Go home and chill," Rob orders and I hear the door close. After that, I hear nothing. Rob is either walking in his quiet way that defies gravity, or he is standing directly next to my door. Either way, I know I want to go back to sleep.

I wake up when I feel the mattress dip next to me. I am awake for a few moments before my eyes actually open. When they do, I see Grandma Mae.

"Hi, GM."

"Hello, my sweetest granddaughter," she coos as she moves hair out of my face and feels my forehead.

"You should get out of here before you get sick," I instruct her.

"Nonsense. I could never leave you alone on your birthday."

"It's what's best for everyone," I promise.

"No. We will share a meal on your special day, so you can just stop fighting it. Alright?"

I chuckle at her determination. "Of course, my sweetest grandmother."

"I'm your only grandmother."

"That doesn't change that you're the sweetest," I reply, echoing the sentiments she has said to me for years. Grandma Mae softens a bit and slides me a loving look. Her eyes even look a little misty before she turns away to pick something up from the floor.

"I brought us a picnic." She pulls up a picnic basket and sets it on her lap. "It's mostly made up of juices and smoothies since you're hideously ill, but I have a few pieces of toast and bagels if you're feeling up to it."

As she is unpacking the basket, I begin to sit up so I can drink and eat whatever she brought me. It gives me a heavy, awkward feeling in my head, but I ignore it. I definitely know I need some fluids and probably some sustenance.

"So, I've been thinking about the company, and what I said you had to do to receive it," she opens. I have absolutely no idea what is coming next. I'm not sure if it's because I am sick and my brain isn't functioning correctly or if I just don't know what to expect from her anymore.

"Go on…" I encourage her even though I'm not positive that I am up for this conversation.

"Well, I know I said you needed a partner, someone to ground you. But… I'm having second thoughts," she admits.

"Is that so?" I ask her with an air of confidence, but I'm completely suspicious. I take a little sip of Gatorade.

"Yes," she answers with a tone that lets me know I shouldn't push my luck. "I've seen how dedicated you are and how well you've been doing at work. And all the while, you seem to be happier." She takes the tiniest bite of a sandwich that I have ever seen a person take. "Maybe

———

having a partner is an antiquated notion that I need to let go of."

I am stunned. I still don't trust that this is the full conversation. I feel like this could be leading up to something bigger. "It's funny you say that, because I've been thinking the opposite." She questions me with an eyebrow lift. "I've been thinking that a partner, someone to be around, wouldn't be the total end of the world."

I can tell my grandmother is hiding her excitement. "Did you have someone in mind? As your, uh, partner?" She is not making eye contact with me and is staring at her sandwich with too much concentration.

"No, of course not." I reach for her hand and squeeze. "There is no one in the picture, I am just saying I am more open to the idea."

Grandma Mae smiles at me with the adoration only a grandmother can give. We look at each other for a minute while we let our feelings transmit without speaking. I'm sure she is feeling excitement for my future and curiosity about what changed my mind. I am highly disturbed by what is on my mind: Colt.

February 15th

I'm aware I am conscious. Without opening my eyes, I can see my eyelids are lighter than normal. They are light, like there is sunlight hitting them. I hear a faint sound in my living room, but I don't open my eyes. I listen some more but hear nothing else. Before opening my eyes, I take inventory of my body. I start at my toes and notice they feel fine. I quickly move on to my legs, which also feel remarkably normal. Without moving, I focus on my midsection and it feels alright. I don't feel any nausea or cramping, no heaviness or discomfort. I am gaining momentum, and skip my arms to move right up to my head. It also feels decent. Maybe a little tired, a little bleh. Otherwise, everything feels good!

After realizing I am probably over my illness, whatever it was, I am still reluctant to open my eyes. What if seeing the light of day brings all the feelings of horror back to me? What if opening my eyelids is just turning on a lightswitch for illness?

Very slowly, and very carefully, I open my right eye. I pause halfway and I still feel alright. I continue the rest of the way until my eye is fully open. So far, so good. Everything appears normal in my room. I open my left eye in one quick pop. My bedroom looks like it ordinarily does. There is nothing out of place and no one is there with me.

I try sitting up and find that feels good, too. I give it a minute for my eyes and body to adjust. When everything settles, I know I have gotten through the worst, if not most, of my illness. My body feels ridiculously better and my mind seems to be much sharper. I hear a gentle rustle from my living room and wonder who is there. Mae? Rob? Gina?

After using the restroom, brushing my teeth, and freshening up, I feel ready to leave my bedroom. I open the door at a snail's pace, giving the person on the other side a warning. I certainly don't want to catch my security team, or my *grandmother*, in any sort of compromising position.

After moving as slowly as possible and finally opening the door, I am surprised to see Colt sitting on my couch. I'm also not very surprised, though. On second thought, I'm not surprised at all. He is sitting there, watching the TV on mute again.

"Hey, feeling better?" Colt asks without taking his eyes off the television.

"Yes, actually, I am." I walk to the kitchen and get myself a glass of water.

"That's a good idea, I'm sure you're dehydrated." Colt turns the TV to a new channel and turns on the volume.

"Right, I probably am." I look around a bit and see that my apartment looks to be in order. Colt makes no move to get up or to leave. "So, what's going on? Why are you here?"

"Oh, uh, Rob isn't scheduled to be back on until 5:00 tonight, so I thought I would hang here until then," Colt explains. He never takes his eyes off the screen and barely

—

notices me, and yet he is basically telling me he is here to watch out for me. I don't understand.

"I'm sure everything will be fine." He doesn't acknowledge me. "I'm sure you have somewhere you need to be, or something you need to do today?"

"Nah, I'm good," he reassures me.

I'm more confused than ever so I fill my water glass again and head back to my bedroom. I get my laptop out to see if I've missed anything important or have any urgent emails waiting for me. I take my time and don't hurry through these tasks, simply because I don't need to. It's nice to work at a leisurely pace for once. After spending all the time I would like sifting through my inbox and sorting emails, I move on to my upcoming schedule and make notes of anything that I need to get done before the meetings that are heading my way. I notice that I still need to do my annual one-on-one with Colt about the marketing department. It's scheduled for Tuesday, but I'm tempted to bite the bullet and try to get it over with today since he is currently sitting twenty feet away from me and doing nothing.

I think about this for a few minutes. Should I interrupt this day by asking Colt to work from my kitchen table? Just as I start thinking it might be out of line to ask this of him, my bedroom lights flicker.

"Ok, ok, I get it. Don't ask him to work," I say to the room. I know my parents are here. They've been with me the entire time I was sick and it brought me a great deal of comfort knowing they were close by.

"What's that?" Colt calls from the other room.

"Nothing, never mind," I respond. I close my laptop and sit back on my bed and relax. I close my eyes and let my mind settle down and forget about work.

A few minutes later, I hear the TV go silent. My eyes pop open, expecting to see Colt pass by my door to leave. I check the clock and it's almost noon, I wonder if he called Rob to come in early for his shift. I'm surprised to see him amble up to the threshold of my room. He has his hands in his pockets and he leans his big body on the doorframe.

"How ya feeling?" he asks, looking around my room.

"Much better, like I said before," I say as I watch him look at every item in my bedroom.

"Just making sure the good feelings are here to stay," he tells me. He stops looking around and makes eye contact with me.

"So far, so good."

"Well, I, uh, was thinking maybe we could go get some food?" He looks horribly uncomfortable, he is shifting his weight and pulls a hand out of his pocket to scratch his jaw.

"Food?" I repeat.

"Yeah, I'm starving and you don't have shit to eat around here. If you're feeling better, let's go somewhere and eat lunch." He is still looking at my face.

Understanding dawns on me. "Oh, I see. You want me to come with you to get food so that you don't leave me alone here in the apartment and you don't want to eat anything I have here." I roll my eyes and cross my arms across my chest.

He lets out a loud sigh and clears his throat. "Honestly, if that were the case, I would just have food delivered." Good point, I hadn't thought of that. "But I was thinking more of just two people venturing out of this apartment that, by the way, could use a hefty dose of Lysol, to get something to eat. It doesn't have to be work, or romantic, or anything. I'm hungry and you haven't eaten in two days. It makes sense."

I search his face for some clue to what is going on in his head. All I see is his calm expression, waiting for my response.

"You're proposing that the two of us act friendly and go get lunch?" I need clarification.

"Yes."

"No funny business?"

He chuckles. "Of course not."

"No work?"

"God, I hope not."

"Ok, ok, I can do that." I nod my head a bunch of times as I process that Colt and I are going to get food together like actual *friends*. "Let me get dressed."

He gives me a very tight lipped smile and nods once before shutting the door.

"So where are we going?" I ask him ten minutes later as we are walking down the freezing sidewalk. I'm wearing jeans and the largest sweatshirt I own along with a giant coat, hat, and a scarf that is wrapped around my head four times. I hope it's nowhere with a dress code.

"Not sure. What can your stomach handle? Anything sound good?"

I think about this for a moment. "Mashed potatoes."

He barks out a laugh. "Mashed potatoes? OK, I know just the place."

About a dozen blocks later, I am warm from the walk and we have finally arrived. It is the cutest diner I have ever seen in my life. I've never been here before but the nostalgic feel it has going on will have me returning soon.

"Wow, this place is so cute," I say as I look around in awe.

"I know, I love this place. It's not far from my apartment and it has the best comfort food. The cook, Tom, makes the best potatoes," Colt tells me.

"Mashed potatoes, right?" I double check. After declaring mashed potatoes as my food of choice, I have not stopped thinking of creamy, buttery potatoes. My mouth is already watering.

"Any type of potato. Mashed, fried, baked, in a casserole, you name it and Tom can make it."

Colt chooses a booth for us along the frosted windows. There is an old, tiny jukebox on the table that is now holding the salt and pepper shakers and the napkins. It's adorable. I take off my giant coat, hat, and unwrap myself from my scarf before sitting down in the booth.

"Your cheeks are so pink." Colt lets out a soft laugh.

"Well, in case you didn't notice, it's fucking freezing outside," I say as I scoot over on the bench. Colt sets a menu in front of me and begins looking at his own.

"Sorry that your birthday was ruined yesterday," Colt says after we've ordered. He ordered a bacon cheeseburger and curly fries while I ordered two servings of mashed potatoes and toast with butter.

"Eh, it sucks but it's fine. Luckily we didn't have anything really planned." It's odd to be sitting so close to Colt with no sort of buffer. We don't need to keep looking at our notepads or portfolios like we would be doing at work. If he walks me home, he doesn't usually stay long and we never *chat*. His eyes are even more blue than I remember. The scruff on his jaw looks fantastic. I blink and look away to clear my head.

"That's good. I was wondering if I just didn't get invited to the party this year." He is giving me a half smile, only the right side of his mouth is turned up.

"Ha, no. No party was planned for this birthday. My only plans were to eat and go shopping with Mae. That's usually how we spend my birthday."

"Rob said she came over for a bit yesterday, hopefully you still got to eat with her."

"Yeah, I did. Thanks." I am playing with my straw wrapper, working up the courage to ask him questions that I've been wondering since we left my apartment. "Were *you* at my apartment yesterday?"

"Oh, uh, yeah, just for a few minutes." He scratches at his jawline while he looks over my shoulder at the rest of the restaurant. I try my hardest not to find him sexy. I am failing.

"Did you have a date to get to?" Ohmygod, that was horrible. I said it all in one giant breath just to get the question out. Now I can't make eye contact while he answers. Why do I care if he has a girlfriend? Or a date? I completely shouldn't.

He laughs and looks down at the table. "No. No date," Colt says quietly.

"So… either you don't have a girlfriend, or if you do, she is super pissed at you," I hedge. I want more information. Learning about the personal side of Colt is like a drug. It's addicting and it doesn't feel like I've had enough.

"No girlfriend. No date." He shakes his head and looks up at me. His eyes squint in confusion. "You really think I have a girlfriend and I watch your door camera like a hawk?"

"Hmm, that's a good point. I guess I hadn't thought of that." It had never occurred to me to wonder if Colt had a girlfriend, and if he did, how she would feel about his actions toward me. Looking back, I guess I just assumed he did not have a girlfriend simply because he never brought one up. He never brought a girl to happy hours or my birthday parties. He never mentioned one at work. No one at work said anything about his relationship status. Not even an uncomplicated, carefree thought like "I wonder if Colt will bring his girlfriend?" It seems pretty obvious that he has not had any sort of serious girlfriend over the past couple years.

What's worse, though, is how self-absorbed I've been when it comes to Colt. I pride myself on being generous and thoughtful with my friends and Mae. I try my hardest to demonstrate to them how much I care about them, their lives, their partners, and their careers. Over the past year especially, I have seen Colt on a regular basis. I have never once asked him about his personal life or anything further than a plain inquiry about how he was doing on any given day. Not only am I ashamed of my actions on a human level, I am mortified as a boss. I cannot believe I know so little about someone I am directly supervising.

I can tell you all about Frederick's life, the head of Research and Development. I know about his wife, Lillian, and their children, Lewis and Danya. I know about their home in New Jersey and that he flies to Arizona to visit his wife's parents every Memorial Day and Thanksgiving.

I know even more about Julian. He is in charge of everything to do with Finance. He lives with his partner, Marc, in the city. They have a second home in Rhode Island that they visit often. Julian has three sisters and Marc has four. They have a slew of nieces and nephews and I can tell you every one of their names. I can probably come close on their ages, too.

I am equally informed about Rosa in HR, Deena in Corporate Sales, and Frank in Customer Service. How have I never spoken to Colt about his personal life? Am I so despicable that I have never once asked him anything about his life? I think I must be.

Horrified by my behavior, I know I must try to rectify it as best I can. I can feel how red my face is, betraying me and showing my embarrassment. Luckily, Colt has taken an extreme interest in his coffee, swirling it around in endless circles with one of those tiny, red stirrers. I do not want to imagine what he must think about me. I hope his opinion of me isn't any lower than my own, currently, which is just about as low as it has ever been.

"No girlfriend, hm? Is there anyone you're seeing casually?"

His eyes fly from the coffee to my face. He is surprised. His jaw goes from tight to relaxed in the blink of an eye. "Nope." He shakes his head just a bit from side to side.

I take a sip from my coffee cup, it's incredible. I expected it to taste stale and bitter, but it's unbelievably good for such a small diner. "So, do you have any brothers or sisters?"

Now he's suspicious of me. He leans back against the bench and just stares at me for a moment. His brows are drawn in and his eyes are moving all over my face. He's trying to figure out my motive for these questions.

"Yes, I have two brothers."

"Oh, that's nice. What are their names? Do they live in the city?" I prod further.

"My older brother is Dale and my younger brother is Clyde. No, neither live in New York." He is still staring at me.

I lean forward, placing my elbows on the table. I rest my chin on my hand, fully interested now. "Oh really? And what do they do for a living?"

"Dale is a police officer and Clyde is a teacher." He is still eyeing me with doubt.

"Wow, very respectable jobs. Do they have families?"

He's had enough. Colt sits up straight and leans toward me. "What the hell is going on here? Why are you giving me an inquisition?"

I put my hand on my chest in an innocent gesture. I'm about as innocent as a raccoon caught in a garbage can, but Colt doesn't need to know that. "I'm just curious about your life." When he doesn't respond and continues to glare at me, I feel the need to explain. "I was just sitting here realizing how little I know about your personal life and I wanted to find out more about you. Is that some sort of problem?"

His eyes bounce all over my face again before he finally leans back once more. "No, it's not a problem." He itches his cheek with his hand before speaking again. "Dale is single. Clyde is married, but no kids yet."

Before I can drop some more questions on him, we are interrupted by our server. He sets our food on the table and then returns quickly to freshen our coffees. I decide to give Colt a break from his quiz and eat some of the monstrous pile of mashed potatoes that is sitting in front of me. Not only do they look delicious, but they smell divine. I close my eyes and inhale a huge whiff. I try to commit the smell to my long term memory, because this heaping plate smells unlike any other plate of mashed potatoes I have ever had before. When I open my eyes, Colt is looking at me and smiling.

"What?"

"Nothing, nothing." He dips some fries into the ketchup on his plate. "I just don't think I've ever seen someone enjoy the smell of their food so much." He tosses the fries in his mouth. He closes his mouth and starts chewing politely and then wipes his mouth with his napkin. I find the whole process mesmerizing.

"Well, maybe you've never seen someone who hasn't eaten in two days get served their most desired food. Because let me tell you sir, these mashed potatoes are *epic.*" I scoop some off my plate and get them into my mouth as fast as I can. My eyes roll back in my head, I let out some sort of weird moan, and I drop the fork on the table as I fall back on the bench. The smell is absolutely nothing compared to the taste. "Fuck, these are good."

I open my eyes and begin loading my fork again. When I look up, Colt is still watching me. He's done chewing and I can't tell if he's swallowing what's left of his fries or if it's just a whole river of saliva. Either way, his throat is moving and much slower than I thought possible. His smile is gone and his lips are pressed together and his eyes have gone a little dark. What is going on over there?

He licks his lips. Fuck, that looks almost as good as the mashed potatoes. "They sure must be something."

"Trust me, they are."

Colt insists on walking me home, and I in turn, insist he not stay until Rob's shift at 5:00. It seems ridiculous for us both to just sit in my apartment for hours waiting for Rob to show up. Eventually, Colt gives in. Before leaving, he searches every room and opens every door to make sure no one is hiding anywhere. I promise not to leave my apartment and to set the alarm the moment he leaves. He agrees and finally, a half hour later he leaves.

I set the alarm and walk into my bedroom.

One of the main reasons I wanted Colt to leave was to be alone while I set intentions for the next year of my life. I do not want or need any company for this process, other than my parents. I want to speak with them and look forward with them for the first time as an adult. I am pretty excited about having them here to weigh in on my thoughts and goals.

I turn on the lamp next to my bed and lie down, leaving room for both of them to sit. My dad at the foot of my bed and my mom next to my head. I give them a few minutes to get settled before I begin speaking to them.

"Thanks for being here and for staying with me through this weird sickness. It's been lovely knowing you are here with me. Usually on the day after my birthday, I figure out what I want from the next year of my life. I sit here and think about the future and what I need to do. There are a few intentions that are just standing intentions now. The first is to continue to grow at MaeDay and just get better at my job in general. The next is to be a good granddaughter to Mae and make her proud. The last is to be a good friend and person." I pause and let the feeling of understanding roll over me. "Now that you've heard them, and I've said them out loud, I don't think I ever need to say those again. Those are just givens for my future life. I'd love a sign if you think that's a good idea."

I wait in silence. I give it almost a minute before giving up and guessing they want me to say these goals every year. But then I hear it. And feel it. A spring pops on my mattress, even though I haven't moved since I laid down. I know they've heard me and we're all on the same page.

"OK, great. Moving on." I bite my lip, not sure how to verbalize what I'm feeling. "I'm humiliated by my actions toward Colt. Even though he is unbearably annoying, he has been nothing but kind and protective toward me. I need to change my behavior toward him. But it's not just that. I feel like I've failed on a human decency level by not realizing what an ass I've been to him for *years*. I think my real intentions this year need to be around looking deeper at myself. I need to figure out who I want to be. How I want to treat others. What boundaries I want to put up. I also need to figure out why I treated Colt the way I did and, oddly, no one else. I want to do some work on me as a person, on my personality, on my character, and check my moral compass. I don't want a boss that doesn't care about me and I can guarantee that no one at MaeDay does either."

The lamp on my nightstand turns off. I smile, knowing my parents agree and want this to be the end of my intentions. I close my eyes and let my head sink into my pillow. I feel relaxed for the first time in a long time.

"Ok, I hear ya. Let me take a nap and maybe by the time Rob gets here, we can have a glass of Prosecco to celebrate the birthday I missed yesterday," I promise them. My mom loved to drink anything with bubbles.

———

I let myself drift off to sleep, thinking about how I am going to take a hard look at myself in this upcoming year and make some changes. It's time for some personal growth and there is no time better than the years in my life as I inch toward thirty. Time to evolve.

Twenty-Seven

February 13th

Are you ready to be surprised? I know you are… I have a boyfriend. I also know what you're thinking, but no, it's not Colt. I still find him incredibly attractive, but what's the phrase? Don't shit where you eat. Yeah, that's the one. It doesn't seem like a good idea to get involved with someone at work.

But anyway, my boyfriend is Fisher and he is an accountant. He wears the best gray suits I have ever seen. His body is perfection, he works out for hours every day and eats perfectly. If I had to pick a downfall of dating Fisher, however, it would be his diet for sure. He never wants to cheat or eat anything that could possibly contain more than three carbs. It's actually annoying as hell, but he's super fun and if refusing to get pizza with me makes him happy, then who am I to try and stop him.

I love hanging out with him, we always have a great time together. He is super adventurous and always wants to try something new. If we're not rock climbing somewhere Fisher just found out about, we're ice skating in Central Park, or going to see whatever is new on Broadway. If I mention wanting to try something, or see a movie that's out, within minutes Fisher has bought the tickets to make it happen. He's very thoughtful and does not care how 'girly' an activity might be. He's all in.

In all honesty though, I try to avoid eating with him. Not only does he make completely perfect food decisions for himself, but he tries to get me to order with him. He claims it is because he is worried about my health and wants me to live as long as I can. I suspect the real reason is that my food is a temptation. He always stares at me while I'm eating in the weirdest way. For instance, one day last week he was watching me eat a croissant at a cafe and I was worried he was going to grab it out of my hands because the look he was giving me was so… primal. I offered him a bite and he looked away in disgust. After that I was worried about the croissant's wellbeing so I hurried up and finished it so we could drink our coffees in peace.

I'm not going to be able to avoid it tomorrow, though. He and Grandma Mae have planned a huge dinner for me and all of my friends and their Valentine's dates. We are eating at some new restaurant downtown and everyone is very excited. We've all been shopping for our outfits for weeks. I knew my dress was for me the moment I saw it; it's red and long sleeved, but the sleeves do this weird thing where they defy gravity above my shoulders and poof out in different directions, it's very interesting. The rest of it is like a second skin and I love it.

Grandma Mae and I are skipping tradition and going out to lunch today so we can buy her a dress afterward, since she'll be attending with Annie. As you can guess, Mae is obsessed with Fisher. She thinks he walks on water.

I walk out my front door and turn to wave at the camera. Yes, Colt still watches. Yes, Fisher knows that Colt still watches. I honestly cannot tell how Fisher feels about it. He says he's fine, especially given all of the information about the note and Rich showing up at my house. He says he wants as many people worried about my safety as possible. But, sometimes, after Fisher has had a few vodka on the rocks or a few red wines (only the healthiest alcohols), he'll tell me that Rich hasn't made an appearance in years and he doesn't understand the big deal. While I partially agree, I also completely disagree. It's been years, but I could never let go of my safety net. I can't disregard my alarm system, my camera, my *tape* - these are all the things that give me comfort and make me feel safe. It does not matter how much time has passed without contact, I cannot return to my previous, exposed life.

———

I speak to Gene on my way out, he compliments my yellow overcoat and tells me how Mary Jo is doing. I head out to the car where Hank is patiently waiting for me. Once inside, I am ecstatic to see Mae waiting for me.

"Darling, you look gorgeous," she praises. She leans over and kisses me on the cheek. I close my eyes and allow myself to enjoy the way she cherishes me. Not everyone has someone in the world that loves them the way Grandma Mae loves me. I let her love and warmth surround me. It feels so good to be near her, like nothing can go wrong.

"Thank you, GM." I pull back and look into her eyes. "It feels like I haven't seen you in forever, even though it's only been a few days."

"Oh, stop that." She dismisses me with a wave and a "psh."

"So where do you want to go to find your dress?"

"Prada, of course."

Two hours later we are sitting, a little buzzed, inside the Prada dressing rooms. Mae is having a hard time getting in and out of dresses without falling into fits of giggles. I can't help but giggle with her. Grandma Mae clearly chose a restaurant offering a champagne lunch and Prada has not been shy about the drinks either. I'm not sure if that's because my grandmother is a nail polish tycoon or it's just their normal practice, but the champagne is definitely working on us. Mae has five dresses set aside to buy so she can wear them all tomorrow. She insists on having wardrobe changes. Once she sobers up, I know she'll decide to wear her favorite of the bunch and return the other four. She isn't one to have things she doesn't need lying around.

By the time we are getting ready to check out, Mae has six dresses for herself, two for Annie, and a bunch of random items she insists on buying for me. She picked out a pair of heels with a beautiful floral pattern, a necklace with different colored shiny stones, a shirt she insisted looks amazing on me, and the most luxurious robe I have ever seen. It's incredibly soft and long, and feels like you are wrapping your body in heaven. It has faux fur around the collar and the hood. It has tiny pieces of velcro on the robe tie so that when you wrap it around yourself, it stays wrapped. It is what I am most excited about. I want to wear this robe all day, every day.

We leave Prada and I go home to have dinner with my parents. I'm eager to relax at home and enjoy a quiet night before all of the birthday and Valentine's Day celebrations that tomorrow will bring.

"Mom, Dad, I hope you're happy wherever you are," I say to the empty seats at the table across from me. It's been a couple of hours since I got home and I am now enjoying dinner in my kitchen, hoping my parents are sitting with me.

I stop eating and close my eyes. I let my body relax and I think of my favorite memory with my parents. I'm six or seven years old and I had just started dancing lessons. I was demonstrating all of my new moves to my parents one night in our living room. They were sitting on the couch and I was performing in front of them. For whatever reason, that evening no one was working, or doing homework, or having dinner with friends. Mae was not visiting that night and we had nothing to do. The three of us were alone together in our home. That was a rare occurrence given how quickly my mother was climbing the ladder at MaeDay and the odd hours my father would work as a sculptor. He had been commissioned to make sculptures all over the city and he was getting to be pretty famous, or so I'm told. But his creativity never struck at convenient times. My mom and I knew that once he disappeared into his studio, he was not to be bothered.

That night, though, it was just the three of us. There were no sculptures, no nail polish. They watched me with such intensity. I will never forget how their eyes followed my every move. They had smiles on their faces and I would like to think their expressions were full of pride. I know they truly did not care if I could dance or not, but I hope now, and hoped then, that they were proud of me for being me. After I finished dancing, they applauded and kissed me. I felt such untouchable joy.

My dad turned on the music and the three of us danced together after that. Sometimes we all held hands and danced around the room. Sometimes I danced with my mom and my dad would do silly dances around us to make us laugh. Other times, I would dance with my dad and he would spin and twirl and dip me. I was delighted to dance with him, as was my mom. She watched us with her hands at her mouth, looking as if she were holding back tears. Finally, to end the dance session, my mom and dad slow danced together, cheek to cheek. I was in between them, swaying as they swayed. I held on to my mother's waist and let her body lead me. We fell asleep in my parents' bed watching a movie that night. I've chased the feelings of content, unconditional love, and blissfulness I felt that night ever since.

As I sit in my chair at the kitchen table, I slowly open my eyes and realize I am crying. Tears are flowing down my cheeks. I even have some spots on my shirt from fallen tears. I sit up and look around, almost expecting to see my parents. They're not there, but I don't feel sad or disappointed. I feel happy. I feel rejuvenated.

"I want a family," I say to the room. "I want a family that I love as much as we loved one another. I want a husband that loves me the way you loved Mom, Dad. And I want to love him the same way in return!" My voice is getting louder. "Now I know. I am certain that I do want to find a partner. I want someone to love."

February 14th

I wake up and I am so full of love. My heart feels like it could leap from my chest. I sit up in bed and reach for my phone. The ding of an incoming message notification woke me. I look at my text messages from friends and co-workers sending me birthday wishes. I respond to them all, my heart growing even fuller.

I jump out of bed and get myself ready for a winter run. I wear my regular shorts, but bulk up on top a bit more since it is especially frigid today. Gene is not there on my way out of the front door; it is one of the part-time doormen that I do not know very well. I give him a quick hello and I'm out the door.

I decide to do an out-and-back style run to ensure I complete all seven miles. I anticipate eating and drinking quite a lot at our big dinner tonight, so I'm trying to get ahead of all the calories I plan to take in later on.

A nice long run like this allows my mind to wander. Which is a little form of therapy. I spend a lot of time thinking about Grandma Mae and how wonderful she is. I wonder what her retirement will look like and what the company will do. We're still eight years away from that point, but I know it's exactly what we are working toward.

I also think about my friends and their lives for a while, which is the absolute best way to pass the running time. I think about how happy Amy and Mackie are. I am so glad Amy was finally able to let Mackie in. Their happiness is another inspiration for me to find love for myself. I want to be as happy as they are in their relationship. Also, Nisha is becoming more and more serious with Max and it's incredible to watch their progression. Ansley is bringing a friend from her lab. She insists that's all they are, friends, but he looks at her like he wants to be more than friends. We're not sure if Ansley is just in denial or she is completely oblivious to Jake's affection for her. A dinner on Valentine's Day should certainly be interesting for them. Robin is also bringing someone and we are all excited to meet him. He is her neighbor and she has had a crush on him for months. His name is Andre and he travels more than he is at home. He happens to be in town right now and accepted Robin's invitation. According to her, he is tall, dark, and handsome. It goes without saying, his attendance is highly anticipated.

I hit my halfway point and run a little further to do a nice loop around a street sign. I'm heading home and very happy to be on the second half of my run. I let myself settle into a nice pace and enjoy the sights of the city while I run. It's freezing out but it's sunny and the way the light reflects off the buildings is beautiful.

———

I see my building sooner than I expected to and that is a total victory. As I get closer and closer, I see a man standing outside. He's leaning against the building, just outside the door. He shifts his weight and I recognize him immediately. Fisher is waiting for me. At first, I am a little worried about why he would be waiting for me. I am not expecting him and I have not heard from him yet today. I pick up my speed to finish as quickly as possible and figure out what is going on.

"Fisher? Hi," I say, breathless. I lean over taking in huge gulps of air. I can feel the sweat streaking down my face.

"Lenni, hey," he looks at me and pauses. "Where have you been?"

I look down at my attire and my heaving chest, as I try to catch my breath, thinking the answer should be pretty obvious. "Running," I answer, breathless.

"Right, I mean, yeah." He waves a hand up and down my body. "The new doorman wouldn't let me up and I couldn't get a hold of you on the phone and I don't have a key to your apartment or anything, so I just had to wait outside."

"Oh, sorry," I say with a little shrug. I'm not sure how any of this is my fault, since I had no idea he was planning to come over. "Want to go inside?"

"Yeah, I'm fucking freezing." He holds the door open for me and I walk to the elevator with Fisher trailing behind me.

"So, um, happy birthday," he says to me once we are inside my apartment. I am taking my top layers off since I am still sweating from my run.

"Thanks."

"I came by because I wanted to give you your gift when we were alone." He suddenly looks very shy. His hands are in his pockets and he is looking at the ground.

"That's sweet," I tell him. I am chugging my first glass of water.

"I was sort of hoping you'd wear it tonight."

"Oh?"

"Here it is," he whispers. He hands me a small velvet jewelry box from his pocket. I find myself hoping there is not an engagement ring in the box. It's way too early for that, right? There is no way he would be proposing today, is there? Or when I'm so sweaty?

I move slowly in his direction and take the box from his hand. My hands are shaking as I pop the lid open. Inside are a pair of earrings. Diamond earrings to be exact, and they are stunning. I stroke them lightly. I am so moved by this generous and incredible gift, I am at a loss for words.

"Fisher, these are unbelievable." I am choked up with emotion.

"You like them?" He is smiling with a hopeful expression.

"I *love* them." I can't stop staring at the earrings. "They will match the necklace my grandmother bought me yesterday perfectly and it all will look great with the dress I got to wear tonight. Thank you, Fisher."

I walk over and hug him with tears in my eyes. After a moment, I pull back and go on my tippy toes so I can kiss him. He deepens the kiss and I don't fight it. I feel my connection to Fisher strengthening and I like it. Maybe he could be the husband that loves me and I can love in return. My oversized heart is still growing in my chest.

"Come on, beautiful." Fisher moves sweaty hair that hangs in my face to behind my ear. "I'm feeling dirty, let's go get cleaned up in the shower together."

Fisher and I spend a wonderful afternoon together. We order in a light lunch of salads, Fisher's without dressing of course, and hang out on my couch relaxing. I wear my new robe the entire afternoon and Fisher is considering buying himself the male version. He can't get over the softness. I make a mental note to buy it for him for his birthday in a few months. After lounging for hours, we get up and get ready to go to dinner together.

It is lovely to have someone to get ready next to. I never would have imagined that to be something I would enjoy, but I truly do. Having him standing next to me in a towel and shaving is fucking hot. The way he watches me curl my hair and stands behind me while I put on makeup, even more of a turn on. So much so, we have a quickie before getting dressed. Maybe I am so eager for love that things I thought would be annoying are turning out to be adorable. Maybe I am so touched by his birthday gift, everything he does is perfect. Maybe I just genuinely enjoy his company. Whatever the reason, I'm excited to give Fisher access to these different parts of my life. I want to figure out what other mundane parts of my day would be better with Fisher's participation.

We arrive at the restaurant still googly-eyed with one another. They take our coats at the door and I wrap myself around Fisher's bicep, not even trying to be demure about my adoration for him. We both have absurdly large smiles on our faces as we enter the private room where our dinner party is being held. Robin's whistles break our trance. I reluctantly pull my eyes from Fisher's face and look at the table. Everyone is seated and we are the last to arrive. For a moment, there is silence as everyone stops their conversations and realizes that we've entered the room.

Everyone begins clapping and yelling "Happy Birthday!" I blow a kiss at everyone, but walk first to Mae. I embrace and thank her while she tells me how gorgeous I look. Annie does the same from behind Mae's shoulder. They both hug Fisher and I show them the earrings he gave me. They ooh and ahh and give him little smiles of pure affection. His ego is thoroughly boosted by the time we move on to Amy and Mackie.

He warmly hugs all of my friends around the table and is polite and welcoming to the men he is meeting for the first time. It feels nothing short of outstanding to have someone to walk around the room with me. We spend most of the time arm in arm and every so often I feel him kiss my hair. I did not believe my heart could grow any larger today, but at this restaurant it has. My heart feels ten times larger than it did this morning, and that is saying a lot.

We finally make our way around to our seats and once we sit, Fisher lays his arm along the back of my chair.

Something else I unexpectedly find irresistible. I am ecstatic to see someone has ordered drinks for us. A glass of something bubbly is in front of me and a tumbler of what appears to be bourbon is in front of Fisher.

"I hope you don't mind, we got you both drinks so we could cheers Lenni's birthday immediately," Robin explains.

"Of course not! You know you can always order for me," I tell her with a wink. Everyone holds their glasses toward the center of the long table. We're all too far apart for everyone's glasses to meet, but we hold them to the center and yell "Cheers!" Everyone, that is, except Fisher. I look over and he is sitting quietly in his chair, not holding his drink to the center of the table. Not touching his tumbler at all, in fact. My mouth turns down and my eyes flick to his in a question of why he's not joining. He just gives me a small smile in return.

"What's wrong? You don't like bourbon?" Max asks Fisher.

"Nah, not my drink," Fisher replies.

"Well, it's sort of bad luck to not drink after everyone has done a cheers," Amy offers with a sly smile.

"I'm not going to put something with so many chemicals into my body," Fisher explains. Everyone's eyes are on me now and I feel completely uneasy. Everyone is taking quiet sips and looking around, more awkward than my friends and I have ever been before.

"You all are not going to believe this amazing robe that Mae bought me yesterday," I say, trying to change the subject.

"Oh yeah?" Ansley to my rescue. "Tell us more!"

After Fisher orders their pure tequila and Jake offers to drink his untouched bourbon, our group returns to normal. We are all chatting and laughing just as we should be. Mae planned the dinner weeks ago and set up for us all to enjoy a ten course meal, small dishes of course. If you chose, as all the females and Andre did, you could also have a wine pairing with each course. The dinner is a leisurely and fantastic affair. They give us plenty of time between dishes to finish our wine and enjoy each other's company before bringing out the next taste explosion. Each plate is better than the last, which seems impossible since they are all phenomenal.

As expected, Fisher only eats the items from each plate he deems to be full of nutrients or protein and leaves the rest. Some courses he eats every bite and others he barely touches. My friends being who they are, eat everything he does not. If there is something on your plate that you choose not to eat, it is passed around the table until it finds a good home. We are all using our forks to eat off one another's plates, drinking any extra wine, and sharing anything and everything. The closeness of my group of friends, and their partners, again makes my heart grow.

After the last course is served, Annie and Mae announce their departure. Even though we all groan and beg them to stay, no one is surprised. Those of us with the wine pairings are sufficiently merry and excited to continue the night. Max tells us about an amazing bar down the street and we all bundle up and leave the restaurant to face the cold.

I press myself against Fisher as much as I can. I try to spread as much of his body heat to me as possible and I'm still high on love and drunk on wine. I don't feel ready to say that I *love* Fisher, but you get the idea.

"I hope this place is close, even my balls are frozen," Fisher says as he pulls me close. I chuckle and squeeze him tighter.

"Maybe if you had a little more body fat, you'd be able to stay warmer," I say without thinking. My wine-infused brain thought it was a good idea to tell my boyfriend he's not fat enough. I feel Fisher tense up and he doesn't say anything. I want to feel remorse that I've upset him, but I've had too much wine to care. It's my birthday after all, he can't stay mad at me all night.

Now, I know I had a glass of bubbles and a wine pairing with each course, let's make a note here that they clearly were only tastings of wine and not full glasses. Who could survive ten glasses of wine? And I know the alcohol is making my eyes and mind fuzzy. With all of that being said, it is unquestionable, indisputable, beyond a shadow of a doubt that Rich is standing across the street. Even if I had a tiny glimmer of suspicion of this man's identity, it is gone the moment I make eye contact and he smiles at me.

My entire body changes when I see him. It is cold out, yes, but my entire body freezes and goes numb. I feel the chill of his eyes through my entire body. The only thing that brings me out of the staring contest with Rich is my phone vibrating in my hand. It vibrates, not once, not twice, but three times.

> *Happy Birthday!*
> *I hope you're having a great day!*
> *Make it home safe tonight.*

All three texts are from Colt. What are the chances he texts me the exact moment that I see Rich? When I look back across the street, Rich is gone.

"Lenni, why did you stop walking?" Fisher asks me. The rest of our group is half a block ahead of us. I hadn't realized my legs stopped moving. "Valentina?"

"Fisher…" I'm not even sure I say his name out loud, it might only be in my head. His eyes search mine.

"Let's get you inside," he says as he ushers me down the sidewalk.

"Valentina, what happened out there?" Fisher asks once we're inside the crowded bar.

"Rich, I saw Rich." Instel'm "He's gone, when I looked up he was gone."

"Maybe he wasn't really there then. Maybe it was someone else?"

"No, he looked right at me and smiled."

"Fuck. I'm gonna go look for him."

"Fisher, don't. You don't even know what he looks like. He's gone. It's pointless."

He searches my face. "OK, don't worry. I'm with you all night. I won't let anything happen to you. We can go back to my place tonight if you want. If that will make you feel safer."

I nod and walk to the bar. I want to go to my apartment where my parents are. I don't want to go to Fisher's but I don't tell him that. I'm afraid he won't understand about my parents. We'll worry about all of that later. For now, I am just going to watch my door camera until we go home.

February 15th

We wake up in my apartment. I can hear and feel Fisher's slow and sleepy breaths behind me. He still has his arms wrapped around me, I don't think we've moved once during the night. I'm grateful to be in my own space and to feel good here. I wasn't the most exciting company after the dinner. Not that it could have been helped. Seeing Rich shook me to my core.

I watched the door camera and its playback for an hour at the bar before Fisher insisted we leave. I couldn't blame him. I was absolutely zero fun after I saw Rich. He tried to get me to go back to his apartment, but I told him I'd be even more worried to go home without him eventually. He could see how serious I was and finally he agreed to go to my apartment. Thankfully, we never saw Rich, there were no notes, and no motion on the hallway camera. We went in and got changed for bed. At first, when we walked around my apartment together looking for any clues he'd been in my apartment again, Fisher seemed a bit annoyed. It felt like he saw the process as silly and unwarranted. Once we finished and brushed our teeth, though, his attitude returned to his normal, caring personality. He sat on the edge of the bed waiting for me to finish in the bathroom, looking sexy as hell in only his underwear. We climbed in bed together and he legitimately tucked me in. He made sure my head was comfortable on the pillows, put the covers all around me, and then he held me close and I fell asleep feeling safer than I have in a long time.

My current need to pee is excruciating. As much as I would love to lay here for another hour, my bladder has other priorities. I inch as slowly as possible toward the edge of the bed. I slide out from under Fisher's arm without waking him, which is miraculous. I tiptoe to the bathroom and shut the door silently. I am impressed with my own stealthiness when I return to the bedroom a few minutes later with an empty bladder and fresh breath.

There is no hope of climbing back into bed so I go to the kitchen and start some coffee. The smell of it brings a smile to my face. I am standing patiently, watching the coffee pot brew when I hear Fisher's approach.

I turn to face him. "Morning," I coo. I give him a sweet smile and pucker my lips in anticipation of a good morning peck.

"Eh," he grunts. He stops at the counter and stares down at the coffee pot. Ok, so clearly Fisher is *not* a morning person.

I nuzzle against him. "I slept so well with you last night." I look up at him through my lashes in an attempt to be early morning sweet and sexy.

'Yeah," he sputters out some coughs and clears his throat in a manner that is so aggressive, it's unattractive. "Me, too."

Being cute and affectionate this morning is definitely not going to work. I give up trying and wait for the coffee. Once it's done, I offer Fisher cream or sugar. He denies both, a man after my heart. We move to my couch and sit to enjoy sipping our hot coffees.

I give him a few minutes to wake up and let the caffeine kick in before attempting conversation again. "So, what are your plans for today?"

"I dunno. You tell me," he says while looking at the blank TV screen.

I'm thoroughly annoyed at his behavior. "Well, you can get dressed and go home while I figure out my plan for the next year of my life. Feel free to take a mug to go." I stand up and walk into my bedroom. I shut the door and walk into my closet. I take my dirty laundry basket and go into my bathroom, where the secret compartment for my washer and dryer are located. I start my laundry and when I walk back into my bedroom, I'm surprised to see Fisher standing there, still just in his underwear.

"Hey, Lenni, I'm sorry. I'm super grumpy in the morning. It's not something I'm proud of and definitely something that I need to work on." His apology seems sincere enough.

"It's alright," I reassure him. Even though it really isn't. I just want him out of my apartment.

"Can we spend the day together?" His voice is sweet. He moves toward me and takes my hands in his. It's a nice gesture and I waver in my decision for just a moment.

"I think I am going to spend the day alone, figuring out my next moves in the upcoming year." I go up on my toes to kiss him on the cheek. "Let's have dinner this week."

"Really?"

"Really."

He pauses, looking back and forth between my eyes. "Are we ok?"

"Yes." This statement is true. I just need a break from him.

"OK," he says. He drops my hands and starts putting his clothes on from yesterday. I sit on the edge of my mattress and watch him get dressed and gather his things. He kisses the top of my head before walking out the front door without saying another word.

I fall back on my bed and once the memories of the night before flood my brain, I hop up and double check each lock on my door and turn on the alarm system. I plop back on my bed and curl up into a ball. Out of fear, I text Rob and Gina to see if anyone is available to pick up an extra shift today. Neither are available and I contemplate calling Colt. I know he would come sit at my apartment, albeit awkwardly, if he knew I'd seen Rich. I just can't bring myself to contact him. It feels like I am cheating on Fisher by calling Colt and that is the last thing I want to do. I know Fisher was annoying and rude this morning, but it wasn't anything unforgivable.

I decide that I am safe in my apartment. I know no one is here. The alarm is on and I know Colt is still watching my door camera. I check to make sure all the windows are locked and then I make the best decision I know I will make all day: I put my new robe back on. It's a little ridiculous how excited I am to put this robe on. I think that speaks only to how amazing the robe is and has nothing to do with how pathetic I am.

After wrapping myself in my new robe and the second best Snowshoe Hare blanket, my first goal for the next year is easy. Buy an oversized chair for my room. My room has the best view from my apartment and I have nowhere to sit, other than my bed. I would love to start drinking my coffee while overlooking the city in a giant, comfy, cozy chair.

My next intention won't be so easy. Figure out my relationship with Fisher. I am teetering on the cliff of our relationship. I could very easily fall in love with Fisher. He is hard-working, thoughtful, generous, full of adventure, and I have so much fun with him. It would not be difficult for me to stop fighting it and just let myself fall.

On the other hand, I feel as though Fisher is replaceable. Is there anything extra special about him that I cannot live without? I guess I'm not entirely sure. I need to do further investigation to make a decision about this. That's exactly what I need to do in the upcoming months, dive further into my relationship and see how I feel.

I have a few tiny goals within this broader idea of Fisher. I would like to get Fisher entirely out of his comfort zone, some scenario where he cannot exercise for a day and must eat greasy food. Or something along those lines. I want to see what will happen. Will he give in and enjoy the moment and rebound just fine? Or will he be even more stubborn than I suspect he already is and refuse to eat anything and do butt clenches when he finds a spare moment?

My next goal for the year is to figure out what to do with my money. I have been making decent money at MaeDay for years now. I purchased my apartment with the money my parents left me and I don't have a car payment so most of my income is disposable.

I have been using Mae's financial advisors for years and I have been saving a majority of each paycheck, but there has to be a better place for my money than a savings account. Or the stock market. I'm certainly not opposed to buying and then subletting another apartment. I refuse to leave my current apartment. It's for me and my parents. End of story. Or maybe I should hire someone to do some property investments for me. I don't know what my money's future is exactly, but I do know I need to think it through and make a good plan while being involved in the process.

I anticipated being much more anxious and angry as I inch toward thirty, but I'm excited. I am happy to gain perspective and life skills! I love my job, I have the best friends, and a supportive, superb family. I am a lucky woman. This leads me to my last goal. I am going to share my luck.

Twenty-Eight

February 13th

"Tell me, my dear, do you think he's going to propose tomorrow?" Grandma Mae asks me while we are working in her office. "It seems like the timing couldn't be more perfect."

"I actually don't think he will," I inform her without looking up from the folder I currently have my nose buried in.

"Whyever not?" Mae gasps.

I lower the folder to my lap and look at my grandmother. "It just doesn't feel right."

"But you've been dating for nearly a year and a half!"

"Two of those months don't count! We broke up!"

Over the summer, I did do a little relationship testing with Fisher and had him spend some time with me in Sag Harbor. On our third weekend in The Hamptons, he refused to eat anything at the Mexican restaurant I love so much and then also refused to pick up two separate dinners to eat together at home. He would only eat at a restaurant he chose and thought would be the healthiest option, which led to a pretty decent sized fight. We both said some stuff we shouldn't have and he disappeared. He left me at Mae's place alone and since he drove us, I was stranded. He called to apologize the next day, but to say I was furious would be an understatement.

My parents rarely even raised their voices, let alone got angry. I am not one to be enraged or over the top with my emotions. But I do have one memory that mirrors the outrage I felt when Fisher left me.

On my first day of Kindergarten, the bus driver dropped me off at the wrong bus stop. Luckily we knew the house he dropped me off at and they immediately called my mom to come get me. I've never seen anyone more angry than my mother that day. She called every principal in the school, the transportation department, my teacher, the school board, the school nurse, the custodian, everyone. If you dared to answer the phone, you were going to receive a wicked tongue lashing from my mother. When people stopped answering their phones, she went to the school and refused to leave until everyone heard what she had to say. By the end of the night, she had completely lost her voice and it took nearly a week for her to sound normal again. It was a spectacle, the likes of which I have never seen again. My anger at Fisher rivaled my mother's fury at everyone that day. I refused to answer the phone and my rage was just barely contained as I called Robin to come and get me. She convinced me to stay in Sag Harbor and get drunk with her and we both called off work that Monday. It turned out to be a great way to improve my mood, but certainly not my feelings toward Fisher.

I told him to leave me alone, and he did for a while. He respected my wishes and did not smother me. He would send a text about once a week asking if I was ready to speak to him yet. I never once responded to those texts. I was not only pissed that he abandoned me, both physically and emotionally, but I was heartbroken. How could someone who cares about you just leave? He drove for hours back to the city, knowing he was leaving me alone and without a vehicle and never once turned around or even contacted me. Could I be with someone who seemed to care so little for me?

I was not pleasant company during those months and I spent a lot of time in the coffee room at Mae's Sag Harbor house. I learned about the joys and benefits of working from home while staying at her house for a week during the hottest part of July. After a bit of rest and escape, I needed to get back to the city. Not only did I miss simple human interaction, I also missed my friends, my grandmother, even my co-workers.

During my week-long Hamptons getaway, I learned something very important. My parents are always with me. I thought I could feel them but I began second guessing my parental intuition. I couldn't take it any longer and I stopped in the middle of the hallway that leads to the kitchen one morning. I calmed down and let my body relax and my head fall back. I closed my eyes and concentrated on the memory of my parents' faces.

"Are you here? Can you please give me a sign if you are?" I took a deep breath, opened my eyes, and continued walking. I hadn't taken more than three steps when I tripped over the end of the rug. It was turned up and it caught my foot as I passed by. I knew it had not been flipped up earlier that day and I was the only person in the house. I laughed, knowing my dad would do something silly like that to make me laugh when I was feeling so gloomy.

"Wait, that was you, right Dad?" I asked the empty house, still feeling just a bit unsure. As soon as the question left my mouth, the timer on the oven began to beep. It didn't stop until I went over and pressed the cancel button about six times. "Ok, ok, I got it."

It brings me comfort to know that my parents are with me even if I'm not at my apartment. It doesn't mean that I am any closer to being ready to sell my apartment, but it still makes me feel content in a way that I hadn't before.

Anyway, after my week away I returned to the city to find Fisher waiting outside my building. He's lucky that he's about six inches taller than Rich, otherwise I might have called the cops.

"Hey Valentina."

"Hello Fisher."

"Can I, uh, can I help you get all this upstairs?" He waved his hand in the direction of the trunk that contained my suitcase, work bag, and laptop bag.

"Yeah, why not?" We would have to speak sometime and there's no time like the present.

Once in my apartment, we went back and forth about our perspectives of the situation. I was upset about his inflexibility, his stubbornness, and mostly his abandonment.

He felt unsupported and bullied by my demands for him to eat something he didn't want to. He felt I was forcing him to do something he wasn't comfortable with. Honestly, I couldn't disagree with him. That was precisely what I was doing. I wanted him to do something out of the ordinary, I thought this would show me how much he cared for me. In hindsight, it seemed like a ridiculous way to ask someone to demonstrate their feelings.

We apologized to one another for our actions regarding the dinner and the fight. But I had saved the big kahuna for last. This discussion wouldn't end so easily and might even lead to a final breakup. There was no way I could just forget about him deserting me.

"Everything you're saying is right. I should never have left you there. I should have stayed and fought for us, for you. I was upset and... I don't know, I guess I was triggered when I felt like you were bullying me. I just had to get away from the situation. I'm sorry. I was completely wrong. I couldn't have handled it any worse." Hmm, that was interesting. I felt like he was telling me something without saying it out loud.

"Triggered? By feeling bullied by me? Fisher, were you bullied when you were little?" The light bulbs were starting to go off in my head at record speed.

He scrubbed a hand down his face. "I mean, this isn't exactly my proudest confession. It's also not a time to withhold the truth." He paused and looked at my face for a long time. "Yes. Yes, Valentina, I was."

"I'm so sorry, Fisher. How bad was it?" My hand reached out to his and he let me squeeze his joined hands.

"Bad," he said with a nod. He pressed his lips tightly together and looked down at our hands.

"Did they hurt you?"

"Yes."

"Physically?"

"Yes."

"Even worse than physically?"

Fisher drew in a deep breath and pulled his hands away. He ran them through his hair before looking into my eyes again. "Listen, let's not rehash this. I really don't want to talk about it. It was a long time ago." When I didn't say anything he continued. "Let's just say it was worse than most of the things your imagination could make up that a bunch of teenagers could do to torture one loser."

My hands flew to my face and a tear fell down my cheek. Fisher caught it. He gently took my hands away from my face and we embraced. It all made sense then. All of his issues with his body, control over his food, his exercise. His stubbornness and his reaction to me trying to force him to do something against his will. Every puzzle piece fit together and knowing the full story. I felt like a monster.

"I'm so sorry, Fisher." I sobbed into his shoulder.

"I am, too."

After that hour-long hug on my couch, we never spoke of his bullying or his leaving me again. We both silently understood those issues were to be left there on my couch and left alone. I felt I understood everything about Fisher's personality approximately one million times better after that day. He seemed happier not keeping the secret and sharing his past with me. I was definitely happier now that I could see the reasons behind his actions.

By the time August rolled around, we were inseparable. Nothing could keep us apart and we spent every night together. I barely remember September through Christmas because one day rolled into the next and every day was filled with bliss. We finally came up for air in January and started spending at least a little time apart again.

It felt good and bad at the same time. I was happy to do things alone with my friends or by myself, but I always missed Fisher when we weren't together. I was fully aware how annoying we were to my friends, but when you're infatuated with someone you just don't care.

Around October I was starting to feel bad that Fisher had shared such an intimate and tragic secret with me and I had not shared anything with him about my parents. He knew they died when I was little, but that was the extent. He seemed uncomfortable bringing it up, even though I love talking about them. The main reason I avoided bringing up my past life with my parents was due to fear. I was petrified to confess to Fisher that I communicate with my parents in my present life. I had no idea how he would take that information or what he would do.

I became obsessed with the thought of his reaction and tried to find ways to gauge what his acceptance level might be. I would ask him questions about what he thought would happen after we die. I would pick movies that had ghosts in them so I could watch his expressions and ask him questions. I asked him endless questions about any topic I thought could give me some insight to his thoughts. These questions included but were not limited to his religious upbringing, his current religious beliefs, who he follows on social media, has he ever watched *The Long Island Medium*, has he ever had a psychic reading, does he own or know anyone who owns Tarot Cards, does he believe in aliens, what percentage of our minds does he think we use, and what does he want to happen to his body following his own death? His answers were inconsistent and contradictory. They left me more confused than ever.

This is why, when Grandma Mae asks me about our possible engagement, I find myself hoping he does not propose. I need to share this secret with him that I am carrying around before I could even think about marrying him. Another worrisome issue is that he has mentioned, on multiple occasions, that we should both sell our apartments and buy a bigger one together. Fuck my life. I need to be honest with my boyfriend and stat.

"Well, I still think he might propose. You've been so happy with one another," Mae declares.

"I mean, I guess there is always a possibility. I just don't think it's going to happen now," I partially agree.

"If you say so." Mae hums. She clears her throat and straightens her back in her chair. "What are you two doing for your birthday?"

"Well, as you already know, you and I are going to lunch." She nods in agreement. "Then he and I are going out for drinks. After drinks he booked us an indoor shuffleboard court and then we are getting tapas." I am ecstatic about the plans that Fisher made for the night. It is not a traditional dinner date and has lots of different places to visit and activities to do.

"That sounds lovely," Grandma Mae says with a smile.

"Yes, I agree it does. It will be my first birthday spent with just a boyfriend."

"Very true." The sly smile she gives me makes me concerned that she is up to something.

"What is going on in that head of yours?" I ask her.

"Nothing, I am just happy for you. I'm happy you're seeing the value in having a partner. I'm happy you're happy." Her misty eyes look at me and she can't hide her emotion.

"Thanks, GM, I *am* happy. I love you very much and I hope you feel as fulfilled in your life as I do in mine."

"You have no idea, my dear. You are the light of my life. Your happiness is reflected in me. My only path to happiness is through you."

Knock, knock.

"Come in," I choke out with tears in my eyes.

"Hi, I hope I'm not interrupting." Colt has half his body leaning into the room and the other half is still in the hallway, hiding behind the door.

"Of course not, dear, come on in," Grandma Mae instructs him.

"Thanks, I was just hoping to go over this new campa-" Colt freezes. He watches me dab my finger under my eyes and looks to Mae. "Is everything alright?"

"Yes," Mae and I say in unison.

Colt's eyes move between us. "Are you sure?"

"Well, I suppose we could use a joke or two to ease the tension," Mae says, using delicate fingers to indiscreetly wipe at her nose.

"A joke?" Colt is taken aback.

"Yeah, ya know any?" I laugh and look down at the papers on the desk.

There's a pause where no one speaks, or even moves. I expect Colt to walk out of Mae's office since we are all so awkward and unsure how to proceed.

"What's the difference between a snowman and a snowwoman?" Colt asks. Mae's eyes and mine fly to Colt's face in shock that he is actually telling us a joke.

"What?" Mae replies in awe.

"Snowballs," Colt deadpans.

Mae and I erupt in laughter that we don't recover from for at least an hour.

February 14th

I spent the night before my birthday with my parents. I chatted with them about my fears of telling Fisher about our relationship. I felt better after saying the words out loud. I'd like to think that my parents understand and are supportive. Of course, there is no way to know this for certain but my heart tells me it is true.

After a lovely lunch with Mae, where we fawned all over each other once again and told each other how much we love one another, we shopped for a new birthday outfit.

I am dressed in pleather pants, a cropped green sweater, and heeled booties. I curled my hair and put on makeup that makes me feel sexy. I am ready to go when Fisher picks me up at 5:00.

"Hey! Want to come in for a drink?" I ask him when he calls to tell me he is downstairs.

"Nah, I got us reservations for drinks. Let's go to the bar," he says nonchalantly.

"Ok," I agree. It feels a little like he took the wind out of my sails. I wanted to tell him about my parents inside my apartment, but I tell myself that it doesn't matter where we have the conversation, as long as we have it.

I go down to the lobby and see Fisher waiting for me, looking hot as hell. His hair is gelled perfectly, he is wearing a camel colored overcoat. His pants are black and his button-up shirt is red.

"Wow, you look amazing," I tell him as I approach and give him a kiss on the lips.

"Thanks, same to you," he replies with a smile. "Let's get out of here."

We take an Uber to a new rooftop bar. Fisher rented us a pod to sit in so the bitter cold on a thirty story roof wouldn't give us frostbite. It is so warm and cozy in the pod. We have a big couch to cuddle on while our server brings us drinks. It's fantastic, the pod is even clear so we can still see all the city lights.

"This is great, Fisher, thank you."

"You're welcome. Happy Birthday."

I snuggle closer to him and inhale his scent. He is wearing cologne tonight and he smells delicious. After two drinks, Fisher tells me we need to wrap up if we want to make our shuffleboard reservation. Fisher asks the server for the bill and after he pays he tells me to finish my drink while he goes to the bathroom. We will meet at the host stand in five minutes.

I take the last couple sips of my wine and I see the white receipt sticking out of the leather folder on the small table in front of the couch. I have no idea what possesses me to open it, but something inside of me tells me I absolutely *must* look at the bill.

I slowly pick up the leather folder and open it. What I see on the inside shocks me. Fisher has written "0.00" on the tip line and confirms it with the total amount written at the bottom. Fisher did not leave a tip? Has he stiffed every server we've had? I suddenly feel like crying.

I pull out my purse and put fifty dollars inside the leather folder and walk to the host stand in a daze. If Fisher has not left a tip at any other restaurant or bar we have visited since we began dating, I will be mortified. I decide, though, that more research is necessary. I will check at the shuffleboard place and again when we get tapas. It's possible this was some sort of fluke. Could he have found our server on the way to the restroom and given her a cash tip then? I hadn't even thought to check the receipt to see if a tip was included. How dumb of me, perhaps in the reservation of the pod, they had included a tip. Surely that must be the case.

I shake off my feelings and see Fisher waiting for me just past the host stand, near the elevators. We move right along, take another Uber to the shuffleboard bar and have a great time playing against another couple. We make friends with the couple and buy them shots and drinks and thoroughly enjoy their company. After hours of playing, Fisher requests the check so we can make our reservation at *El Gallo* for tapas at 9:00.

When Fisher is saying goodbye to Mark, the man playing next to him at shuffleboard, I sneak a peek at the bill. Again, a big, fat zero on the tip line. I double check to make sure it's not included. It's not. Fuck a duck. My worst fears are being confirmed in front of my eyes. What sort of hideous person doesn't tip?

I have one more stop to either make or break Fisher before I confront him about his tipping behavior. If Fisher does not tip at the tapas restaurant, there is no way I can continue our relationship without speaking to him about this. If he does tip, then I will just be flabbergasted.

We go to our final location and order five or six tapas and they are all to die for. We mmm and ooo over each plate and the flavor explosions happening in our mouths. We praise the server for his attention to detail, he asks us about our need for further drinks and fills up our water before the glasses are empty; he also brings out one plate at a time so we can enjoy it before he brings another. He is the best server we've ever had and if Fisher denies this man a tip, I am going to lose my shit.

We sit at the tapas bar for hours ordering more plates and more Spanish wine. We laugh and indulge and just, in general, have a good time. It's a little after midnight when we decide to finish the last bites and drink the rest of the wine and head to my apartment.

I watch, with bated breath, as Fisher signs off on the bill. Sure as shit, he leaves another big fat zero. And again, for the third time tonight, I throw cash on the table to cover.

We get into the Uber and I am disgusted. Doesn't he know that's how servers make a living? Doesn't he know that servers have to give a percentage of their total sales to bartenders and the people who clean the tables? Does he realize that when he shorts the server, the server then in turn still has to pay others at the restaurant? That, in fact, they are going to have to pay for a portion of our bill by his neglecting to tip? The whole thing makes me feel sick to my stomach. It's despicable.

We arrive at my apartment and we exit the Uber together, surely without leaving any sort of tip, and take the elevator to my floor. After unlocking my door, disengaging the alarm, and re-activating the alarm I feel ready to speak to Fisher.

"What the fuck, Fisher?" He whips around to look at me in confusion.

"What are you talking about, Lenni?" His eyes look hurt.

"You don't tip?" I let it sound like a question, even though it is more like an accusation.

"So?" His flippance furthers my horror.

"So?! So?! How could you not tip? Don't you understand what you're doing?" My hands are flying in the air and dropping to my sides.

"Yeah, I think tipping is dumb. I already pay for my meal or drinks or whatever. I shouldn't have to tip on top of that." He waves his hand in a dismissive gesture.

"That's how those servers make a living. How could you take money out of their pockets like that?" I am near tears.

"Oh, those servers make plenty of money! More than most careers, actually."

"Because. Of. *Tips*." I spit the words at him.

"No, they get paid well," Fisher assures me.

"No, they get paid tips." I know my face is red with fury.

"Maybe we should just agree to disagree about this," Fisher offers.

———

My hands slam into my hips and I look down at the ground. I cannot believe I have been dating someone for more than a year that does not tip. I am repulsed at my own unknowing actions. I know I need to tell him about my parents and I decide that now is the time.

"Fisher, I need to tell you something."

"Ok..."

"I appreciate how much you've shared about your past with me, and I want to reciprocate."

"I would love that," Fisher encourages me.

"Ok, well, as you know my parents died when I was very young." He nods. "In a car crash."

"I'm sorry, Lenni, I didn't know how they died." He looks genuinely remorseful.

"It's ok, it's been a long time." I pace back and forth in my living room a couple times. "But I need to tell you that a couple years ago, I started communicating with them."

"What? Communicating?" It's clear by his expression that he is completely dumbfounded.

"Yes. One night I was very frustrated and out of total desperation I screamed to my dad for help. He helped. Ever since, I have found different ways to communicate with them. They flicker lights, make noises, you know - ghost stuff."

"Whoa. Valentina, what are you saying?"

"I'm saying that my parents are here. With me. And they were the most generous, kind people on the planet and I don't know how they would feel about me dating someone who isn't even generous enough to tip." The lights flicker.

Fisher looks distraught. "Lenni, this is a lot to take in. I think I should go home and process this information."

I'm fine with this. In all honesty, I don't want to be around him right now. "If that's what you think is best."

He walks over and kisses me on the cheek. I don't move under his touch. He walks to my front door, enters the code he has now memorized to disengage the alarm. He opens the door and looks over his shoulder.

"Happy Birthday, Valentina."

I wake up unsure how to react. Fisher may or may not be an awful human. Do I want to continue dating him? Do I want to discuss his bad habits and make an attempt to correct them? Is he worth all of this?

I check my phone and have no correspondence from him. I'm not surprised.

I decide to get up and make coffee to wake myself up.

Once I am fully caffeinated, I know I need to get to work on my intentions for the upcoming year of my life.

Aside from the usual goals of making my grandmother proud and growing within the company, I am going to set another familiar goal: figure out my relationship with Fisher. I first need to dive deeper into his morality. Who is he as a person? How does he view kindness and generosity? After I figure out those questions, I next need to see how he feels about my parents. He didn't seem too open to the idea last night so I need to navigate where we go from here.

I am moving at rapid speed toward thirty. It's time to make some changes in my life.

Twenty-Nine

February 13th

Welp, as you have probably guessed, it's been a tumultuous year. It took almost a week for Fisher to talk to me again. He was totally freaked out by the thought of me communicating with my parents in any way. It helped once we sat down and I explained it all to him, how it began, how it progressed, and how I feel about it. It didn't help entirely and he is still terrified to come into my apartment. This is, of course, ridiculous because my parents are always with me, but I choose not to bring that up.

Once he was able to have a rational conversation with me, we moved on to this tipping business. He told me he was raised not to tip and didn't understand the importance. I explained how the restaurant industry works and how the server "tips out" other people and how not tipping them affects their lives. He seemed to take it pretty seriously. When we are together now, he always tips. I'd like to believe he tips when he is eating out alone or with others, but I'm not entirely sure about that.

We spent the spring barely talking but still staying committed to one another. This was not difficult for me, I just went back to working the crazy hours I was working before Fisher. Work kept my mind off him and focused on my financial future. Mae would tell me to leave early and go see Fisher, but it boiled down to that I simply just never wanted to. The honeymoon phase was long over and I couldn't bring myself to fuss over him the way I had the year prior.

As spring rolled into summer, we began to see each other more. He would spend weekends with me in Sag

Harbor and work from home with me in his tiny, hot apartment (he still refused to step foot into mine). Our bond was rekindled and we remembered what we loved about one another.

The heat of summer dissipated and the cool fall breeze blew in. With it, blew in Fisher's pettiness. Maybe we were cooped up too much together or he just missed the sunshine and the beach, but either way Fisher got grumpy. Everything set him off. He was angry if I wanted to pick out pumpkins. He was angry if I wanted to stay at my place for the night. He was angry if I stayed at his place too often. He was angry if I talked about my day, he was angry if I was quiet at dinner. It didn't matter what I did or didn't do, he was crabby. Sometimes, he was even downright mean. At some point, around Thanksgiving, I had had enough. I left and didn't answer his texts or calls. I knew he was too afraid of my parents to come to my apartment, so I just hid there. Finally, he got the message and stopped contacting me until Christmas. Around the New Year, he began trying to get in touch with me again and I agreed, with the intention of breaking it off. When we met up in the beginning of January, he told me how much he missed me over the holidays and how desperately he wanted me back. The conviction with which he spoke convinced me to give our relationship one more chance.

Here we are, at our one more chance. We've been seeing each other every week for the past five weeks, trying to work it all out. Tomorrow night, my friends and I decided to go clubbing. Yes, you read that correctly. This is our last Valentine's Day, and my last birthday, before we all turn thirty. No one has any children yet, and even though two of us are married (I feel as though I should mention here that Nisha eloped with Max in Vegas on Halloween) we thought it would be good to hit the town one more time before we are in our thirties and probably parents.

Mae has agreed to accept the fact that the outfit we are going to buy after lunch tomorrow will be a bit more risque than normal and she is actually on board. She wants me to enjoy my youth while I have it. Those are her words, not mine.

I'm closing out my workday and finishing it all up when Colt walks in.

"Hey, Valentina, you have a moment?"

"Hey Colt, sure. What's up?" Based on my notification and access alerts, I know he still watches my front door. He has not, however, randomly stopped by or walked me home in over a year. I still have Gina and Rob in the background, but I think Colt must think I am in a safer place now that I have a man consistently visiting my apartment. Or, at least I used to.

He looks nervous and puts his hands in his pockets. "So, I, uh, I'm sorry, this is awkward. I just wanted to check in and make sure you're doing alright?"

"Doing alright"

"Yeah, you know, life? Work? Friends?"

I feel touched. I cannot believe Colt cares enough to check in with me.

"Yes, everything is good. Mae is great. Work is great. My friends are amazing as always. I appreciate you asking, and just you in general." I shuffle a couple papers around and file them. "How are you? How are your brothers? Are you an uncle yet?"

"Actually, yes." Colt chuckles. "Clyde has a son now, and Dale is actually expecting."

I stop messing with the papers and give Colt my full attention. "Wow, Colt, that is wonderful. Congratulations! Do we know if Dale is expecting a girl or a boy?"

"We do not, and there is a lot of money riding on it." He smiles at me in a way that makes my knees quiver, just a little. "For the sake of my bank account, it better be a girl."

It warms my heart to hear about all this fun and shenanigans with Colt and his family. "Hmm, this sounds interesting. I might need to get in on this action."

"Nah, you don't want to get involved with a bunch of degenerates like us."

"Maybe I do."

"Well, anyway, I'm glad you're doing well. We hadn't talked for a while so I just wanted to see how it all is going."

"As much as I appreciate your concern, I didn't miss that you evaded my betting attempt. I'll let it go, whatever the reason." I turn my computer off and rise to look at Colt again. "I was serious about appreciating you, though. You've always been thoughtful and kind with me. It means a lot."

"Of course. Anytime."

"I'm off, do you have any plans for Valentine's Day?"

"Nothing too exciting. I hope you have a great birthday."

"Thanks, Colt. Me, too."

February 14th

Mae said she was comfortable buying me something that showed more skin than normal, but that was not entirely true. When I came out in the outfit that I knew would be the one I purchased, she did not seem very pleased. In fact, she refused to buy it. This was fine, I purchased it myself, with my own money. Mae apologized about ten minutes after we left the store.

Even though over the past two years, I have purchased five different properties and sublet them all, I am still finding ways to spread my wealth. I donate a lot of it, but I also want to find other people like Mae who have a great idea and just need some help. This is something else I need to address with my financial advisors.

Regardless, I have no shortage of finances and it's not an issue to pay for my own outfit. Even if I did buy it from YSL. The sequined skirt and low-cut bodysuit left me with no choice. Even *I* thought I looked great, which is really saying something.

While I am getting ready, I get a text from Fisher saying he is running late and will meet up with me later. I have no idea what that means and I don't even respond. If he intends to blow off my birthday fun, we will be having words tomorrow.

I am fully coiffed and ready to go. In my excitement, I estimated incorrectly and I am an hour ahead of schedule. I think about pouring myself a glass of wine, but that feels silly to do at my house, alone. I am dressed and looking very hot, if I do say so myself. I decide to head to the first bar and await everyone's arrival.

It's especially frigid out tonight so I layer up as much as I can and order an Uber as I walk down the stairs. I wait in the lobby for just a moment before my car arrives and I am able to run into the backseat. The driver cringes when I open the door and the blast of cold air hits him.

"Christ, it's cold," he mumbles.

"I know," I agree.

We take off and the heat gets moving around the car and I forget what is just outside the windows. When we pull up to the bar, I hesitate to open my door and the driver laughs. He tells me to just get it over with as quickly as possible, so I take his advice and bolt. I'm inside the front door of the bar in less than five seconds after leaving the car. I tried to shut the car door as quickly as possible so the driver wouldn't feel the cold. Judging by his shriek, I was not as successful as I hoped.

I walk to the bar and plop down at a barstool in the middle. There are plenty of open seats and it's not too crowded. It seems New Yorkers aren't very anxious to get out and about on a freezing Valentine's Day.

I immediately order a pineapple martini. As the bartender starts shaking the concoction, I see someone sit next to me. Elated, I turn to see which of my friends has arrived. I gasp.

"Hi Valentina, how are you?" Rich says to me. He holds up a finger to the bartender and then points to a vodka bottle on the shelf behind the bar.

"Rich?" I am stunned, too stunned to be scared. Yet. "What the fuck are you doing here?"

"Well… I wanted to wish you a happy birthday and I honestly wasn't expecting to see you here." He takes a swallow of the clear liquid as soon as the bartender sets it down.

"You know it's my birthday?"

"Of course I do." Another swig of his vodka.

"Well, you've wished it. You can go now." I pull out my phone and open the app that allows me to call someone. I start to dial 9-1-1 when I feel his hand on my arm.

"Don't be like that."

"Rich, I do not like you. I do not want you near me. Please leave and leave me the fuck alone." I aim for my voice to be forceful and strong. Instead it sounds squeaky and scared.

"Oh baby, you don't mean that! If I can just show you how great we can be together, you'll want me around for all of your birthdays." He reaches a hand up to my face. I smack it away with as much strength as I have. I pull out my phone to call for help.

"Everything ok over here?" The bartender interrupts. Before I can register what is happening, Rich is off his chair and out the door. My skin prickles at the wave of cold air and I turn back to the bartender.

"No. He's a fucking creep. If I see him again, I am calling the police. You should do the same."

I act on instinct and pull out my phone to shoot off a text.

Colt, I'm sure you're busy since it's Valentine's Day and all, but I am sitting at a bar and Rich just appeared. I don't want to admit it to him, but I'm scared.

He immediately calls my phone, but I don't answer. I know my voice will betray me and I don't want to start crying on my birthday

I can't talk right now. Text only please.
Why can't you talk? Is he still there? Where are you?

No, he's gone. I'm at Cousins.
Hang on, I'm calling Rob.
Don't. It's fine, he's gone now. I want to tell him I am hoping he'll come be near me the rest of the night, but that

doesn't seem to be an option, or appropriate. Fuck, he's probably with someone.

I'm calling Rob. Why can't you talk to me?
I just can't.
Missed Call - Colt
Please answer.
I don't want to.
Please answer.
FINE

"Hello?"

"Valentina? Are you ok?"

"Yes, Colt. I'm fine."

"You don't sound fine."

I put my head down on my forearm. "Well, Colt, some man who is apparently stalking me just walked up and sat next to me telling me he wants to wish me a happy birthday. How would you be?"

"Fuck! Goddamnit, fuck!" Lots of rustling. "What else did he say?"

"Not much, I think the bartender scared him off."

"The bartender? Are you alone?"

"Yes."

"Goddamnit, why are you alone?" I hear more rustling.

"I was early."

"Please put the bartender on the phone."

"What?! No!"

"YES!"

"NO!"

"Valentina, listen to me. I drove to Massachusetts to visit Dale and I am at least three hours away from you. Put the fucking bartender on the phone. Now." His voice is an angry growl and now I understand why he's not offering to come to me.

"He's gone into the back. You don't need to speak to him. All my friends will be here soon." I reach for my martini and see how badly my hands are still shaking. I want Colt. My fear is acting as binoculars. It was as if it was too far away for me to see it before, but in this moment when I want someone near me, someone I trust and will make me feel safe. I want Colt. Not Fisher. This is an interesting realization but I can't focus on it now.

"That's something." He pauses and I hear a turn signal. "Where's Fisher?"

"He's running late. Are you in the car?"

"What a fucking moron." Now, I hear a horn blast.

"Colt, if you're driving we should hang up." I'm worried he'll be driving distractedly and get into an accident, or hurt someone else.

"What do you mean 'if'? Of course I'm driving. I'm driving to you." I hear another person talking in the background.

"What? No! You're far away, don't come to me. All my friends are coming. And Fisher eventually. Call Rob if you want. But stay in Boston, or wherever you are."

"Valentina." His voice is a low rumble. "I am coming to you. I am going to ask you for something and I'm also going to ask you to please do this for me. It's a big ask but it's short term."

"What? What are you talking about? What do you want?"

I hear him take a deep breath. "I want you to share your location with me. Just until the end of today, or until I get there. Whatever comes first."

At first, I am shocked. Sharing my location with him seems awfully personal, but it is also comforting at the same time. I don't share my location with anyone. It might be nice for someone to be able to locate me if needed.

"Colt…"

"Listen, it's entirely under your control. You can stop sharing at any time. All I'm asking for is tonight. Until we're in the same city again, please share your location with me." I can hear the desperation in his voice and I give in. I take the phone away from my ear and press the button to share my location. A follow up question pops up asking if I want to share for one hour, the end of the day, or indefinitely. I surprise myself by pressing 'indefinitely.'

———

"There. Are you happy now?" I ask him.

"Absolutely not, but this will do." There's a pause again. "See you in two hours and forty-eight minutes." He disconnects.

I put the phone back in my purse and reach for my martini again. After a shaky drink, I set it down and take a deep breath.

"So, instead of calling me, you called him?" I turn and see Fisher standing behind me.

"What? Hi, uh, no. Fisher, hey, I, uh, didn't call him. He called me."

"Why did he call you?" Fair question.

"Well, I texted him that Rich just showed up."

"Ohmygod, if I hear *one* more word about fucking Rich." He runs his hands through his hair in exasperation.

"What do you mean? He just showed up and sat next to me."

"So?"

"So?! So, the man who is stalking me shows up at a bar where I am sitting alone and you don't think that's a problem?"

He shakes his head and rolls his eyes a little. "I just think 'stalking" is a strong term."

"It is. And that's what he's doing."

"Listen, Lenni. It's complete and utter bullshit that you called him when you thought you could be in trouble instead of me." He throws his hands in the air in a dismissive gesture. I don't disagree with him, but it speaks volumes about our relationship.

"Listen, Fisher." I stand out of my seat, really fired up now. "I *was* in trouble. I am still in trouble. The fact that you refuse to believe it is the exact reason I chose to call someone besides you. You can take your bad manners and your fucking horrible attitude and leave. Do not contact me again."

"You can't be serious," Fisher scoffs. He draws back as if I've hit him. His surprise at my reaction only buoys the sinking feeling of fear in my stomach. Just twenty-four hours ago I was thinking of what it would be like for Fisher to propose, and now I am dropping him over a thirty second conversation. The thing is, though, that the conversation shows me his true thoughts. I've been dealing with, worried about, and randomly seeing Rich for years. For Fisher to think Rich showing up at this bar, where I am meeting all of my friends, on my birthday, when I am alone is not a big deal tells me that Fisher is not for me. He doesn't care about me, or my safety. If he did, he would have a much higher level of concern for Rich and his interactions with me.

It also says quite a bit about my feelings by who my gut told me to call. And that surely wasn't Fisher. It was Colt. My heart knew I wouldn't feel safe with Fisher here, but I absolutely would if Colt were here. All of these thoughts rolling around in my head, and my heart as well, tell me all I need to know about my relationship with Fisher. I have a fleeting thought about how disappointed Mae will be that I've just dropped Fisher like a bad habit, but I don't have time to dwell on this line of thinking. I have a super pissed man standing in front of me wanting an explanation about why I just told him to get lost.

"Fisher, look, I'm sorry," I try to speak in a calm tone. "Wait, scratch that, I don't like the way you just treated me and I'm honestly not sorry. I just don't think this will work with us. You don't seem worried about me at all, and I want someone who can't breathe if they even think I could possibly be in any sort of danger. And that's not you. That is fine! All that means, is just that our relationship will need to come to an end."

"What are you even saying? Of course I care about you and I'm worried about you!" His voice roars through the bar and people are starting to look at us. I see the bartender making his way over to us. Poor guy must be so confused.

"I know you care about me, but it's not enough. I want more. I *deserve* more."

"Wow, Valentina, I can't believe you. This is fucked up!" Fisher throws his hands in the air. The bartender, sweet man that he is, moves closer to me and I put my hand up to let him know I'm fine.

"It's not, though. This is exactly why you need to leave." I point to the door and turn back to my martini. I am shocked at how carefree I am about this breakup. I am not upset in the least at dismissing Fisher from my life. I guess that's just another sign this is all for the best.

Fisher lets out a huff before throwing his hands in the air again. I keep my eyes on the martini as he storms out the door. I hear his boots clomp across the floor as he makes his exit. I close my eyes and wish him a silent goodbye.

Three hours later, I see Colt walk through the same doors Fisher left through.

"Ohmygod, you're here," Colt says as he wraps me in a hug. I can feel the cold coming off his coat as he hugs me and it makes me shiver.

"Yeah!" I'm feeling the martinis and am entirely too loud. He lets go of me and steps away after I yell in his ear. "Of course I'm here!"

Colt gives me a knowing look. A look that has his mouth pressed together and his eyes looking at me from the corners and this look lets me know I'm busted. His face is saying what his mouth is not: You've been sitting here for three hours and doing nothing other than drinking martinis.

"I'm glad. I was a bit worried you'd just left your phone here to throw me off your track." Colt looks around the bar. His eyes search every face he sees.

"He's not here," I inform him. My eyes search his face. Fuck, he's handsome.

"I can still check."

"Sure, sure, have at it!" I wave my hand wildly around. My gestures cause a bit of liquid to slosh over the edge of my martini glass that is being held by my other hand. "It won't change the fact that he left hours ago and hasn't returned!"

"Right." He looks back to me. And for the first time, his eyes focus on me. He looks me up and down. "Wow, you look great."

"Thank you," I slur.

"Are you alright?" His eyes jump all over my face before looking over my shoulder. "Where is Fisher?"

"No idea." I pick a piece of pineapple out of my martini and pop it in my mouth with a sloppy smile.

"He never showed?" Colt looks pissed. Not surprised, but pissed.

"Oh, he showed alright," I mutter as I turn back to face the bar. I wave my hand at the bartender, motioning for another drink even though mine is half full. "What do you want to drink?" I ask Colt.

"What do you mean he showed up? Where is he now?"

"I told you, I don't know where he is!" The bartender is just a foot or two away from me now. "I'm sorry sir, can we please have another pineapple martini and a bourbon for this guy?" I point over my shoulder. The bartender gives us both a sly smile and disappears for a moment.

"Valentina, tell me now. Fisher came here," Colt demands.

"Yes, yes he did." I look him in the eyes.

"Then what happened?"

"Then, he was a dick so I dumped him."

"You broke up with Fisher?" Colt is stunned.

"Yup."

"Tonight."

"Yup."

"On your birthday?"

"Yes."

"What happened? How was he a dick?"

"Oh, you know," I say with a wave of my hand.

"No, I don't know, that's why I'm asking." Colt's voice is still calm and kind, but the way he shifts his weight and his jaw ticks just once, I can tell he is running out of patience.

"He just didn't care about me." I climb back up on the barstool. I'm actually taller this way, closer to Colt's face. "He was *uber* pissed that I texted you before him about Rich."

"You texted me first?" His voice is sweet and he seems genuinely surprised by this.

"Well, uh, yeah," I reply, feeling insecure about the whole thing for the first time. I guess it is odd that I didn't first reach out to my boyfriend, but it just didn't feel right. "He doesn't think Rich is anything to worry about."

"What do you mean?" Colt asks, eyebrows furrowed.

"He thinks Rich is just a normal guy, living his normal life, and the notes, the appearances, everything is just a coincidence. Fisher was… irked when I used the word 'stalking' in reference to Rich."

"Irked? He was irked you called Rich a stalker? When he's stalking you?" Colt's eyes are now wide and his jaw is ticking like crazy.

"You got it," I point at him with my pointer finger that is holding the martini glass before taking a sip.

I can almost see the steam coming out of Colt's ears. He throws back the entire tumbler of bourbon and raises it to the bartender to signal another. It takes the bartender only a few seconds to pour him another glass and slide it across the wooden bar.

"Thanks, man," Colt yells to the bartender so he can be heard over the music. He takes a twenty out of his pocket and tosses it onto the bar. "Keep it."

The bartender picks up the twenty and holds it up as a gesture of thanks. Colt nods and picks up his bourbon to take a swig.

"Where are your friends? I thought they were coming?" Colt asks.

"Oh yeah, they're here somewhere. Everyone but Amy and Mackie, they left already." I look around the room. "Ansley is down there pretending she isn't in love with Jake and flirting with that guy who she could never like. Robin is by the bathrooms talking with that bachelorette party, who she'll probably end up leaving with soon. And Max is feeling Nisha up, all the way down there at the end of the bar." I point to each one in turn.

"None of them are watching out for you?"

"We were all playing games together when Mackie and Amy were still here. Then when Robin went pee, we lost her to the bachelorette group and everyone started going their own ways. It's fine!" I move on to my next pineapple martini.

"How many of those have you had?" Colt points to my martini.

"It's not cool to count drinks, Colt." I take a defiant drink. "Especially not on someone's birthday. And the day they broke up with their boyfriend. And Valentine's Day."

Colt chuckles softly and takes a sip of his own drink. "Very true."

Colt holds his drink up to the bartender and points at it again, asking for another. I'm surprised since his is basically full. The bartender brings it over and Colt gives him another twenty with a nod.

"Dale!" Colt yells. He is facing the door and holding his hand up to get someone's attention.

An older, possibly hotter, version of Colt walks over. "Thanks," Dale says as he takes the drink from Colt.

"Valentina, this is my brother, Dale. Dale, this is my boss, Valentina." Colt gestures to each of us as he introduces us to the other.

"Hi Dale," I hold out my hand for him to shake. He takes it and gives me a gentle squeeze while our hands move up and down in unison. "Good Lord, you're so handsome."

Both men laugh. Their combined laughing rumbles are sexy as hell. "Thank you. It's nice to meet you. Colt did tell me you are beautiful, but wow," Dale says and lets out a low whistle.

"Alright, enough you two," Colt says. His expression lets me know he's uncomfortable but his jaw lets me know he is angry.

"Colt! You told your brother how gorgeous I am?" I say too loudly, again. I flutter my eyelashes at him in an exaggerated flirting gesture.

Colt shoves Dale's shoulder. "Fuck, man." Colt looks truly upset.

I shove Colt's shoulder. "Don't hit your brother! And it's fine, everyone knows you have a crush on me." I bump Colt with my shoulder and giggle at my own joke. Dale and

———

Colt both lose their smiles and look at one another in a weird silence. I look back and forth between them, the whole situation is now awkward.

"Dale, what brings you to town? Wait! Isn't your wife or girlfriend having a baby?" The memory of Colt telling me this rushes back to me.

They share one more secretive look before focusing on me. "Yeah, my baby is due in May." His eyes flick to Colt and then back to me. "But I'm not involved with the mother."

"Oh, gotcha." The tension is still so thick, I feel like breathing is more difficult than normal. "Are you excited to become a father?"

"Oh yeah, I can't wait," Dale says, finally giving me a smile. "I can't wait to meet the baby."

"Aww, that's sweet!"

"What's sweet?" Robin asks. I was watching both men so intently, I missed her approach. She wraps her arms around me and waits for my response.

"Dale, here, is going to have a baby in a couple months." I wave my hand in Dale's direction. "Robin, this is Dale. Dale, Robin."

They shake hands and I can already tell by Robin's expression that she finds Dale attractive. Honestly, I can't blame her. He's smoking hot. Since he is a police officer, you can imagine that the gorgeousness of his body rivals the handsomeness of his face. "Nice to meet you, Dale."

"You, too."

"How do you know my little Valley Girl?" Ugh, I hate that nickname.

"I just met her actually. She knows my brother." Dale stuffed one hand in his pocket but never took his eyes off Robin.

"Oh yeah? Who's your brother?"

"Colt," Dale replies. He nods his head in Colt's direction. It seems impossible that Robin didn't notice Colt standing on the other side of me. But I guess therein lies the proof of Dale's beauty.

Robin leans around me and the shock on her face makes it evident she had no idea he was there. "Colt! Hey!"

———

153

"Hi Robin," he says with a low tone. He takes a sip, looking horribly uncomfortable.

"I'm going to grab a drink, you want another, Dale?"

"Sure. I'll come up with you."

Colt and I turn simultaneously and watch as Robin and Dale walk to the bar.

"Uh oh, we're in trouble," I say out of the side of my mouth.

"What do you mean? With those two?"

"Yes, with those two! Robin's already doing her flirting stance." Her laughter breaks through the crowd. "Oh! And look! She's already touching his arm!"

"Did she just squeeze his bicep?" Colt asks.

"Probably," I reply. My attention is back on my martini. I take another sip.

"You feeling ok?" Colt asks me.

I debate how I want to answer his question. I, technically, feel fine. I know that I've had a little too much to drink and tomorrow I will pay for these martinis, but I feel good right now. My mood has lifted significantly since Colt's arrival and that realization is not lost on me. I see how much I enjoy his presence. I hate to use this outdated and pathetic word, but it's the one that works best, I *longed* for him. The moment I saw Rich in that chair next to me tonight, I wanted Colt. I wanted him close to me, to be with me, to talk to me about it all. I'm not sure why all these feelings flooded me at once. It could be that I wouldn't let myself feel them before when I saw him primarily as a co-worker. Maybe I was blinded by my infatuation with Fisher and simply busy with our relationship. It could also be that seeing Rich face-to-face again was so unexpected and overwhelming, it was a catalyst for these feelings. Whatever the reason, I know now, standing in this bar, that I have it bad for Colt Arden.

Should I make a move on Colt? My status as his boss makes me think twice about this option. I sure as hell don't want to leave him alone in this bar with all of these single women around. He looks sexy as always and certainly should not be left alone. Especially not with his equally hunky wingman at his side. No sirree.

———

154

"I'm fine, maybe a little tired, but fine," I tell him. I went with honesty.

"Want me to take you home?" Colt offers.

"What about Dale?" I point in Dale's direction. He and Robin are already wrapped around one another, whispering in each other's ears.

Colt smiles. "I think he'll be alright for the night. If not, he knows how to get into my apartment." Colt looks at me and shrugs. "Come on, let's get you home."

"Ok, let me text the group real quick."

While I'm texting, Colt gets our coats from the hooks by the door. I slide my arms in while he holds it against my back.

"Thanks. Do you need to tell Dale?"

"I already texted him and he told me to stop distracting him." This makes me laugh.

We wait for the Uber under the heaters outside of the front door. Once it arrives, we run in as fast as we can and rub our hands in the back of the cab trying to warm up.

Once we're sufficiently warm and settled in for the ride home, Colt casually lays his arm across the top of the backseat. His hand lands behind my head and I can feel the heat of him coming off of it. His heat feels like a magnet and, suddenly, I am desperate for him to touch me. I look over at him and he is looking out the window, paying me zero attention. I decide to take matters into my own hands and lean into him, into the crook of his arm. At first his body goes stiff at my touch, but once I snuggle even further into his body, he gives in.

"Are you cold?" he asks. He drops his hand from the back of the seat and uses it to rub my shoulder.

"No." His hand stops rubbing and freezes on the outside of my arm. "Thanks for coming tonight. I know that was a lot of driving."

Colt is silent for a moment. His hand starts rubbing my arm again, this time in a more slow and sensual way than in a 'I'm trying to warm you up' way.

"No problem. I'm happy you texted." He lets his arm rest around me. I nuzzle him again, just trying to get millimeters closer.

We say nothing for the rest of the car ride and when we arrive at my apartment, I don't want to get out. I make no move to exit the car when it stops in front of my building. Colt taps me and I groan. He chuckles.

"Come on, I'll help you get out and then I'll carry you," he offers.

I sit up, get out of the car, and stand on the sidewalk waiting for him. "It's not that. I was just comfortable."

He climbs out of the backseat, shuts the door, and walks right up to me. "Yeah. Yeah, me too." He puts one arm around my shoulders and we walk into the building together.

We both wave to the camera as we enter my apartment. I go in and take off my coat and shoes and head into the living room. When Colt isn't next to me, I look around. He is still standing at the door, in his coat and shoes.

"What are you doing at the door? Come in, take your coat off." I move to the kitchen. "Want a nightcap? Something warm to drink?"

"Hey, Lenni, listen, I'm not sure -" Colt is interrupted by the loud ding of my phone.

"Sorry, Colt, hang on, just want to make sure this isn't one of the girls needing help."

"Oh yeah, of course, please check it," he says with a furrowed brow.

When I read the text I feel all the color drain from my face. My legs feel shaky and my heart starts beating a mile a minute. I stumble over to the kitchen table and sit down in one of the chairs.

"What's wrong? Does someone need help? Should I go back?" Colt moves to my side.

I shake my head.

"Then what is it? What's wrong?" Colt is kneeling in front of me now. I hand him my phone out so he can read the text that came through from an unknown number.

Now you're sleeping with a second man? Does your boyfriend know about him? Ur nothing but a whore and a tease u little slut.

Colt bolts upright. "Whose number is this?"

"No idea." I'm in a fog.

Colt begins pacing back and forth. "You have to change your number."

"I know."

"I'm not kidding, Valentina."

"I'm not either, Colt."

He walks around, checking every window and closing every blind in the apartment. He triple checks that the alarm is on. I walk into my closet and start putting on my fuzzy pajamas. I hear him mumbling about security and new alarm systems.

"Good idea, let's get you into bed," Colt instructs once he sees me standing in my bedroom.

"Stay with me," I say, just above a whisper.

"Yeah. Of course, I'm staying." Colt nods and walks with me to my bed.

"Stay in here with me."

Colt runs a hand through his hair, clearly unsure. "I, uh, yeah, sure. I'll stay on the floor and keep an eye on things."

"No." I shake my head from side to side. "Sleep in my bed with me."

"Valentina…"

One frustrated, scared tear escapes. As it slides down my cheek, I see all of the resolve leave Colt's body. He deflates and begins nodding again.

"Yeah, ok, come on." He climbs in, still wearing his coat.

"Please don't wear your shoes and coat in my bed."

"Oh, right." He leaves my room and returns seconds later not wearing a coat or shoes. But still wearing his pants and sweater.

"You can get as comfortable as you like," I say and motion to his clothes.

———

"Yeah, I don't think that's a good idea."

"Suit yourself," I say and climb under the covers. Once we're both in, I scoot over and cuddle against him.

"Lenni, I don't think this is a good idea. Maybe you should sleep on your side and I should sleep on mine?"

"Why?" I ask. He lets a frustrated growl loose.

"I don't know, because you just broke up with your boyfriend five hours ago, you have someone stalking you, and I -" Colt stops talking. I hear him rub a hand down his face. "I just don't think we should."

"How can I be sure you won't leave me alone in the middle of the night?" I ask with a weak voice.

"Oh, Valentina, if you've ever trusted me at all, then trust me now when I tell you that I promise with everything I have that I will not leave you alone tonight."

I say nothing and roll away from him. I hear as he releases a huge sigh and tosses and turns for a minute. I am about to tell him that I've changed my mind and I want him to go sleep on the couch when I hear him cough and sigh again.

"Oh, fuck it," he whispers. He rolls toward me and wraps an arm around and pulls me against him. My back is flush with his front. "Goodnight, Lenni."

February 15th

The next morning I wake up alone in my bed. The light is glaring in through my curtains and I roll over to see the bed empty next to me. Disappointment hits me like a brick wall. How dare Colt promise not to leave me, and then leave me? I climb out of bed and once I'm done cleaning up in the bathroom I leave my bedroom in search of coffee.

As soon as I open my bedroom door, I see him. He's standing in my kitchen, sipping coffee, shirtless. His hair is tousled from sleep and his eyes are heavy. God, he's sexy as hell.

"Morning, Colt," I manage as I walk toward him.

"Morning, Lenni," he replies sweetly. He hands me a full mug of coffee. I close my eyes and let the scent of the coffee lift to my nose before taking a sip. It's delicious and I repeat the process again. I open my eyes and see Colt staring at me.

"How long have you been up?" I ask.

"Not long." He smiles at me from behind his coffee mug. He clears his throat and gets rid of his perfect smile. "I do want to talk to you about a few things."

"You usually do," I mumble and take another sip.

"First things first, without question, you need to change your number today."

"You'll get no argument from me about that."

"Great. I also think we need to beef up your security. More cameras, maybe some floor sensors for the alarm system." He looks at me as if he's going to get some sort of fight from me on these topics. He's wrong. I still agree.

"Ok to everything you mentioned." He tries to hide the shock that crosses his face.

"Perfect. Let's sit down for the last item on my list."

We walk over to the kitchen table and sit down. I sit in the chair I always sit in and ironically, he sits in the fourth chair. The only chair I never picture either of my parents sitting in. It's as if he let them sit in their chairs and then took the only spot left open.

"Listen, Colt, if this is about the location sharing, I will leave it on," I tell him.

"You will?" His voice squeaks a little in surprise.

"Yes, it was actually sort of comforting to have someone know where I am." He is still silent, staring at me with his mouth open. "Don't get me wrong, you abuse this privilege in any way and I will end it. Immediately."

"Of course. I understand." He shakes his head a little.

"Great. Was that all?" I ask.

Colt searches my face and stalls for a moment. "Not exactly."

"Oh?"

"Yeah, I, um, wanted to talk to you about the apartment."

"The apartment?"

"Yeah, Lenni, I know you want to stay here because of the connection with your parents and their money. I completely understand and respect that. Please know the only reason I'm about to broach this topic is because I am worried about you. Worried about your wellbeing." His head falls back and he growls softly. "Worried about your life."

"Alright, go on." I'm not sure where this conversation is going but my newfound attraction to Colt has me fully engaged.

"I want you to move."

"Colt, no."

"Lenni, yes. It's not safe for you here. He knows where you live. He knows how to find you. You don't have to sell this place. You can do anything with it. Leave it the way it is, just move somewhere else. You could sublet it. Whatever you want. It just isn't safe for this to be your one and only home."

As much as I hate to admit it, I don't hate his proposal.

"Colt, I understand exactly what you're saying. I will never sell this apartment, but I am willing to move into one of my others."

"Your others?"

"Yes, I have been buying property for years and I have a management company that runs it all. They just deposit whatever profits I've earned into my bank account every month."

"Wow. Nice. That's great, Lenni."

"I'll look and see if any properties have expiring leases anytime soon. If not, I will buy another." I look around and feel tears fill my eyes. "I will never let anyone else live here, though."

"I understand."

"I don't think you do, Colt."

"What do you mean?"

"I'm about to come clean to you about a few things. I am not sure you can handle it, but I want to give it a go." I give him a small shrug and take a sip of my coffee while I wait for some sort of response.

"Ok, I'm game." Colt nods his head in encouragement.

"First, I think I could possibly like you. *Like* you, like you." The bombshell of my bluntness is written all over his face. "I think you're great and while I'm worried about how it will play out at work and if it will interfere, professionally, with us, I'm not sure that I care about any of that. I wouldn't mind seeing where it goes, but before we even consider moving forward in any way, I have to tell you more about my parents."

"Your parents?"

"Right. My parents. This is going to sound… odd." I pause, gathering my courage. "I communicate with them."

Colt's face is curious, not mean or disbelieving. "Communicate with them, how?"

"Well, I speak to them and then I get some sort of response. Sometimes lights flicker or the oven beeps or my feet tickle." I stop and smile at him. "They find a way to help or convey their feelings to me."

Colt sits for a long while in silence. He is thinking, I can see his eyes moving rapidly back and forth. After a few minutes, he looks up at me. "This makes so much sense."

"It does?" I am flabbergasted at his response.

"Yes! So many things have happened in this apartment. One time when you were sleeping, I was watching TV. I heard you move around in bed a few times and then the volume on the television stopped working. No matter what I did, I couldn't get it off mute."

"No shit." I laugh.

"And another day, the alarm was acting funny when I was waiting for Rob. After about twenty tries, I just left it on and waited for Rob to get here. He was stuck in traffic that day and was almost an hour late. Who knows what would have happened if I had left?"

"Wow," I say in awe. I never would have thought I would need to hear someone else feel the same things I feel in this apartment. Colt speaking these words to me elates me. I'm not crazy, they are here.

"I can't tell you how happy this makes me," I confess with burning eyes and a tight throat. My curiosity is taking over my entire body. "I'm so glad you're accepting of my parents. But, I have to know. What about the other part?"

Colt looks directly into my eyes. He does not look away or break eye contact. It's so intense, I almost need relief. I hold strong and keep looking into his eyes as long as he's looking into mine.

"Lenni, as wonderful and amazing as you are, I can't."

I recognize this for what it is, a rejection. I want to fight it and demand to know why. I want to figure out what it is about me that repulses him. I want the nitty gritty. The fatigue, both mental and physical, from the day before and seeing Rich and dumping Fisher has me drained. I have nothing left in me to fight, though. The only two options for me are to sink into his acceptance or to rest away his rejection. Clearly, it is going to be the latter.

"I understand." It's all I can bring myself to say.

"Let me explain," Colt starts. I hold up my hand to stop him.

"It's fine, I understand." I rise from the couch and grab both of our coffee mugs from the table as I go. "I'm going to take a shower, I think you should go while I'm in there."

"No, I'm not leaving you. Rich could be sitting right outside your apartment," Colt says, his voice contains just a bit of panic. He waves wildly toward the windows.

"Then, you'll see it on the camera when he comes up and you can call the police. I'll handle it when he gets here." I've never been more sure of anything in my life.

"Lenni, no. This is all wrong! You broke up with Fisher *yesterday*, I can't go there - "

"Colt, fine, I understand. I'm not upset. This will have no affect on your work compensation or reviews or anything.

Like I said, though, I am going to take a shower and when I get out, I want you gone." I turn on my heel and walk the opposite direction before he can see the tears streaming down my face.

<h1 style="text-align:center">Thirty</h1>

February 13th

Remember how years and years ago I was trying to figure out my "type" of man? Well, as it turns out, my type is Colt. And only Colt.

This is not due to a lack of trying. Believe me, I tried to find men attractive this year. My friends and I went out every weekend. We went anywhere in New York City you would think you could find a good, fuckable man. We went to sporting events, libraries, hardware stores, outdoorsmen shows, cooking spotlights - you name it, we went there. Not one single man spiked my interest. Every man I saw only made me wish I was there with Colt.

I am so pathetic, I even smell him from time to time when I'm alone. My mind conjures up his presence or something. In my new apartment my parents still talk to me and it still smells of Colt, even though Colt has never once stepped foot inside my new apartment. Oh, I moved by the way. I agreed with Colt and the text from Rich really did freak me out, so I told my parents I needed them to come with me and I went apartment hunting. I decided not to move into one of my existing apartments. After all, I deserve it! I've been working so hard at MaeDay and started this property side business. It's one of the reasons I can afford my new, swanky place. Honestly, the hardest part about moving is not seeing Gene every day any longer. I stop by when I can to see him and ask about Mary Jo, but it's not the same.

Colt and I have been nothing but professional with each other over the past year. And I mean, *strictly* professional. No flirting. No smiles. No funny business whatsoever. I fucking hate it.

I know he still watches all the cameras that have now been installed in all of my properties. They are all linked to the same account that he has access to. I did stop sharing my location with him, though. He was clearly pissed at me for a few days, but I refused to give in. We were barely speaking, why would I let him know where I was at any moment of the day?

I did my regular one-on-one with him yesterday and I am itching to get out of the office today. Tonight, I am meeting up with my fab four for dinner and drinks. Tomorrow I am having an epic birthday party at my new apartment so tonight it will just be the five of us.

I sneak out of work a few minutes early, not even saying goodbye to Mae. I have Hank take me to the restaurant to meet my friends. Ansley is already sitting at the table, waiting for us all. She stands as I approach and we give each other a quick cheek peck and a long hug. Within a few minutes, everyone else arrives.

The wine is flowing and we're all laughing and drinking as we discuss my party for the following night.

"I'm obsessed with the theme for tomorrow," Amy confesses.

"Me, too!" Ansley agrees too loudly, the wine is working.

"I mean, it's just Dirty Thirty," I say.

"Right, but the fact that you have to dress up and actually be dirty, that's fucking awesome," Nisha chimes in. "What are you all wearing?"

"I'm going to be someone from The Walking Dead," Robin says with a giggle. All eyes swing to her. "Clearly once the zombies are here and the grid is gone, there are no showers." We all laugh and have to agree.

"I'm going as a zoologist," Ansley tells us. We all look at her with confused expressions. "What? I have a hot zookeeper outfit."

"Mackie and I are going to dress as porn stars," Amy says. "It literally won't get any dirtier than us!"

"What are you going to wear, Lenni?" Ansley asks.

I take a deep breath before responding. "Ladies, I've lived this past year in agony. I want Colt and he wants nothing to do with me."

The table explodes into rounds of "fuck him" and "he doesn't deserve you." I wait until they are finished before I continue.

"But I'm done with all that. I'm going to look so unbelievably good tomorrow, he won't be able to keep his hands off me." The ladies all erupt in hoots. "Unless he can, and then my hotness will just drive him berzerk!"

"So, what is it? What are you wearing?" Robin asks.

"I'm going to be Jane."

February 14th

I'm standing in front of the mirror in my bedroom in just scraps of fabric. I hired a glam squad to make me up for tonight. I didn't want to miss an opportunity to look amazing for Colt. I want him to want me. This outfit should do it since I'm nearly naked.

I am wearing a leopard print skirt, but skirt is a loose term. It is jagged and frayed and barely covers my vagina or buttcheeks. I have on thigh high boots and a matching leopard print crop top. Again, the crop top is much more cropped than normal. It's also cut up and uneven, appearing as though I've been living in the jungle with Tarzan. I'm secretly hoping Colt arrives dressed as Tarzan. Wouldn't that be something?!

Aside from my leopard skin and boots, I had the glam squad make my hair big and wild. It's sticking out, but in a sexy way. They even stuck a few twigs they found in my yard in my hair. My makeup is dark and seductive. I'm wearing fishnets, under my skirt and boots, that are ripped in all the right places, of course. Finally, the team put fake dirt swipes all over my arms, chest, and back, and a couple on my face. I look like the dirtiest *dirty* thirty-year-old woman there ever was.

I've never worn anything so revealing in my life. I stand in front of the mirror, gathering all of my courage. After a few deep breaths and a shot of tequila, I leave my bedroom for the party downstairs.

Amy and Mackie are waiting for me outside my bedroom door. I know they said they were going to dress up as porn stars, but it's more correct to describe them as a sub and a dom. I don't need to say anything more.

After them, I meet up with Ansley and Jake. Ansley looks adorable in her zoologist costume and she even talked Jake into dressing up as a lion. When prompted, Jake will tell you that lions are dirty animals that love to roll in the dirt. Then they participate in social grooming. We are all desperate for Ansley to realize that he loves her.

Robin, as always, looks great. She looks like a zombie, but her dark makeup and the red dripping from wounds all over her body really work. She looks like some sort of Hollywood actress.

Once Robin catches sight of someone dressed in the same genre as her, and isn't truly even in the same genre, she's gone. The man is dressed as a vampire, but according to Robin both vampires and zombies aren't completely alive and both feed on living humans. She sees him, and I know it's likely I won't see her again for the rest of the night.

I sense him. I know he's here somewhere. I look around and then it happens. Just like in a movie scene, the crowd parts. The people move away from the center of the room. Everyone on the right side walks to the right, and everyone on the left side walks to the left. It's like the parting of the Red Sea. And at the end, there he is. Colt.

As much as I wanted him to be dressed as Tarzan, he's not. He's infinitely hotter. He looks better than I've ever seen him look in my entire life. He is a baseball player. Hang on, hear me out. He's got on a super tight baseball shirt. You know, the one with the white center and blue sleeves. Fucking hot. Then he has on actual baseball pants, gray ones. Equally as hot. I'm staring at those pants so intently, I've found the outline of his penis. He's also wearing high white baseball socks. No hat, but his hair is messed and gelled to perfection. I can see the outline of every muscle in his arms and legs in this outfit. It makes me feel desperate to see what's underneath. He's got dirt rubbed on his clothes and his skin and he is hot as fuck. I might have mentioned that already.

It takes a few minutes for his eyes to catch mine. I don't mind. I just take him in. I inspect every inch of his body while I wait for him to notice me. He's talking with co-workers and friends, chatting up the people standing around him. I just wait. I know he'll see me eventually and I want to watch his face when he does. Will he be attracted? Unaffected? Turned on? Turned off?

I know the moment he sees me and every fear I've had over the past year of him not liking me or me not being good enough for him flies out the window. His eyes catch my body and I can instantly feel his attraction to me, it feels like he is shooting fire at me. Every body part he focuses on is warm. He catches my bare midsection first and his eyes take their time roaming my torso. Then he moves down to my legs. Again, he takes his sweet ass time examining those. His eyes then jump to my chest, lingering, before moving up to my face. I get the pleasure of watching his perusal. When his eyes finally find mine and I see the look of trepidation cross his face, I'm able to hold it together and give him a seductive smile.

He makes no response other than to start looking into his drink. I walk toward him and when I enter his vision, he immediately looks up and watches my approach.

"Hi Colt. Thanks for coming."

He clears his throat. "Sure, right, no problem."

"I hope you have a great time. I'm not sure if you've been to the bar yet or not," he's clearly holding a drink, "but, it's fully stocked."

"Great. Thanks." Colt's struggle to look only at my face is obvious.

"Ok, well, enjoy the party." I lift my hand next to my face and give him a little wave. I turn and walk away from him, moving my hips from side to side just enough that he can't tell I'm doing it on purpose.

"Patrick!" I scream and pick up my pace to head toward my cousin. I jump into his arms and he easily lifts me into a huge hug. Colt has no idea Patrick is my cousin, and he certainly doesn't need to.

I talk to Patrick for a few minutes before I feel someone standing behind me. Patrick's eyes keep jumping to whoever it is back there. I finally give up and turn to see Colt.

"Valentina, can I speak to you for a moment?" Colt is glaring at Patrick while asking me the question. Patrick holds his hands up and walks away, he's never been one for drama.

"Sure, Colt, what's up?"

He looks around the room and nods in the direction of my bedroom. This is happening faster than I expected, but I'm not complaining. I lead the way into my room. He walks in behind me and locks the door.

"Why are you wearing that?" he asks while still looking at the closed door.

"It's a dirty thirty party, and I'm dirty." I know what he's asking me, but I'm not done playing hard to get.

"Lenni, I can't even concentrate on having a conversation with anyone while you're wearing that." He finally turns to face me and to his credit, his face does look a little pained.

"I don't know what to tell you, Colt," I say as I turn and walk away from him.

"Why are you doing this to me?"

I whip around and look at him. "Doing what to you?"

"This!" He waves his hand in the air up and down in front of my body. "You know staying away from you is hard enough already, why are you torturing me?"

Confusion riddles my body. It's at least a minute before I can move again.

"What the hell are you talking about? Torture?"

Colt turns away from me and walks in a circle, sinking the heels of his palms into his eyes. "You know!"

"I don't! What are you talking about?"

Colt walks right up to me. We are heaving chest to heaving chest. "You told me at the bar you knew."

"Knew what?" I search the back corners of my mind for the memory.

"Knew how I felt, for Christ's sake!" The night comes back to me all at once. I told him we all knew he had a crush on me. Is that what he's talking about?

"The crush? You had a crush on me?" He turns and paces in the other direction.

"More than a crush..." he mumbles.

"Colt! Stop!" He stops pacing and looks at me. I know my eyes are too wide and I am excited and anxious. "Colt, are you saying that you had feelings for me?"

"No, not *had*." He shakes his head.

It's all I need to hear. I walk up to him, again pushing my chest against his. I don't miss the way his eyes flutter shut when we make contact. I pay attention to the groan that leaves his mouth when I'm inches away. I can feel the way he is pressing against me. I know he wants me.

I lean in, as close to his mouth as I can get without kissing him. Remembering his rejection, I want to make him suffer for just a few moments more.

"Why did you make me wait? Why did you torture *us*?" I whisper.

"Because I'm the dumbest man alive." He breathes. I can smell his breath, it's mint and bourbon. I want to taste it on his tongue.

"You're a fucking fool," I whisper again.

"You're fucking right," he admits. He is still hovering and I realize he is scared to make a move. I don't want to remember my last birthday, when he turned me down, and I don't want to think about what that means now. I just want to act.

I move my hands up to his chest, just below his nipples. His eyes close at my touch. I gently slide my hands up his pecs and over his shoulders. His eyes are rolling to the back of his head now. I reach around and grab the hair on the back of his head. It's barely long enough for me to grip, but I make do.

"Don't *ever* do that to me again," I demand as he breathes on my face.

"Fuck. Never. I promise."

I put us both out of our misery. I crash my mouth into his. It ignites a fire inside of him and he instantly takes over the moment my lips make contact with his. One of his hands goes to my back and pulls me flush against him. The other goes to the back of my head and maneuvers it anyway he wants so he can gain better access.

The only way to describe the kiss is 'wild.' He is everywhere. His mouth is everywhere. His hands are everywhere. And without even realizing it's happened, we're lying on my bed. He's lying on top of me and kissing me, hard. I am trying to catch my breath when I hear the door open.

"Colt?" It's the vampire.

"Get the everloving fuck out of here, Dale!" Colt's voice is deep and scratchy and scary. I look around his shoulder to see the vampire, who is apparently Dale, and Robin giggling and closing the door. It all makes sense now.

"I'm so sorry, I thought I locked it." Colt is kissing up my neck.

"I'm sure you did. Robin knows where the key is." It's hard to formulate real and true thoughts when he is kissing me like this.

"Hmmmm, well that makes sense." His grumble across my skin sends a lightning bolt down my body.

"Colt, get up."

He immediately takes all of his weight off of me and backs away. "What's wrong?"

I didn't want him to stop touching me entirely. I move forward and straddle his lap. "I just need to know why you rejected me last birthday before I can be with you on this birthday."

His eyes move to my hair. He pets my hair and moves it away from my face. "I want to tell you everything. But I'm afraid, first, that you'll fire me and second, which would be so much worse, you will be scared and leave me."

I ponder this for a moment. "What if I promise to do neither?" I look in his eyes. "I promise, just like you promised to me last year, that I will not leave you alone tonight."

His face softens. "Lenni, rejecting you was the hardest thing I've ever had to do. You had been drinking so much and you had just broken up with Fisher. Not to mention, Rich scared you and made you feel vulnerable. The whole situation felt wrong. I felt like I would be taking a cheap shot if I allowed anything to happen between us. Plus, I was doing a little self-protection since I couldn't be sure how serious the breakup with Fisher was."

"Hopefully, you can see now that the breakup was serious. And I've only had one drink tonight so you should see how serious I am about us."

He starts playing with my hair again. "The truth, Valentina, is that I *had* to protect myself because I was in love with you. I am in love with you. I've *been* in love with you."

I'm taken aback by his words. I'm not scared or worried, I'm flattered. Even though thoughts of Colt have dominated my mind for the past year, I don't feel ready to tell him I love him. It's not out of the realm of possibility that I *do* love him, I just want to spend a little more time with him. More… personal time.

"Colt, I have no idea what love feels like. All I know is that I think about you all the time. I want you with me all the time." I search his eyes. "I miss you all the time," I whisper.

He moves my hair around and kisses my forehead.

"It could be love, I'm not sure. Either way, I want to figure out whatever this feeling is with you. I want you."

"Thank fuck, because I want you," he says as he leans into me, putting his hand behind my head and pulling my lips against his.

Forty-five minutes later we unlock the door and emerge from my bedroom. We didn't do much more than kiss and some fondling, but he is going to stay the night. It took all of my willpower to pry myself off of him long enough for both of us to calm down enough to become presentable and able to leave the privacy of my bedroom. As badly as we both want one another, listening to our friends talk and laugh over the blaring music with only a wall between us does not exactly sound like a conducive environment for first time lovemaking.

"How long are all of these people planning to stay?" Colt whispers in my ear.

"Seeing as it's barely ten o'clock, probably a while." I giggle at the noise Colt makes in response. It lands somewhere between a growl and a whimper.

"Pull the fire alarm?" I let a small cough of laughter escape. When I turn to look at his face, I see that he's not laughing. He's completely serious.

"As much fun as clearing out the entire building into the snow and having a dozen firefighters rush through my door sounds, I have a better idea." I kiss his cheek and squeeze his butt lightly before turning around. He wraps his arms around my waist and the way they are already starting to travel toward indecent areas of my body, I know he won't make it much longer.

I look around the room until I find exactly who I'm looking for. I walk up to Robin, leaving Colt hiding his lower half behind my kitchen counter.

"Hey, let's take this party to the city!" I fill my voice with as much enthusiasm as I can bring to the surface. Robin looks me up and down, a suspicious expression on her face. Her mouth is drawn tight and to the side. She looks around and sees Colt watching us so intently, his eyes might actually bug out and fall onto my kitchen floor.

"You don't want to go to the city," Robin says. She shifts her weight and points at me. "You just want *us* to go to the city so you can stay here and fuck Colt."

"Pretty much, yeah." I shrug. I see no point in hiding the truth. It is what I want, desperately what I want, and all the girls will eventually find out anyway.

"You little sex kitten!" Robin whisper yells at me. She pulls me into a hug and bounces around in excitement. "I'm so happy for you!"

"Thanks! Happy enough to get everyone the fuck out of my apartment?" I ask from over her shoulder in the middle of our hug. She pulls away from me and rolls her eyes.

"Hey, go tell everyone we're going to go to the bar down the street that has those weird chairs and all the ladders," Robin orders Vampire Dale.

"Thanks, girl," I tell her sincerely. She winks at me and walks away. Within five minutes, she has everyone out of my apartment. On her way out, she could smell my desperation to be alone with Colt and was able to weasel the promise to either show up at the bar later or call her with details tomorrow.

As soon as I slide the lock into place, Colt is on me. He is standing behind me as I enter the code on the alarm system. It's surprisingly sexy to have him standing there, rubbing his front against my backside, and holding my hand as I type in the numbers on the alarm panel. I spend way too long moving from one digit to the next and I can tell it's driving him crazy. I love it. I even *accidentally* mistype a button and have to start over. The animal noise that leaves his throat when I press 'cancel' and start fresh is not only a tad funny, it's also almost pornographic. I move my fingers across the alarm pad even more slowly the second time, but Colt plays dirty this time around. He starts moving his hands up my shirt and down my pants and I feel like I'm close to combustion. So much so that I genuinely make a mistake this time. I give up on the alarm and try to turn and suck Colt's face, but he's having none of it.

"Enter the code, baby," his gruff voice whispers in my ear.

"I don't even remember it," I rasp. There is no way I can remember my name, let alone my alarm code, when his hand is now inside my underwear and moving south, quickly. "You're distracting me."

"You can do it. I believe in you." His voice is another level past gruff now. His hands are driving me insane. I am melting into him. I can't form words to even respond. I moan instead. I feel him growing even harder, if that's possible, behind me.

"Come on," he encourages me. Removing his hand from my shirt, he lifts my arm back to the alarm pad. Silently instructing me to begin pressing numbers. He gently slides his fingers down my arm, along my ribs, along my upper abdomen, and back under my shirt. I moan again. "Go on," he encourages once again.

"Fuck the alarm," I breathe. There is not one thing I care about more than having Colt inside of me. I'll unlock the door for Rich to come in and watch us at this point. I have never been this turned on in my entire life and I can tell Colt is loving every second of this torturous foreplay. I have no idea if he actually cares about the alarm being on or if he is just enjoying what he's doing to me. Either one is entirely possible.

"Go on," he whispers a second time. "Turn the alarm on and I'll make you come."

My eyes fly open at his promise. I move an inch closer to the alarm, as if seeing the numbers better will help my concentration. I clear my throat and give it a go. The first try, I type at lightning speed and hit numbers out of order. I cancel it out and try again. This time, I do a better job of making sure I am efficiently pressing the numbers in the correct order. After typing in the second number, Colt finds my nipple and I no longer even know there's an alarm panel in front of me. I try to turn to him again, but again he stops me.

"Come on, beautiful. Enter the code." His voice is a little more forceful, a little more anguished. The way his hands are moving in my underwear and over my breast gives me hope that he cannot hold out much longer either.

"I don't care about the fucking alarm, Colt," I say with a throaty voice.

"I do. Turn it on so we can be mindless and lost in one another without having to worry. Come on, Lenni, finish the code." His mouth is on my neck now, his hands still doing very naughty things to the rest of me. My head falls back to his chest, giving him easier access to my neck. After he licks, and kisses, and blows on my neck, I'm so close to finishing I can't focus on anything else. "No, no, no my sweet girl. Stand up and finish the code."

He takes his mouth off my neck and before I have time to think about it too much, I punch in the last two numbers. After the alarm beeps, alerting us that it has been activated, Colt spins me around. He removes most of our clothing and takes me right there against the wall.

Three hours and many orgasms later, Colt and I are lying in my bed and drinking a glass of my birthday bubbly. The past three hours have been blissful and I feel so close to Colt. This has been the best birthday of my life. I am wrapped in my favorite robe and Colt is only wearing his boxer briefs.

"I had no idea an alarm turned you on so much," I say before taking a sip of my Cava. I look at Colt over the top of my glass as I sip. He cocks his head to the side and gives me a 'don't be ridiculous' look.

"We both know the alarm had absolutely nothing to do with my arousal." He takes a sip and squeezes my thigh. "There's a little fox right here in front of me that is fully to blame."

"Thanks to you, I'm probably going to get horny every time I set my alarm," I confess. This earns me a huge smile. It's a great smile, possibly the best I've ever seen. I can see all of Colt's teeth with this smile and it's fantastic.

"I like that," he admits. My legs are spread across his lap. I am naked under the robe and he is moving it up inch by inch, exposing more of my skin.

"I'm so pissed you made us wait an entire year to do this," I tell him and take another sip.

"Nah, it's good for you." His eyes are glued to my bottom half. He's done messing with the robe now and has moved on to caressing my legs.

"A year of nothing but professionalism was *not* good for me," I argue.

"A year of foreplay was," he counters. His hands are riding higher and higher up my thigh. His eyes are still on my legs. "Fuck, you're so gorgeous."

———

"So are you," I reply with honesty. I haven't taken my eyes off his abs since we got into my bed. I thought his body was great with clothes on, I had no idea what I was missing underneath.

He props my right leg up so my foot is flat on the mattress and my knee is bent. With the mattress as the base, he's made a triangle with my leg. He lowers his head down toward my foot and raises his champagne flute to my knee. When he touches the mouth of it to my leg, it's cold and I flinch.

"Don't move," he commands, making eye contact for the first time since he began touching my legs. I nod in agreement.

He pours just a swallow of Cava on my leg, right below my knee. The cold path it makes down my unmoving skin makes me feel restless and excited. Gravity pulls the liquid down my shin and into Colt's waiting mouth. His tongue is resting on my leg and once he catches most of the wine, he slowly licks his way up the trail it just traveled down. I've never seen something so erotic in all of my life. I just watch, mouth open and breathing heavily.

Next, he lifts my foot off the bed. He holds it in the air in front of him and pours Cava down my foot, it trickles down and travels to the ends of my toes. As the droplets fall off the tips of my toes, Colt catches the drops of wine in his open mouth. Once more, he licks my foot and toes to follow the trail of wine.

He reaches for my hand, and without realizing it, I see I had moved it to open up the chest of my robe. My nipples are not exposed, but my cleavage is, and Colt takes a nice long look before moving to his next destination. He repeats the same process with my right arm, letting the wine slide down and around my arm to drip from my elbow. He catches every drop and licks the trail all over again. I can't believe how turned on I am given the number of orgasms I have already experienced tonight.

He climbs on top of me and unties the belt of my robe. He moves the sides away just enough to expose my center. He tips my head back with a light touch of his fingers

———

and pours the bubbles in the crevice just below where my collarbones meet. Since I am propped up on pillows, gravity once again leads the liquid down my body. This time it heads toward my belly button but Colt catches it first. The noises I make during this round of his sensual Cava game let Colt know how much I enjoy it. He repeats the exact process again. This time getting a little more liberal with the amount of Cava and where the trail starts and ends. He sets his glass of Cava and mine on the nightstand and pulls me flat on the bed.

"Colt, what are you doing to me?" I am breathless.

"Hopefully, making you mine," he replies.

February 15th

"Lenni... Valentina," Colt whispers in my ear. "Wake up, baby."

"Need more sleep," I respond without opening my eyes.

I hear Colt chuckle. "But I forgot to give you your birthday gift yesterday."

"You're all the gift I need," I tell him, leaving my eyes closed.

"I'm not falling for that. Time to wake up, beautiful." Colt starts maneuvering me so I am sitting up in bed. I'm still naked, so when the covers fall away, I shiver and wrap my arms around myself.

"Oops, sorry," Colt says and he grabs my robe and wraps it around me.

"Much better," I say and snuggle into myself.

"Ok, are you ready?" Colt asks. His eyes are dancing, he is clearly excited.

"I told you, you don't need to get me any gifts." I rub my sleepy eyes.

"Too late." He is bouncing on his toes in front of the bed.

"Ok, ok, I'm ready," I say. I open my eyes fully and straighten my posture to demonstrate my readiness.

———

"Hold out your hand."

I do as Colt asks and he pulls an envelope from behind his back. He lays it softly in my hand and sits on the bed. I give him a questioning glance and he waits for me to open it.

"I don't understand," I admit after reading through the printed piece of paper. "What is this?"

"I made you an appointment. With a medium. Today." Colt's expression is falling rapidly. I can see the insecurity and fear creep into his eyes.

"A medium?"

"Yeah, you know, one of those people that can communicate with people who have passed away? I thought you could go talk to your parents." His voice is shaky and unsure.

"A medium?" I repeat.

"You don't have to go, I just thought you might like it. I'm sorry. I didn't know if you'd be into this sort of thing or not. I should have asked first." He takes the paper and the envelope from me and starts folding them up. I grab his hands.

"Stop!" I scream. His eyes fly to mine. "Stop! Don't crumble that!"

"Do you want to go?" He's hopeful again.

"Of course I want to go, you lunatic! I was just shocked that I had never thought of this! Give me the paper!" I am scrambling to his lap and all but tackling him in an attempt to get the piece of paper with the appointment information on it.

"You had me worried," he says as he holds it out of my reach. I climb on his lap and try to grab it, but his arms seem to be twice as long as mine.

"Colt, give it to me!"

He kisses me instead, still holding it far enough away that I can't grab for it.

"Will you come with me?" I ask, trying to make my eyes look as big and innocent as possible.

A smile spreads across his face and his muscles relax just a bit. "If that's what you want."

"It is what I want." I nod to emphasize my point. Still straddling him, I let my hands travel up his chest. I feel his muscles begin to dissolve under my touch. I kiss him again, this time licking his bottom lip. He wants more, but I keep my tongue at his mouth's entrance.

"Give me the paper, Colt," I murmur against his lips.

"I don't think so," he responds against mine.

I repeat the kiss, and this time I grind against him.

"Nice try, Valentina." His voice is going husky, I know victory is near.

I let my robe fall off one shoulder. His eyes instantly move to the exposed skin. While he's distracted with my bare shoulder, I loosen the belt. I let the robe fall open and lean into Colt. He lies back on the bed, still holding the paper away from me. With my robe open, I begin piling my hair on top of my head, both arms raised. It's all Colt can handle. Without thinking he moves his hands toward my exposed body. Just as his hands are inches from my body, I grab the paper from him and jump off the bed.

"Hey!" I hear him yelp from the bed.

"Time to get up, Colt!" I sing as I tie my robe and walk toward the bathroom.

"Oh, I'm up Valentina," he grumbles. "Come on back over here and finish what you started." He puts his hands behind his head and he looks like a damn Greek god lying on my bed. I poke my head around the bathroom door. He's grinning at me.

"You'll have to catch me, first," I say, hearing the entertainment in my own voice. Colt's up for the challenge and his eyes sparkle in return.

"You're gonna need a headstart," Colt promises.

"I'm so nervous, thanks for coming with me," I say to Colt. We're sitting on the couch in the waiting room of the medium's office. Would you call it an office? Room? Lair?

"Of course. I'm happy to be here," he replies. He lifts our entwined hands up to his mouth and gives my fingers a soft peck. "I hope your parents like me."

"Do you really think that's possible after all the ways you defiled me over the past twenty-four hours?"

Colt's face loses all its color. "Wh- wait, what? They were *there*?" I can't help but giggle.

"I would hope not! I told them long ago to get lost when I have a boy over." I nudge him with my shoulder, but his face is still pale. "But I guess we're about to find out," I say as I nod my head in the direction of a woman standing in the doorway.

"Come on in, Valentina." The woman is tall and slender. Her long, brown hair has natural and frizzy waves. She has minimal makeup on, but she is wearing a bold reddish-purple lipstick. It looks perfect on her. Her clothes are casual and loose, but look expensive.

"I'm Mary," the woman introduces herself. "It's nice to meet you."

"It's lovely to meet you as well," I say. There are two chairs and a couch inside the office. Colt and I eye one another before sitting together on the couch. Mary sits in an oversized chair across the room. She folds her legs up underneath her and gets comfortable. "I'm Valentina, and this is Colt."

I was a hair's breadth away from referring to Colt as my boyfriend. It almost just rolled right off my tongue, but my brain worked quicker than my mouth. Given that Colt told me yesterday that he loves me, I'm decently confident he wants to be my boyfriend. We haven't had the conversation yet, though, and it seems like jumping the gun to call him that without discussing labels first.

"I'm her boyfriend," Colt offers. My head swings to look at him in surprise. After all my thoughts and internal debate, he throws the term out there as if he's been using it for years. He leans back against the couch, resting his arm behind me. He winks at me and I can't help but smile.

"It's new," I tell Mary.

"Yes." It's a statement not a question.

"Is it alright if he stays?" I ask.

"Absolutely! Anyone you want to be present is welcome." Mary smiles warmly at us.

"Ok, thank you."

"So, Valentina, have you ever visited a medium before?" Mary asks.

"No. No, I have not," I say and shake my head.

"Ok, wonderful. Let me tell you a little about how it all works," she offers.

"That would be great." My leg is bouncing up and down.

"As we talk, people will come forward. They will make their presence known. I am able to see and hear them, but sometimes I need a few seconds to let them finish talking. Sort of like a translator, does that make sense?"

"Yes, definitely."

"Great, we will call them spirits, unless you have a different name that you prefer?"

"No, spirits are fine." I nod in agreement.

"Wonderful. You might want to record this on the voice notes on your phone. You won't remember all of it later and I'm sure you'll want to look back at some point." I can see Colt setting up his phone to record next to me. I give him a small smile. "Well, I can tell you right from the beginning, you have a strong female spirit with you." I feel Colt rub my back.

"I do?"

"Oh, yes." Pause. "She is telling me that she rarely leaves your side. She loves to be with you." Pause. "She really enjoys watching you at work. Do you work at a large, huge corporation?"

"Yes! Yes, I do!"

"Yes… she is showing me a very large office building and putting you on the top floor. I'm guessing you are a leader in the company?"

"Yes! I am!"

"Mmmhmmm." Pause. "She loves seeing you take charge. She loves to see you rising to your potential." Pause. "Do you have a mentor? An older woman? Someone close to you?"

A tear falls down my cheek. "Yes," I reply with a shaky voice. "My grandmother."

"Ahh, that makes sense. I am getting a strong feeling of love between you two." Pause. "This person is happy about your relationship. She loves the bond you share." Mary has been looking in front of me, and for the first time, she looks up and meets my eyes. "This woman is young, maybe in her thirties. She has long, blonde hair, very straight. She is wearing tight jeans and a large, loose sweater. She's beautiful. Is she familiar to you?"

I nod as the tears stream down my face. "It's my mother."

Mary nods in understanding. "Oh, she's excited. She's telling me…" Pause. "Telling me that she loves to ride in the black car with you to work. She thinks that's a lot of fun." Pause. "She loves eating with you?" Mary looks at me in confusion and I nod to let her know that's correct. Mary giggles. "She thinks you're very funny. She likes it when your friends come over." Pause. Mary's eyes bore into mine. "She's fiercely proud of you."

"She is?"

"Oh yes! She is so proud of who you are as a person and all that you've accomplished." Pause. "Hang on, she's showing me a memory." Pause. "I think it's little you, and her and a man dancing. You three are dancing in a living room. Does that make sense to you?"

"Yes, yes, it does. That is my most favorite memory of my parents."

Mary nods again. "It's her favorite, too." Pause. "She leaves you tokens to let you know she's near."

"She does?" Colt has his hand flat on my back, full of support.

"Mmmhmm, she says she leaves you butterflies."

"Butterflies?"

"Yes." Pause. "Sometimes real butterflies, sometimes drawings or stickers." Pause. "She wants you to know when you see one, it's from her."

I nod so much my head hurts. "Ok. Thank you, Mom," I say. Colt rubs my back.

"She wants me to tell you not to be scared."

"Why would I be scared? Scared of her?"

Pause. "No, not of her." Pause. "There's going to be something that is coming up, some sort of conflict." Pause. "She's saying that you should not fear the outcome. She just keeps saying 'Let him handle it.'"

"Let who handle what?" I ask.

Mary shakes her head. "I don't know. That's for you to find out."

We sit in silence for a few moments and Colt is rubbing my back again. Squeezing my neck and offering every possible version of non-verbal support he can.

"She's hugging a man, now," Mary says. She's back to looking in front of me instead of at me.

"My dad?"

"He's very tall. Long, shaggy hair." Pause. "He has on old, ratty shoes. He keeps saying he refuses to take them off."

"That's my dad!" I nearly jump off the couch.

Mary's smile is wide. She looks to be on the verge of laughter. "What's with these shoes?"

I laugh. "He hated buying new shoes for some reason. My parents rarely fought, but when they did, it was about my dad's disgusting, smelly shoes." Colt laughs quietly.

"Yes, they are smiling but arguing about his shoes now," Mary relays.

"They're together?" I ask. The tears are really rolling now.

"Oh yes, they're together."

"Are they happy?"

"They're very happy," Mary nods. "When they crossed over, they brought all of their love for each other, and for you, with them." Pause. "Did they die together?"

I nod.

"Yes, I see that." Pause. "They are showing me it was too early, unexpected."

I nod.

"Their love for you is very, very strong." Pause. "Your dad is trying to say something, it's difficult for him." Long pause. "Ok, he is saying, no, he is wanting me to tell you that he *promises* they will wait for you. They will not return to a body until you're with them again." Pause. "Oh, and anyone you want to wait for, as well."

"Return to a body?" I'm confused. Is she talking about reincarnation?

"Yes, Valentina. Our spirits, our souls if you will, choose when they return. We all choose where and when we are born. Lots of spirit families travel together. They will wait until you cross over before returning."

"Spirit families? So if I have children, are they part of my spirit family?" I wonder aloud.

"Yes, most definitely."

"Do you know? Will I have children?"

"Let me ask your guides," Mary says.

"My guides? What guides?" I'm more confused than ever.

Mary refocuses on my face. "We all have spirit guides and angels guiding and assisting us. They are all around and will do their best to give us the best case scenario. We all have free will, of course, so sometimes we get in our own way. If you are ever in real trouble, don't be afraid to call out to your angels and ask for help."

"Just yell out for help?"

"Make sure to make it known you are asking angels for help, then yes, just yell out for help. They cannot interfere with our own free will unless we ask for them to do so."

"Hmm, interesting."

"But, back to your original question." Mary smiles at me. Yes, you will have children."

I'm surprised by the amount of joy that brings me. "Really?"

"Yes, your guides are showing me a scene from your future. You have a very happy family." Mary is smiling at me and nodding.

"Mary, if I speak out loud to my parents during the day, can they hear me?"

"Without a doubt."

"Thank you, Mary." I notice the time on the clock hanging on the wall behind Mary. "This has been wonderful."

———

"You're very welcome. Your parents' presence is so strong, you should know they will never leave you and they love you very much."

"That is very comforting," I confess. I wipe my eyes and stand up off the couch. Colt follows and takes my hand in his.

"Your mother wants me to tell you not to forget to listen to her words. Let him handle it, whatever that means."

"I will, thanks again."

Colt and I walk out of her office and I let go of his hand in order to reach around his entire arm.

"Wow, that was incredible," he says, letting out a breath.

"Yeah, it was." So much just happened, I don't know how to process it all. We take the half flight of stairs up to street level and begin walking toward my apartment. It's so cold we can see our breath in the air. "I can't wait to get home and light the fireplace."

"That sounds great," Colt agrees. "So, what did you think?"

"Honestly, I'm not sure. I would like to believe everything she said. It's reassuring to think that my parents are always with me and they are waiting for me. I like to think that I'll see them again." We walk a few steps in silence. "It's even more reassuring to think we have people, or whatever, on the other side that help us out when we need it."

"Right," Colt agrees. "I like the thought of that a lot."

"Yeah, it just seems hard to believe though, doesn't it?" I ask him.

"How do you mean?"

We stop walking and I turn to face him. "I guess I mean, do we really think that woman was just speaking with my parents and there are angels all around us right now?"

Colt thinks about this. "How would she know all of that about them if she wasn't speaking to them?"

"That's true," I say. He has a point. The session with Mary has worn me out. Or maybe it was all of my sessions with Colt that have me exhausted. Either way, I lean my head into his chest and he pulls me in for a hug. It's hard to hug with winter coats on but we do our best. Colt kisses my forehead.

"Ready to go light a fire?" Colt asks.

"Yup." I pull away from him and when I open my eyes again, I freeze. I feel all the color drain from my face. My hands move to my mouth. A tear escapes.

"What? What is it?" Colt asks me.

"Colt…" I point to his shoulder. Sitting on his coat, in the middle of winter, on a sidewalk in New York City, is a butterfly.

Thirty-One

February 13th

It took me about three days to tell Colt I loved him.

I would like to think we are doing a good job keeping things professional at work, however, that would be a lie. It would be more accurate to say we are doing a good job at keeping it professional at work *when* we're in front of others. If we are in a meeting or sharing lunch in the kitchen, we are as professional as we ever were. This professionalism goes right out the window the moment we are in the building after hours, alone in anyone's office, alone in the stairwell, alone in any room with doors, if both our legs are under a table that no one else can see, on our lunch breaks, or if there is an opportunity for eye fucking.

We try our best, but Colt is so unbelievably sexy that it makes it very difficult for me to behave when we are close to one another. I made the mistake in June of telling him the smell of his cologne drives me nuts while we are at work. I hate smelling it but not being able to touch or kiss him. I'm almost positive the sneaky bastard has been spraying that shit all over my office ever since. I can assure you, however, that he wears that cologne every single day and usually freshens it up at least once during the day.

Two can play at that game. I have made sure in turn to drive him as crazy as I possibly can. When uncrossing and recrossing my legs in a skirt, I make sure my legs stay spread for a moment or two just to give him a peek. I usually unbutton the top button when I know I will see him, then direct my cleavage right to his sightline. I also seem to have butter fingers whenever we're together. It's such a shame that I have to bend over to get my pen a few times every meeting.

It's a fun but risky game. One time we were nearly caught by Frederick in R&D, but luckily my office door was locked and Colt was able to hide in my personal bathroom until Frederick left. Mae did catch us making out, shall we say *passionately*, one time in her office. In our defense she was supposed to be off that day. Regardless, she just gave us an eye roll and left without saying a word. She did give me a stern talking to later about behaving in the workplace.

We've been doing better and just leaving the building altogether when we absolutely cannot keep our hands off one another. Poor Hank has driven us around the city too many times to count and we are all grateful for the divider I had installed in the back.

Don't judge me. We're young and in love.

Outside of the office, Colt is nothing shy of perfect. He eats dinner with me and my parents every night, he even shares about his day as well. He is so thoughtful and considerate with me. He is always surprising me with dates or little things he thinks I'll like. Anytime he sees anything in a store that resembles a butterfly in any way, he buys it and brings it home to me. I have quite a butterfly collection going, as you can imagine. He holds me, he makes me laugh uncontrollably, he cooks for me, he picks up after me, he takes care of me, he loves me.

Looking back, I cannot fathom what I was thinking when I told Mae a decade ago I would never get married. I was so worried about losing my freedom, I just never realized that the right man would *never* take away any of my freedoms. Colt supports and even pushes me at work. He is happy to work 'under me', as he calls it. He wants me to succeed. We both spend time with our friends, separately and together. He always includes Mae and his family invites me to every get-together and meet-up they have. The only freedom I've lost is one I've never enjoyed anyway: dating.

I'm so happy with Colt, I cannot imagine a life without him.

A couple weeks after my birthday, I realized I did not set any intentions for my future year. I also realized that most of my intentions would have revolved around Colt anyway. I am already focusing on my happiness and future, my long-term relationship. It is mostly fun and exciting to be with Colt, but it can also be hard work sometimes. Compromise isn't always easy and I have really had to work on myself in order to be a better partner for Colt. All of this growth is welcome and needed. I am starting to agree with my grandmother, learning how to be in a devoted and loving relationship *will* make me a better leader.

Mae is out of town again this year for my birthday so I am spending a quiet night at home with my parents and Colt tonight. Colt has things planned for tomorrow, but nothing too crazy since we both need to return to work on the 15th. We are in the middle of a huge partnership negotiation with one of the largest department stores in the world and since Mae is in China, I absolutely cannot afford to miss an extra day.

Colt and I are wrapped around each other in bed. He made us an amazing pasta dinner with the best zucchini noodles I have ever tasted. He even made homemade breadsticks. The whole meal was incredible and my belly is still full two hours later. We are watching a movie and sipping from the same glass of wine. This is my idea of a perfect evening.

"So, what are we doing tomorrow?" I ask with drooping eyes.

"I've got a few things planned," Colt hedges. He kisses my forehead and offers me the glass of wine. I shake my head in response.

"I can't be trusted to hold that right now. I am so comfortable lying with you, it's possible I'll fall asleep mid-sip."

"Want me to pour some in your mouth?" Colt chuckles.

"I'm game," I say. I lean my head back, point my nose toward the sky, and open my mouth. Colt tips the wine glass with care and lets just a couple drops fall into my waiting mouth. I hear him set it on the nightstand and he kisses the tip of my nose. I'm astonished he is able to pour it so precisely and accurately.

"How are you good at everything?" I ask him after swallowing the wine.

"I'm not," he argues.

"But you are and it's incredibly annoying," I disagree.

"Beauty is in the eye of the beholder," he says, paired with another forehead kiss.

"True, but everyone at work agrees that you have the Midas touch," I inform him.

"Is that so?" I can hear sleepiness seeping into his tone. He's done with our banter.

"Mmmhmm," I reply.

"Maybe I'm horrible at planning birthday celebrations for the woman I love," he offers and nudges my head with his. He is moments away from sleep.

"Somehow, I highly doubt that."

February 14th

I was entirely correct. Colt is great at planning birthday celebrations.

He took me to brunch at this beautiful restaurant downtown. The inside is entirely covered in vines, leaves, and flowers. It makes you feel like you are in the middle of a beautiful jungle. The food was delectable and Colt made sure my mimosa was always full.

From there we moved on to shopping. We made a quick stop to call Mae and Colt told her he hoped to be doing her proud by trying to replicate her normal birthday routine with me. He told her knows he can never live up to her standard, but hoped to do it justice.

Instead of taking me to expensive clothing stores, Colt takes a nice twist on this shopping idea and takes me shopping at a spa. I know, this sounds ludicrous. But it isn't. At all.

"I know how much you love your robe, so I thought maybe you could use some other luxury relaxation items," Colt tells me when we walk into the boutique just outside the spa doors.

"Luxury relaxation items?" I echo.

"Yeah...isn't that what they sell at a spa boutique?" Colt's brows draw in and I can tell by his jaw that he's clenching his teeth. He's worried.

"I would think so." I look around the boutique. "Honestly, I don't know. I've never purchased anything other than spa services at a spa before."

We walk around and look at table after table of items, just getting the lay of the land. As it turns out, they sell quite a lot of luxury relaxation items. Tables are filled with essential oils, high quality creams and moisturizers, face masks, eye masks, lip masks, anti-aging masks, hair products, skin products, bath salts and bombs, crystals, diffusers, just about anything you could ever think of.

There is one table in particular that pulls my attention. I approach it slowly, almost as if it's too good to be true and if I move too quickly, it will disappear. Almost everything on the table looks like it will match my favorite robe perfectly. I immediately choose the fuzziest, warmest slippers in the world. They are so soft and beautiful, I can hardly wait to get home and put them on. Next, I choose another very soft and luxurious item, a hair wrap. This is followed by a satin sleep mask and a scrunchie that promises not to hurt my head. Every time I look at Colt, he has a huge smile on his face as if watching me shop for myself brings him joy.

Colt insists on buying me some creams and bath products as well, but I am most excited about the slippers. By the time we leave the boutique, we have filled three large shopping bags and I have more items than necessary to keep my skin hydrated and my body comfortable.

"Thanks for that," I say to Colt once we are back in the car. I give him a kiss on the lips. He gives my shirt a gentle tug to keep me from moving away from him. We kiss again and he smiles against my lips.

"You're welcome. I hope you liked it. I know it wasn't usual dress shopping."

"I loved it. It was genius." I flutter my lashes at him and give him a sweet smile.

"Great, because we have more things to do today."

"We do?" I was thinking this was the end of our day.

"We do, indeed."

We pull up to an unmarked building that I have never seen before. Without saying a word, Colt climbs out of the car and walks over to my side of the car. He closes my door behind me.

"Where are we?" I ask.

He doesn't answer, but takes my hand and walks us inside an unmarked door. For the first time, I am feeling a little anxious with Colt. Where in the world did he take me? Where are we?

The hallway is almost entirely black. There are some paint splatters along the walls and ceiling and black lights that illuminate the colors. I cannot see an end to this hallway and instinctively walk behind Colt, letting him lead the way. He reaches out and moves a black, velvet curtain out of the way so we can pass through. He smiles at me and in the black lights his teeth look green.

"Right this way," he says and motions with his hands for me to walk through the curtain. We are greeted on the other side of the curtain with a teenager behind a small counter.

"Welcome to Glow Golf, do you have a reservation?" she asks.

"Yes," Colt answers and gives her our information.

"Clubs and balls are over there. Enjoy."

I look around and take it all in. The outlines of each mini golf hole are in different neon colors, accentuated by the black lights. There are only a few other people playing and their clubs are also neon and lit up.

"We're putt putting?" I ask.

"We're *glow* putt putting," he responds.

"Hell yeah!" I am excited. This looks like so much fun. Who would've thought playing putt putt inside with black lights could be so cool? I didn't before. I do now.

At the end of eighteen holes, Colt is the one thinking that putt putting in the dark isn't any fun. I hit two holes in one and beat Colt by six putts. I am elated. He is clearly upset with his performance and is significantly more quiet than when we began the game. It makes me giggle. It also makes me feel supremely confident about my mini golf skills given that Colt clearly did not let me win.

"Aw, babe, don't be sad!" I nudge him with my shoulder.

"I'm not sad." He pouts.

"Don't be *mad*," I try again.

"Not that either." His jaw is tight and his eyes are hard.

"If you say so," I reply. I'm gonna leave his delicate ego alone.

We wrap ourselves in our winter gear and bundle up in our coats in silence. Just when I am beginning to wonder how we are going to navigate the rest of the day, I hear Colt sigh.

"Wow. You just kicked my butt. Maybe things do come too easily to me." Colt is walking next to me on the sidewalk and shaking his head.

"Told ya," I respond with a smile.

Colt barks out a laugh. "You did."

"Can we both accept this is your life and move on with today?"

"I would love that," Colt agrees. He wraps his arm around my shoulders and pulls me in close. I inhale his scent and relax.

"Where are we going now?" I ask.

"Well, I was thinking we could get some super greasy, yet tasty, appetizers that are incredibly bad for us?" He looks down at me. "What do you think about that?" His warm breath makes a visible cloud in the cold air. I watch it until it disappears.

"That sounds downright amazing."

"Great, I know just the place."

Twenty minutes later Colt and I are seated at a small table at a distillery in Brooklyn. Colt is sitting in a leather chair opposite me while I sit along the wall on a booth bench. The cushions are soft and almost too big for the table. Our table is near the fireplace and the heat coming from it warms our freezing bodies. Once I feel sufficiently toasty, I lean back and let my body rest fully onto the bench.

"I've never been here, but this place is great." I praise Colt on his choice.

"Yeah, I've only been here once before but I thought it was cool." He nods his head slightly as he looks around the room. It's very dark inside and the tables are lit either by candles or the fireplace with a few dim light fixtures hanging from the ceiling. The enormous stone fireplace takes up the middle of the sitting area with tables all around it on either side. It looks like the inside of a castle.

"It seems sort of a romantic place," I say with a questioning squint. "Did you come here with friends?"

"You would say this place is romantic?" Colt clears his throat and looks down at the table in front of him.

"Ah, so it was with a woman?" I push.

Colt scratches the back of his neck and looks around again. His posture is filled with enough discomfort to overflow a truck.

I reach across the table and take his hand. "It's ok, we have pasts. As long as you didn't come here with her yesterday, everything is fine." I squeeze his hand and lean back again.

"Ha, definitely not yesterday," he mumbles out of the side of his mouth.

"Oh no?" I ask. "When was it then? How long ago?"

Colt lets out a heavy sigh and leans back in his chair. "Do we really have to talk about this?" He looks me in the eyes for the first time since we sat down.

"I'm just curious," I reply with a small shrug. I give him the best puppy dog eyes I can manage. At least that is what I hope my eyes are doing.

———

"Oh, fine," he says with a sigh again. My eyes must be cooperating. "It was many years ago, her name was Gwen. She ended up being horrible."

"Horrible how?" I'm intrigued. I've never heard of this Gwen person before and I want to know more. Colt is opening up and I feel the need to jump on the opportunity.

He runs a hand through his gelled hair. "Well, she, uh, brought me here after a long, on-again-off-again relationship. I was in awe of the beauty of this place. I told her how much I loved it and thanked her for knowing me well enough to bring me to a place that fits me and my personality so well." He pauses and presses his lips together. "Then she dumped me."

I feel my eyes go wide at the admission. "Dumped you? Why?"

"Oh, she had her reasons." He looks away from me and back to the fireplace.

"Who would ever dump you?" I'm astonished.

"Gwen."

"I don't understand." I look at him, hoping he'll give me more of an explanation. When he stays silent, I ask another question. "What does this place have to do with your breakup? You told her you loved it and she took you home and ended it?"

He licks his lips and looks utterly relieved when our server shows up. He orders a double and I order a cocktail before I motion for him to continue.

"No, uh, this is where she ended it."

I lean forward on the table. I'm embarrassed that I lean forward so heavily it makes the table shake and the candle wobble, but I power through for the sake of hearing the end of the story.

"She broke up with you here? In the tasting room?"

"Yup." His face looks so sad.

"What a horrible person." I am astonished, once again.

He lets out a sad laugh. "Yeah, yeah she was." He runs a hand down his face. "She even blocked me right in front of me."

"Wait. What?" I cannot believe my ears.

"Yeah, she told me to never contact her again and she was already worried I had become attached so she blocked me. While I watched."

"Get the fuck out of here." Colt laughs. "Why in the world would you ever want to come back here?" I ask.

Colt leans forward and rests his forearms on the table. He takes both of my hands in his and leans forward just another inch. "That's the thing. I loved this place the moment I walked in. I wanted to come here and try all their bourbons and gins and spend the day here, having fun. Then she took that away from me." He lifts one of my hands up to his mouth, careful not to disturb the candle, and kisses my knuckles. "But then I had a thought. Whynot change my mindset? I hated giving her the power to determine where I went and why. The thought of coming back alone was too sad, though. Then I thought, what if I brought you? Who is the only person that has the ability to change the way I see this place? Lenni. I knew if I brought you and we shared a table and had some drinks, I would forget all about Gwen."

"Colt, I…" My eyes are starting to prickle and my nose feels itchy.

"Thanks for coming here with me." He kisses my other hand before leaning back in his chair. "I absolutely had not planned on telling you all that. It's like you could read my mind or something."

I'm still in shock. It's unbelievable that someone could be so horrible to Colt. I know for years I had been blind to his greatness, but I had never been mean or hurt him with any sort of intent. How could a woman treat a man like Colt in such a disgusting way?

What followed his breakup confession still has me on the brink of tears. I mean so much to him that I can erase her behavior? I am desperate for this to be true. I, of course, want to mean that much to him, but even more than that I want his memory to be gone. I want it to scatter and leave like sand in the wind. I want him to forget all about her and her ugly name, *Gwen*. He deserves to be loved and cherished and any idiot that blocks Colt should be struck by lightning. He is the center of the universe and she is some lunatic that had no idea what she had.

I stand from the bench and walk to Colt.

"You ok? Where are you going?" He looks up to me with confusion all over his face.

I say nothing but climb on his lap and kiss him. I don't even try to hold back, I cover his mouth with mine and shove my tongue in his mouth. He responds immediately and deepens the kiss. I continue it for a minute or so before pulling apart and giving him a soft peck on the corner of his lips.

"Remember that instead," I demand. His eyes are wild and flicking between mine. I give him one more kiss on the cheek before settling in next to him on the big, leather chair. There is no need for me to return to my seat.

Colt clears his throat and adjusts his pants. He puts his arm around me and kisses my hair. "Yeah, I will."

I smile at him. "Oh look! They dropped off our drinks!"

February 15th

My alarm blares entirely too early. Both Colt and I groan. We know we need to get up and help with this huge account, but neither of us wants to leave my warm bed. We hit the snooze button four times before I can be annoyed enough to turn it off and get out of bed. When I get out of the shower, Colt is still sleeping.

I'm guessing his exhaustion is twofold. First, I made sure to bring him home and show him how much I appreciate and love him last night. He refused to be outdone. Needless to say, we were both pretty tired by the time we fell asleep last night. And second, because he shared a lot and I know that's not always easy. I'm sure his emotional hangover has a much bigger impact than any alcohol or sexual hangover ever could.

I drag him out of bed and thanks to his much shorter hair, we are ready for work within moments of one another. We pour coffee in our travel mugs and head to the car where

Hank is waiting for us. Colt has yet to say a word this morning and I am starting to worry, just a little. Is he mad at me for asking him about his ex?

Before I can get too deep into my thoughts, Colt nudges my arm out of the way. He lays his head down on my lap and snuggles in. The motion warms my heart and settles my fears. I rub his hair and his face and he moans in pleasure.

Too soon we arrive at our usual spot to drop Colt off. We've been dropping him at the bus stop a block away from the office so that no one sees us arrive together.

He kisses my leg before lifting his head to look at me. "See you inside, beautiful."

After four hours of the legal team explaining the partnership contracts to me, I just want to go to sleep. My brain hurts, my eyes hurt, my neck hurts and all I want to do is go back to my bed with Colt and curl my body against his. I want to wrap my legs up and around his, I want to intertwine my arms with his, I want my head to be one with his chest.

I'm daydreaming of this when Colt walks in my office. He walks in with his usual all-business work stride. I look up and I feel that my brain is two steps behind my eyes. Once they catch up to the sight of Colt, my face melts into a smile.

"Hey," I say, leaning back in my office chair.

"Oh, Lenni, are you ok?"

"Yeah, just tired from the lawyer meeting. It was intense and required way too much thinking. How was your morning?"

"A million times better than that. I think I even got a nap in."

My eyes shoot to his. "A nap?"

"Yeah, I had a budget meeting with Julian and the finance team. I'm pretty sure I slept with my eyes open for at least ten minutes." The sparkling smile Colt gives me is priceless.

I smile in return. "That sounds lovely."

———

"It was." He stalks toward my desk. His hands are in his pockets and his eyes have gone dark. "I had a dream about you."

"About me?" I point to my chest.

"Mmmhmm, you." He walks toward me like a jungle cat. He leans on my desk. His hands are in fists and his knuckles are flat against my desk. His shoulders and arms are puffed out. He looks incredibly sexy. "If you meet me in the stairwell in five minutes, I will reenact it for you."

"Reenact the dream?" My nether regions are waking up.

"Why not?" he asks.

I cannot think of a single reason why I should not meet my gorgeous boyfriend in the stairwell for a steamy lunch session. Except that it's already past lunch, but you get the idea.

"See you there."

Colt has me plastered against the concrete wall of the stairwell when we realize someone is watching us. My right leg is wrapped around his waist and he is milliseconds away from unzipping his pants. My left leg is barely touching the floor, my head tilted back against the concrete wall, my arms around his neck, and his face is in my cleavage. We both freeze the moment we hear the echo. Our heads pop up to attention and look around. Neither of us hear anything else or see anyone, so we rearrange our clothing as quickly as possible. We stay as quiet as we can.

As soon as we are put back together, we make eye contact. We have a silent conversation that one of us will go up the stairs and one down. We nod at one another and step apart.

"I knew it."

We both freeze. I spin to look down the stairs and see Stuart standing on the landing below us. He has his arms crossed and has a smug look on his face. "I knew you two were sleeping together, I just needed the proof. Now I have it." He waves his hand in our direction.

"Stuart," Colt growls.

"No, no, no Colt. You don't get to order me around any longer." He walks up three steps. "I own you now."

"You own nothing," Colt yells. He moves toward Stuart, but I throw my arm out to stop him. He could go right through my arm and attack Stuart if he wants to, but he respects my boundary and stops at my arm. This gives Stuart joy and he smirks at Colt.

"Get the fuck out of here, Stuart." Colt's jaw is so tight, it looks like his skin is going to rip right off his jaw bone.

"Oh, I will. I'll get right out of here and walk directly to HR."

This lights a fire inside of me. "Great. Go. We signed one of those little forms to say we're dating and no one holds the company liable." I swing my arms wildly. Colt steps up behind me and places a calming hand on my hip.

"Is that so?" When neither of us answers, he nods his head. "Ok, I'm sure HR would love to hear about your gross misuse of company time, Colt."

The weasel knows that HR would never approach me about how I spend my time, but they would come at Colt. Stuart has us here and he fucking knows it. The three of us participate in an epic staredown for about two and a half minutes before Stuart clicks his tongue and walks away. Once we hear him push open the stairwell door, I drop my head into my hands. Colt starts cussing, loudly, and pacing on the small landing.

"What are we going to do?" I whisper, dangerously close to tears.

"Nothing, we're going to do nothing." Colt's voice is hard. "HR will question me and we will just go from there." I've never seen his jaw tick like this before.

"Wait, Colt, are you pissed at *me*?"

He drops his head and looks at his feet. "No. I'm pissed at myself."

"What does that mean?" I ask.

"Nothing." He gives my chin the briefest touch with his pointer finger. "I'm going back to my office."

———

Colt walks away and leaves me alone in the stairwell wondering what the hell just happened and how this would affect our future.

Thirty-Two

February 13th

To say the last year was tempestuous would be a disservice to the nastiness that was the year. It was at least eighteen levels worse than tempestuous. It was a main course of volatile, preceded by a huge appetizer of dreadful, and followed with a dessert full of horrendous.

As you can guess, things did not, and still currently are not, going well for Colt at work. Stuart marched himself right to HR the moment he left the stairwell and reported us. After he spoke with HR, he went to every person in the company that would listen and told them what he saw on the stairs. It goes without saying, Colt and I were mortified. We didn't know how to handle it and Colt was especially cold to me after we were caught. Mae ended up leaving China early and flew home to "deal" with the situation.

The first issue was with the paperwork we turned in regarding our relationship. It is required for a member of upper management or someone in HR to sign off on all romantic relationship forms. Being a member of upper management, I signed off on it and I sent it to HR to be filed. In retrospect I see this was a colossal mistake on my part. After Stuart spilled the beans, it became apparent that no one took a moment to read the form I sent to HR and just filed it in my personnel file. There was a secondary issue with the form in that Colt never dated the form, leaving everyone to question its validity. We correctly filled out the form, ensuring every line was dated, and had it signed off by Rosa immediately after we were caught. It didn't help our cause much.

I had to sit through forty hours of HR training about the importance of having the correct person sign the correct forms. Many topics about forms and their legality were included. Naturally, the proper way to sign a form, how to check for correctly signed forms, and how to detect fraud were all covered, just to name a few topics. It was unpleasant, to say the least. I was also subjected to countless lectures from Mae, Rosa, and the entire HR team.

I fared a million times better than Colt. I feel bad even complaining about my consequences after watching Colt go through what he went through. The first, and possibly the worst, repercussion was sitting through the interviews. Colt had to be interviewed for hours on end. I eventually lost count of the number of interviews and the number of people questioning him. They asked him about everything. It started with our relationship and its logistics. The where and when, how often in the office, how many times did we 'have intercourse' in any area of the building, and so on. You get the idea. I'm sure you can also see how foul it was for Colt to sit there and answer questions about our sex lives with his co-workers.

These questions led to deeper questions regarding the power dynamic. Did I pressure him into a relationship? Did I ever use my position to force him to have sex with me? Did I offer him a promotion in return for sexual favors? Again, you get the idea.

Colt was also immediately ostracized at work. People began giving him shorter and shorter answers. They would avoid him and even leave the lunch room when he walked in or scatter like a fart in the air when he would approach. Co-workers that he considered to be friends started ignoring him. They stopped coming by his office or inviting him to happy hours. The less our colleagues spoke to him, the less he spoke to me.

He then had a trial of sorts about his misuse of company time. He brought in character witnesses, time logs, performance reviews, profit and loss statements demonstrating his value, his project reviews, colleague testimonials, anything he thought would help his case. From my point of view, he was a master at defending himself. He got very creative with the proof of his high quality work and how he has moved the company forward.

I wanted to help him. I was determined to help. Colt, however, refused any offer of assistance that I made. He was certain that involving me with his case and the disciplinary committee would only make him look worse and make it look like I was using my power within the company to get him out of trouble. I thought it would make me look like a doting girlfriend, but what did I know?

The trial took months and took up most of Colt's time. We barely saw one another until the end of summer. The trial ended the first week of August and Colt received a three-day suspension. Thank goodness it wasn't anything worse. Colt had only himself to thank for their leniency. He proved many times over that he was and is an asset to the company and MaeDay is lucky to have him. I wholeheartedly agreed.

I asked him to come with me to Mae's Sag Harbor house for a week to celebrate the end of this debacle and try to reconnect, but he turned me down. He said he had a trip with his brothers planned in September and couldn't take a week off of work in August and September after receiving a punishment for misusing company time. I chose not to push the issue.

I knew Colt was exhausted from fighting the largest professional battle of his career and was still upset about us being caught, so I gave him space for a week. I contacted him minimally and decided to go to The Hamptons alone. I worked remotely while Colt worked in the office. I didn't actually plan this, but I see now that it gave everyone a small piece of time to forget about us. When I would return, and Colt and I would be in meetings together or having our one-on-one meetings in my office alone, everyone would stare. Colt and I felt eyes on us constantly, but that week apart did help people to talk and connect with Colt again without my presence and to forget he was involved with me. I could only hope that would help tear down the fence he had put up between me and him.

Another unexpected, albeit great, thing about traveling to Sag Harbor was running into Milo. I saw him the second night I was there at our favorite Mexican restaurant. When he saw me, he walked right up to me and pulled me into a hug. He apologized profusely and told me he couldn't believe how big of a jerk he was when we saw each other in the city. He told me he had been young and full of himself and had felt horrible for years. He was too embarrassed to reach out to me, but he was happy we ran into each other and that he could make amends in person. We ended up eating that meal, and another, together before I left. He seemed like the carefree Milo I remembered from my childhood and I was excited to have him as a friend again. I texted Colt all about it but his only response was a thumbs up emoji.

I knew he was hurting and fighting to regain his footing in the company, so I was patient. I waited for him to come back to me for weeks. I reached out daily, whether or not I got a response. I never pushed back when he was grouchy or short with me. I gave him what I thought was ample time and space to heal from the war he had just finished struggling through. I stayed patient for as long as I could. As it turns out, though, my patience had limits. We reached those limits around Halloween.

He did go with his brothers in September and when he returned at the beginning of October, he was a different man. He was frigid and distant. I began to wonder if we were even still dating. He rarely came over, or responded to my requests to go to his apartment, and he absolutely downright refused to acknowledge me at work. Our October one-on-one was the most uncomfortable experience of my life. He spoke only seven words during the entire meeting. I counted. The rest were grunts or nods and when we reached the end of the agenda, he stood and walked out of my office without speaking a word. Not only was it unprofessional, it was mean and heartless.

It was around then that I knew we might not make it through this. After making many lists of my options, I decided to show up at his house the day before Halloween. I would simply wait until he opened his door. That's all there was to it. I needed to speak to him. Alone. Outside of work.

It took almost two hours for him to return home. When he did, he was looking unbelievably sexy in tight joggers and a ripped up, sleeveless shirt. He was dripping in sweat and it was evident he had been at the gym. The way the sweat glistened on his biceps, I had a hard time keeping my hands, and my tongue, to myself.

When he saw me, he stopped in his tracks. He just stared at me standing outside his door. He took in a deep breath and then let his shoulders drop. He unlocked the door and held it open for me to enter. I was relieved to see he was willing to let me in, but very anxious that he hadn't even greeted me.

Once we were inside, Colt asked if he could take a shower before we got into it. Listening to him for those five minutes, imagining the body I know so well, thinking about him in there naked was a form of torture for me. I was so worried and so sad, my throat got tight and my eyes burned while I fought tears waiting for him to return to his living room.

He got us glasses of wine and joined me on the couch. We talked for almost five hours. He explained to me that he hated seeing everyone at work question our feelings. He hated that he was public enemy number one in the office, and he hated walking on eggshells daily. What he hated most of all, though, was people questioning whether I coerced him into having sex with me. He told me he had wanted me for so long, dreamt about me, fantasized about us being together, and now that people were saying I forced him into it, it all just felt wrong.

He didn't want anyone to mistake that he loved me and that we were happy. Well, happy before Stuart walked in on us. He agreed he broke company rules by misusing the company's resources, property, and time. He was happy to accept the punishment for that. He could not stand, however, the way the people within the company were treating him or, more importantly, me. He felt like they saw him as some sort of prostitute and I was his regular customer.

———

It didn't matter how much I tried to tell him none of that mattered and the *only* thing that mattered were our feelings for one another, he couldn't let it all go. He said he still loved me and never even looked at other women, but he didn't know how to handle these feelings at work. He asked me to give him some time to figure it all out and compartmentalize his life. He wanted me to stop contacting him and only speak to him in a professional manner for the foreseeable future.

By this point in our conversation, I was unabashedly crying. If I tried to touch him, he pulled away as if my hand was on fire. This only made me cry harder. I told him that I could not handle a relationship where we were in limbo. I needed to know, were we together or not? I could not live with the ambiguity. He said if I would make him choose, then he would need to end it for now, but he would stay committed to me. He would continue to love me and he would try to get his own insides organized so we could move forward, if I would have him.

I stood up and yelled at him to not do me any favors. As I threw my jacket on, I told him to sleep with every woman in sight because I would be sleeping with any man that would have me. His face scrunched in pain and his jaw ticked when I yelled that, but I was too far gone into my own misery to care. I stomped away from him, slammed the door, and left.

I called Hank on my way down the stairs and told him to meet me at my apartment in twenty minutes. I threw some items into a bag, including three bottles of wine, and left for Sag Harbor. I called Mae on the way and told her Colt had just broken up with me and I was getting out of the city. She agreed with my decision and supported my leaving. She said to work remotely when possible and she would cover anything needed at the office.

On my drive to The Hamptons, I blocked Colt's number. Not that he had tried to contact me since I left his apartment, but just pressing those red letters that would stop any communication from him felt good. So I did it. I knew I'd have to unblock him in the morning since I would be working remotely and wouldn't have a landline office phone to use. Still, I left him blocked for the night for no other reason than simple spite.

I recorded a video of myself giving a thirty second recap of what happened and where I was headed and sent it to the girls. Their first responses were full of shock and after a few opened mouth emojis, things became darker. Lots of threats were made toward him in the group chat. The girls didn't stop at insincere threats against his life, but they threatened numerous body parts, including his penis. Let's just say, if my phone is ever subpoenaed for any reason, we're all going to be in big, big trouble.

I opened one of the bottles in the backseat of the car knowing Hank would never object. He is like family to me, and while he is always professional, it would take a fool to believe he doesn't listen to my conversations when the partition is down. I left the partition down on purpose, just so he could hear why I called him so desperately. I also VenMo'd him $1000 from the backseat. I heard his phone ding moments after I sent it, but always the professional, he did not check his notification. I hoped it would be a nice surprise for him once we parked. He deserved the bonus for driving me two hours outside of the city late on a Tuesday night.

After arriving at the house, I put on the loosest and softest pajamas I owned and took my wine to the coffee room. I cried for hours. I eventually had to leave the room to clean my face because my eyelashes were crusting together from all of the layers of dried tears. I took my wine to my bedroom where I turned on the television to watch something to take my mind off of the breakup. I started watching one of my favorite rom coms, but it made me even more sad knowing the movie would end with the lead characters in love. I flipped through the channels until I landed on a true crime show. I was terrified through the entire thing, but being scared was much preferable to being sad.

It was an unfortunate turn of events that I frightened myself so badly that I could not sleep after watching the true crime show. It didn't help that the following day was Halloween. Even though it was the middle of the night, I texted Milo to see if he happened to be in town. To my surprise, he responded immediately saying he was. I told him I had just gotten dumped and then watched horrifying crime shows and I couldn't sleep. He came over and sat with me while I told him what happened and cried myself to sleep.

I woke up the next afternoon with a massive headache, cottonmouth, and eyes that were nearly swollen shut. I pulled my laptop close to me to check how many messages and emails I had already received. I was stunned, yet delighted to see that at some point in my stupor the night before, I had put up an away message for the day. It only had one typo. I considered that a win.

I also happened to notice that the little circle next to Colt's name that denotes his status was green. Green means active. If Colt's status is active, that means he is at work and on his work computer and probably doing just fine. I hated him just a tiny bit in that moment. How could he just get up and go to work as if nothing had happened?

I stayed in Sag Harbor for two weeks. I never unblocked Colt's phone number or personal email address. I forced him to communicate through work portals and email only. I barely left the house and worked many hours. I barely ate. Milo would occasionally bring me take out from one of the restaurants in town, but otherwise I couldn't bring myself to put food into my mouth. My diet consisted of numerous cups of coffee starting the moment I woke up, followed by many glasses of water in the afternoon (I was dehydrating myself due to the output of tears), and finally wine at night. I wouldn't even think of wine until I put my work computer away at night, which also happened to be my body's cue to begin the crying portion of my day.

I went on like this until the weekend before Thanksgiving. Robin showed up then and forced me to leave the comfort of Mae's palace. I didn't miss how her eyes watered when she saw me. She helped me shower, then combed through my hair and forced me to put real clothes on. It was then that I realized how much weight I had lost in those weeks. Robin insisted on taking me to town for a meal, which I went and ate. She took me back to the city and stayed with me until Sunday night.

I went back to work on Monday. It was horrible. At lunch, Colt pulled me into the breakroom and told me to unblock him. When I didn't answer and just stared at him with blank eyes, he continued on. He wanted to know why I wasn't eating. I stayed silent. He bumbled and fumbled his words, one moment seeming exasperated and running his hands through his hair and the next moment giving me a list of demands and looking close to tears. I stayed silent through the entire conversation and he finally got so frustrated, he left. I went back to my office and twenty minutes later, he stormed through my office door without knocking. He set a bag of food in front of me, my favorite sandwich and soup combo from my favorite lunch spot. I just looked up at him and blinked once. He said something to me then that shook me a little. He walked toward my door as if to leave, but then rounded back toward my desk. He knelt down in front of my desk and with interlaced fingers, he wagged his hands at me in a praying motion.

"Please, Lenni, please." He closed his eyes when I didn't respond. "Please eat the food." His voice broke halfway through. His eyes were pleading and so full of desperation, I knew I didn't have the strength to fight him. I opened the bag and took the sandwich out. I took a quick bite and looked at him. I wanted my face to look bored, and I didn't have to try very hard. I was bored. Bored of feeling so sad, bored of feeling inadequate, bored with life. I couldn't muster interest in anything other than coffee and wine.

My bad eating habits continued through Christmas. During those weeks, my friends would eat with me as much as possible. I know they were babysitting me, but again, I couldn't bring myself to feel enough emotion to care. Every single day, Colt showed up to work. And every single day, Colt brought me lunch and stayed to watch me eat at least one bite. Sometimes, he wouldn't leave until I ate closer to half of whatever he bought me that day. I never knew what amount of lunchtime I'd have with him and I grew to hate and love those lunches. I despised being close to him when I was not over him. I abhorred having to smell him and see his body and remember how great things were between us for so long.

It was sick and twisted, but I also loved seeing him and smelling him and feeling his overpowering presence. It was a little gift for five minutes every day. One I would cry about every night. Sometimes it felt like he still cared, but sometimes he looked like he hated being in my office as much as I hated him being there. I never spoke one solitary word during our lunches. I would sit there and chew in silence. Sometimes I would make eye contact and sometimes I would just keep working. As far as I could tell, nothing I did determined how long he would stay. I never could figure out his pattern. Our November and December one-on-ones were also done in silence. I filled out the necessary forms. I slid them across the desk to him, he read them, and signed on the correct line, making sure to include the date. I counted the moments until our office closed down for the holidays.

I actually ended up having a phenomenal Christmas with Mae. We stayed together for a week at her apartment in the city and had friends visit every day. Whether it was Annie or one of my friends, someone was always coming to visit and bake cookies or watch a Christmas movie. The week of Christmas was the first time I could feel sparks of myself returning. There would be quick flashes of normal Valentina. They would burn bright for a few minutes and then they would disappear again. I was ecstatic to feel myself returning. I knew the flashes would last longer and longer and I would eventually get back to normal. It would just take time.

That's precisely what happened. After the New Year's celebrations, I began feeling like myself again. I was eating more, I started working out again, and I was seeing my friends more. Ansley and Jake were dangerously close to dating, but I could tell Ansley didn't want to talk about it in front of me. I encouraged her to tell me everything, but I knew she was holding back. I'm sure she was fearful I would fall back into my dark hole and she didn't want to be to blame. I was happy for her though. Robin had also started dating someone, Diego. He speaks six languages and Robin finds his worldliness irresistible. Amy and Mackie are doing well as always and Nisha is pregnant! Being around my friends and their successes really helps me forget about my failures.

Colt still brings me lunch every day, and I still sit in silence. This ritual is completely unnecessary given that I am eating on my own now, but he hasn't faltered and I refuse to ask him to stop.

Which brings me to the present moment. It's a little after noon and I'm sure Colt will be arriving any moment. I am happy to have tomorrow off for my birthday and to eat lunch with Mae, instead of Colt. I am also a little sad when I think of not having Colt watch me eat my first couple bites. I know it's disturbing, but it's just the way I feel.

I'm beginning to worry, and to be honest the feeling is closer to panic, when Colt isn't in my office by 12:30. I try to focus on my computer screen and keep my eyes off my door. I am typing the same sentence I have been typing for the past ten minutes when Colt blows in my office. I'm trying so hard to focus on my typing that his entrance startles me.

He walks over and sets the bag down on my desk. He backs up and sits in one of the chairs on the other side of my desk. This is new, he never sits down. I notice he has his own bag of food. What the hell is happening?

I open the bag on my desk and see my favorite salad from a very expensive restaurant across town. I have no idea how he got there and back in thirty minutes or how he got the salad at all. The restaurant does not accept carryout orders. I decide to ignore all of this and just enjoy one of my most favorite meals, whether he is sitting across from me or not.

We eat in silence and I don't make eye contact with him. I am almost done with my salad when he stands up and walks to the door. He tosses his crumpled up bag in my trash can as he passes it. He puts his hand on the doorknob and looks over his shoulder at me.

"Oh and Lenni? Happy Birthday."

I give him a tight smile. "Thank you." These are the first words I've spoken to him since I barged out of his apartment last October.

February 14th

I wake up and have a quick convo with my parents while I put on my makeup in the mirror. Mae is taking me out for a mimosa lunch and shopping. I am doing everything in my power to forget Colt's twist on our ritual on my last birthday. I am failing. Miserably.

I take my time getting ready and spend as much time as possible in my robe and slippers. I am relaxing on the couch when my phone dings with a text. It's Milo.

Hey Valley Girl! Happy Birthday!
Thanks, Milo. Even though that is the worst nickname ever.
Nah, I could come up with worse, I'm sure.
Agreed.
So, hey, I gotta come into the city for a meeting tomorrow. Wanna grab some lunch? I'll take you out for your birthday.
Sure, sounds good.
Great, I'll text you tomorrow.

I'm immediately filled with worry about how to explain to Colt that I am leaving the office for lunch. Maybe I could just send him an email saying I have a lunch meeting. Or add it to my shared calendar in the hope that he sees it before leaving the office to get lunch.

I'll have to figure this out later because it's time to get dressed for my lunch with Mae. I stop myself from biting my thumbnail in anxiety. Why do I even care if Colt wastes his time and money bringing me lunch? I shouldn't. But I do.

"Valentina! Darling!" Mae reaches out to me and pulls me in for a hug. She kisses me on the cheek and pulls back to look at me. "Sweetheart, you look beautiful."

"Thank you, Mae." I smile at her. "So do you. Do you have a date after our lunch or something?" She swats at me as we both take our seats.

Mae does look beautiful, she always does. I have never seen her look disheveled in my life. I've spent many, many nights with her through my childhood and even as an adult, but she gets out of bed looking fresh as a daisy every day. No one knows how she does it. My friends and I have had quite a few conversions over wine about how Mae manages to look gorgeous at every minute of the day. We are no closer to the answer today than we were ten years ago.

I can't ignore the way she has been looking lately. Her skin sags a little more and looks thinner. Her frame hunches forward more than I remember it used to. Her perfect hair seems to be just a little less full and her fingers never seem to fully straighten anymore. I can see all the signs of aging on Mae and it breaks my heart.

Not only do I want her to stay with me forever, as impossible as this is, but I also want her to be able to age without worry. I know she is worried about me turning thirty-five and still being single. I also know she feels conflicted on whether or not she'll turn the company over to me or not when I am thirty-five and unwed. We still have a couple years, but I see how tired she is. She wants to be done. I want that for her, too. I hate that I am back to square one and this time I'm jilted.

I will never be able to fall so hard for another man like I did with Colt. I know how much it hurts on the other side. It will take me years to be able to love a man enough to marry him and Mae doesn't have that sort of time. Why did Colt have to break us? Why did Stuart have to find us? Why?

I tear my eyes away from Mae's face and look at my menu to stop the tears from coming. I need to change the subject.

———

215

"So no date?" I ask her with a smile.

"You know better than that." Mae doesn't even take her eyes off the menu.

"Why didn't you ever date after grandpa died?" He died before I was born, but Mae never speaks about him. I barely know anything about him.

Mae puts her menu down on the table. "Well, I tried at first. But every man was just wrong. I disliked them all for one silly reason or another. Then one day I found a man I didn't detest."

"What happened?" She has my full attention.

"He kissed me."

"And?"

"And, I cried immediately. I felt like I was cheating on the love of my life. The other man was scarred. I began crying right into his mouth. He ran away as fast as he could." She let out a little giggle. I do the same.

The server approaches our table as Mae and I are holding cloth napkins to our mouths, trying to contain our laughter. We get it together enough to order, but the mimosas do not help our laughing fits.

"I do need to tell you something, my dear." We've just finished our main course and Mae has ordered a piece of cake for dessert.

"Yes?" I am leaning back in my chair, sipping the last of my second mimosa.

"It's about work… and Colt."

"Go on." I'm holding my breath.

"He has resigned and will not be returning to MaeDay." She's gripping her napkin with tight fists. She must be nervous.

"What?!" I set my champagne flute down on the table with too much force. It makes an ugly noise and I'm surprised it doesn't shatter.

"Now dear, it's for the best."

"The best?"

"Yes, he has been miserable and distraught. He needs to start fresh. He packed up his desk last night and he set up an email to go out to everyone tomorrow morning."

Mae's tone is kind but also stern. She is not going to back down and she supports him.

"He left?" I am hurt. I don't have any right to be, but I am. I cannot believe he did not say goodbye or give me any sort of notice. Maybe he does hate me that much. The tears are falling before I can stop them.

"Oh, sweetie. Don't cry." Mae reaches across the table and dabs at my tears with her napkin.

"Mae, he can't do this! He can't throw it all away after fighting so hard!" I am much too loud for a restaurant.

"He can do it, and he did. He needs this, Valentina. Try to understand."

"Where is he going to go? What is he going to do?" My whole body is shaking, I'm a little afraid I'm going into shock. I down the rest of my sugary mimosa just in case.

"I believe he is going to take some time off."

"He doesn't have another job?!" I roar. People are starting to look. Neither Mae nor I pay them any attention.

"Valentina, listen to me." Her voice is harder, more demanding now. "It is his decision to make and his life. Everything will be fine."

"No, it will not! Everything will not be fine! How can the company and our co-workers do this to him? He can't quit, he doesn't deserve that! I'll leave, he can stay and I can go. I'll just work in properties the re-"

"Valentina, get a hold of yourself. You will do no such thing. You will take over MaeDay, do you understand?" Her mouth is taut and her eyes are steel.

I take a deep breath and let it out slowly. "Yes. Yes, I know, I understand. I'm sorry, Grandma Mae." I put my hand on top of one of hers and squeeze. I'm not done with this topic, though. "But how can he quit? How can we let him go? What will he do?" I can hear the shrillness in my voice.

"Valentina, let him handle it."

Her words make my entire body stop. It stops shaking. It stops crying. It stops worrying.

"What did you say?" I whisper to Mae.

Her expression softens to one of confusion. "I said… let him handle it."

Hearing the words that the medium said to me two years ago gives me tingles and goosebumps all over my body. She said that my mom wanted me to know that in the future there would be a conflict and I should 'let him handle it.' I never had even a single guess of what that meant until now. All this time, my mom knew I would spiral out of control over Colt's departure and she wanted me to know he needs to handle it.

My body feels calm, but my eyes are dancing everywhere. My mind is making connections and settling on the conclusion that Colt needs to handle this. I look up to see Mae's worried eyes on me.

"Are you alright?" She reaches for me and I grab her hand in response, still too in shock to say anything.

"Here's your cake!" The server is much too chipper and clearly has no ability to read the mood of the table. He sets the plate down in between Mae and me, which forces us to let go of one another's hands.

"Thank you," Mae says to dismiss the server. "Here let's enjoy." Mae hands me a fork.

But I can't enjoy the cake. I can't bring myself to dig in and eat a bite. I stare at the cake not wanting to disturb the frosting decoration on top. It's a yellow butterfly.

February 15th

I hide in my office the entire morning. Mae wants to talk about who to promote to Colt's position, but I'm not ready for that conversation. The thought of replacing him feels like I'm cheating on him somehow, even though I know this is ridiculous.

Milo texted me to meet him at a café that happens to be near my apartment. It seems like too much of a coincidence to turn down the opportunity to work from home for the afternoon. I pack up my bag and send out a message to the department heads that I will be working from home for the afternoon.

As soon as I walk in the doors, I see Milo in a back booth. I wave and walk to him, we hug before I take off my coat and sit down.

"So, what was your meeting about?"

Milo waves away the question. "Oh, just some case I'm working, blah blah."

"Blah blah?"

"Yeah, you know, it's boring. Let's talk about something that is *not* boring. How's the boyfriend?" Milo wiggles his eyebrows at me and I can't help but laugh.

"You mean *ex*-boyfriend," I correct him.

"Ahh, so he's still a former instead of a current?"

"Yes."

"What an idiot." Milo shakes his head and takes a sip of his coffee.

"I believe he said the same thing about you once." I pick up my menu.

"Touché."

"Well, what about you? Seeing anyone?"

"I have a few exes of my own." Milo seems sad when he admits this. "But there's no one of interest right now."

The server approaches and we place our orders. We chat and laugh with one another for the rest of our meal. It's so nice to have reconnected with Milo and to be comfortable in our friendship. I find myself hoping in the middle of the meal that we'll keep in touch and maintain our relationship.

We scoot out of the booth and Milo is helping me with my coat when I see him enter the restaurant. Colt is staring right at us. I cuss under my breath. I grab my work bag and purse and walk to Colt. There is no reason to avoid him.

"Hello, Colt."

"Hello." He barely grunts out the greeting and gives me a nod.

"I was sorry to hear about your resignation."

"It needed to be done."

I can feel Milo walk up behind me. "I'm sure you two remember each other, Colt, remember my friend Milo? Milo, remember my ex, Colt?"

The men look awkwardly between each other and then me before finally giving each other a nod and half of a wave.

"Hey, I gotta run. I'll see you later, Valley Girl." Milo leans down and gives me a quick peck on the cheek. "Hope you had a good birthday."

Other than feeling the cold air hit my face, I don't notice Milo's departure. I am too focused on Colt. He's dressed in jeans and a sweatshirt, so clearly not working or looking for work. Is he meeting someone here?

"Yes, how was your birthday, Valentina?" Colt asks. His tone is one of forced politeness. I can see his jaw ticking and I can feel the anger rolling off of him.

"It was good until my grandmother dropped a bomb on me at lunch that one of our employees quit without notice." He looks away from me, turning his head toward the wall. "He didn't even say goodbye."

"Huh, so you weren't at work for lunch today?"

I look around like this answer should be obvious. "No, I was here, why?"

"No reason."

"Colt?!" A server yells his name from behind the hospo stand. Colt lifts his hand in response and takes the plastic bag filled with food. He hands the server a tip and turns back to me.

"Bye, Valentina." He leans down and pecks the opposite cheek.

He walks out the door leaving me standing in the front of the restaurant completely befuddled. Why did I need to be at work for lunch? Did something happen?

Without making the conscious choice, I scurry back to MaeDay as fast as possible. I walk-run to my office and I see a bag sitting outside the door. It's a bag of lunch food and there's an envelope stapled to the outside.

I take the food into the break room and put it in the refrigerator. I sit at the table and rip open the envelope. Inside is a half piece of paper.

Lenni -

I couldn't say goodbye. It was too hard. I'm sorry for everything. I hope you'll accept lunches as an apology - both will be endless.

- Colt

Well what the hell does that mean?

I stomp down the hallway and to the elevator, more determined than ever to go home now. What is he talking about? Lunches and apologies? Is he trying to apologize by giving me lunch? I hate the power this man has over my brain and my heart. I can't stop thinking about him. I can't stop missing him, even when he's in the same room.

Maybe it is for the best that he leaves. Maybe the old saying is true and once he is out of sight, he will also be out of mind. One can only hope. I need to figure out a way to leave Colt behind.

On my walk home, I set the one and only intention I have for the upcoming year: Change everything about my sad little life.

Thirty-Three

February 13th

It's been 363 days since I've seen Colt. It has helped with my crying. It has had no effect whatsoever on my love for him. I know, I'm disappointed too.

It doesn't help that he had lunch delivered every day for the past year. It makes it nearly impossible for me to forget him. It makes it incomprehensible that I could ever move on when I think of him every day at noon. I'm still excited to see what he picks out for me to eat that day. I still feel like I'm eating with him, even though he's not there. I'm not proud of my desperation. But I try to counteract my hopelessness with thoughtful actions.

I have worked hard to change my life over the past year. We promoted an amazing young woman from the marketing department to Colt's job. Her name is Tasia and she is so much fun, along with being good at her job.

I have refocused on work and I am now more determined than ever for Mae to retire in two years. End of story.

I realized that a breakup doesn't have to be the end of my world. I certainly shouldn't see it that way. It's unhealthy and ridiculous to have one person be the nucleus of my life. I am a privileged, strong woman and I need to get over it.

I was utterly annoyed with my own behavior and I knew I needed to change. I needed to grow as a human and forget about any problems I thought I had and start focusing on others for a change. So I started volunteering at a women's shelter. There are too many women in this world that need help and it was time for me to put my money where my mouth is. Well, actually, I took both my money *and* my mouth to the shelter. I not only volunteer my time, I also donate lots of money and as many items as I can.

I've met amazing people at the shelter and they have taught me how to make MaeDay more philanthropic. This has been another major project of mine, giving back through the company. Not only do we now give away more of our profits than ever before, I also started an employee volunteer incentive program. For every hour that a staff member volunteers with an approved charity or non-profit, we match it with a vacation hour.

If Colt had stayed, I never would have seen the need to pivot my attention off of myself and on to others. I would have never made changes within myself and my own life. I would have never made changes within MaeDay. And I definitely wouldn't have made any change at all for anyone at the women's shelter. I'm so grateful I've had this year to grow and expand. I can't believe I'm saying this but I am thankful for Colt vacating my life.

That does not mean that I am not horribly sad. Or lonely. I am both, but there does not seem to be any light at the end of any tunnel for my loneliness. I choose not to dwell on my own feelings of isolation and anguish. If I begin to feel sad, I call one of my friends who are all now in happy, committed relationships.

Jake couldn't take it any longer and basically kissed the shit out of Ansley one night while we were all playing trivia at a bar in Brooklyn. She jumped on his lap, right there at the bar in front of everyone. We were all shocked by shy Ansley grinding against Jake, but it was long overdue. We sent the two home and no one heard from Ansley for almost two weeks. We were and are very happy for her.

Robin is officially dating Diego. They both love to travel and are currently in Australia with the pygmies and watching the toilet water flush in reverse.

I am taking a lesson from Robin and Diego and I have decided to go on a short trip for my birthday. Alone.

I've always wanted to see the coast of Maine, so I rented a cabin and Mae rented me a private jet for my birthday. I am going to spend three glorious days being completely disconnected from society. I am going to enjoy nature, read some books, and give meditating a try. I can't wait.

I forgot to get a few travel sized things, so I need to run to a drug store in the morning, but otherwise I am packed and ready to go!

I'm forgoing tradition and not having a meal with Mae, or anyone, tomorrow. Once I am packed, I am heading to the airport where three days of solitude await me. It's going to be magnificent.

February 14th

I wake up and jump out of bed. I am so excited to go to Maine all by my lonesome, I can't wait any longer. I take a quick shower and get dressed to go to the drug store on the corner for my last minute items.

I hustle down to the corner and get dry shampoo, chapstick, and a small container for the moisturizer I use daily and am embarrassed to admit how much I spend on it. Trust me, it makes my face feel so soft.

I climb the stairs as fast as I can to get back to my apartment. I feel my face smiling and I am so excited for my getaway to rest and recharge. I notice the red light flicker on the camera outside my door. I haven't paid any attention to the cameras lately and I errantly wonder if Colt still has access? Once Colt became a regular in my life, we moved Gina and Rob to an 'as needed' basis and I never thought to restart their contracts once we broke up. Clearly, I still have cameras and security systems but I haven't thought much about any of that lately. I make a mental note to check on Colt's status on the account and remove access, if he even still has it.

I bounce into my apartment on my toes, too excited to walk like a calm person normally would. I turn the alarm off and turn to go to my bedroom to finish packing so I can head to the airport. I have all the blinds closed since I won't be home for a while and it is still pretty early in the morning and dark in my apartment.

When I turn, I walk into something. There was nothing in the hallway when I left thirty minutes ago? Is that a person? I back up and turn on the hall light. It *is* a person. It's Rich.

I'm flabbergasted to see him. I haven't seen or heard from Rich in *years*. He hasn't shown up, left any notes, nothing. There has been no contact since I moved. At first, I'm in such an astonished state, I can't find my voice. I try to breathe, but nothing happens. I gasp in a ragged breath. He watches me struggle the entire time. He just stares at me with the smallest hint of a smirk pulling on the corners of his lips. He looks completely satisfied with himself.

"R-Rich? What the fuck are you doing here?" My voice is shaky and sounds much less severe than I anticipated.

"It's nice to see you, too, Valentina."

"*Nice* to see me? You broke into my fucking apartment! Get the hell out!" I point toward the door, glad my voice is cooperating and using a more aggressive tone.

"I was hoping we could talk." Rich pouts just a little.

"Listen, you've lost your everloving mind. We went on two dates, I don't like you. You need to leave, *now*." I move to the alarm and he grabs my hand with more force than I was expecting. I yelp in pain and he smiles.

"Don't do that. Actually, it's fine if you do - I can just dismantle it since I saw you enter the code when you came back in." When he sees the panic in my eyes, he looks me up and down. "OK, let's sit on the couch and talk, huh?"

"It doesn't appear I have a choice," I hiss through my teeth.

"True," he agrees.

We walk over and sit down. "Why don't we start by telling me how you got in here in the first place."

"Oh, that was easy. When you left this morning I grabbed the door after you left. Simple as that."

———

"What about the alarm?"

"Oh, Valentina, you have sixty seconds to leave before it engages, remember? I was inside with the door closed and locked with forty seconds to spare. I knew if I waited long enough, the other guy would stop coming around. I knew he wasn't right for you." Fuck, Colt was right. A man *was* the best deterrent. The thought of Rich watching me all these years gives me chills. I don't like it one bit.

"What do you want from me, Rich?"

He looks astounded. "What do I want? How could you ask that? I want us to be together of course."

"Together? You think we're going to be together?" My common sense is telling me that I probably shouldn't anger him, but I can't help it. He has violated me in too many ways. I am vibrating in fury with some fear mixed in.

"Clearly. We're both beautiful, fun people!" He holds his hands out and smiles as if this should be obvious. "You will continue to be the beauty mogul you were born to be, ruling the world and making all the money. Don't worry, I'm not threatened by a strong woman." He stage whispers the last sentence.

"What will you do while I'm out making all of the money?" I am seething.

"Run the house, of course! I'll take care of our children eventually, but for now, I'll just enjoy the life of a stay-at-home husband."

"Now we're married?" This guy has lost his mind if he thinks I am going to marry him.

"We will be soon."

"Soon?"

"Yes, I have someone capable of performing the service on the way."

"What the hell are you talking about? I would never agree to marry you! We also don't have a marriage license!" I'm standing now. He motions for me to sit and just as I think of diving for a kitchen knife, he stands and walks over to me before I can act. He puts his hand on my shoulders and pushes me back to the couch. He sits next to me and places a heavy hand on my thigh. I hate the way the weight of his hand feels against my leg, even with my jeans separating our skin.

"You will say all the right words and agree and cooperate." When he sees me start to argue, he holds up a hand to stop me. "If you don't, I will kill Mae."

I gasp in horror. My hands fly to my face. "You wouldn't!"

"I would. I know where she lives, I know where she works, I know about her Sag Harbor house, I know about her driver, Jake. I know it all, babe." He reaches up to move a piece of my hair behind my ear and I scramble out of his reach. He drops his hand and looks at me with a soft expression. "You'll come around. I will do whatever it takes to get what I want."

"What do you want?!" I screech, frustrated and terrified.

"You."

After three attempts to run to the kitchen or the alarm, Rich now has me tied up in my bedroom closet. I don't normally suffer from claustrophobia, but being stuck in this closet is really starting to grind my gears.

Knock, knock. "Sweetheart, are you ready to come out?"

"Yes, please!" I'm desperate to get out, I'll play nice.

He opens the door and helps me to my feet. He walks me into the living room. He has set up some cheap, fake flowers and has fake white petals all over the floor. I hate it so much. I am willing to say the words and marry him to end this, though. I'm hoping if I can get through the wedding, I can talk him into going out to celebrate. Once we're out of the apartment, all bets are off and I will raise hell to get attention and help.

"Are you ready?" Rich asks.

"Yup." It's all I'm capable of right now.

"Great. I'm going to hold the door open for my friend, Keith. He's ordained in the state of New York and he will perform the ceremony." Rich pulls a piece of folded paper from his pocket. "I am so lucky he also works at the courthouse and could help me with the marriage license."

I don't even care if it will be legal. I can fight it later. I just want to be away from Rich. He taps my nose with the paper and I'm disgusted. He turns and walks to my front door, which is a miracle. I could not stand being near him one moment longer.

I look around seeing if there is any sort of weapon I can find close enough to grab. Something I can hide in my pocket or up my sleeve, but I don't see anything. I notice that even the knives are gone from the counter. The bastard must have moved them.

I remember then what the medium said to me years ago. She told me if I am in trouble all I have to do is ask my angels for help. They can't interfere with my free will, but they will help if I ask them to. I take a quick peek down the hallway and see that Rich is still holding my door open for his friend. I drop my head back and close my eyes.

"Angels, if you are here, please help me!" I feel a single tear stream down to my ear. When I open my eyes, I see the living room camera looking down at me from the corner of the wall where it meets the hallway to the front door. I've never turned it on. It was installed but we all agreed to only use the exterior camera. Could I turn it on now? Surely it would alert anyone who has the app on their phone. Is there any chance Rob or Gina would still have the app downloaded? I quickly reach up and press the button on the side. Thankfully, I have messed with the outside camera enough to know where the power switch is. The little light in the front immediately starts blinking bright red. I close my eyes and will it to stop before Rich returns and notices it. I open my eyes and now it is a dull red. I know this means it's recording. I check Rich again and he is still waiting. I look directly at the camera and wave my hands. I mouth "help" as clearly as I can. Then I use my hands to try and spell each letter, H-E-L-P.

Just to be thorough and because it cannot hurt I ask again. "Angels, please, *please* help me. Do whatever you have to do. Save me from this man."

I hear Rich speaking to someone but it's not loud enough for me to hear what they're saying. I close my eyes and take a deep breath, trying to calm myself for what's to come. The door closes and two men walk toward me in the living room.

"Valentina! My bride! Please meet the man who is going to marry us, Keith. Keith, this is Valentina." He motions between us in a grand gesture.

Keith looks around the apartment, seemingly confused. "Hi Valentina, it's nice to meet you." He dips his brows in concentration. "Is this your apartment?"

"Is there a problem?" Rich asks.

"No, not at all." Keith is speaking too quickly. Is he scared of Rich? Is he nervous? Who is this man? "It's just a very beautiful apartment."

"Indeed," Rich agrees. "Soon, we will be able to make it our own."

I work to keep the disgust off my face, I can only hope I succeed.

"Ok, let's get started!" Rich claps his hands together loudly. He takes my hands and turns us so we are facing one another. He is focused on my eyes and staring at me with serious intent.

I do my best to ignore his eyes on me and focus on my getaway. It is almost as if I can see my escape before I enact it. I know his undivided attention on me is an opportunity.

While he is looking into my eyes, I move as if I'm adjusting my weight and he ignores the motion. I use the momentum of my movements to take my one shot. I swing my leg with as much strength as I have directly into his crotch. I can only hope I mangle his penis and testicles. He sucks in breath in pain and surprise. He drops my hands, his eyes go wide, and he instinctively reaches for his groin.

While his eyes are bugging out in agony and he is leaning toward me as he tries to regain his breath, I take two fingers and poke them into his eye. I ignore the wetness I feel, I ignore his screams, I ignore Keith, and I bolt. I bolt out my front door and slam it shut. I am sprinting down the hall as fast as I can when I hear the elevator ding. I hope it is a neighbor I know so that I can use their phone since Rich took mine when he locked me in the closet.

As soon as the doors begin sliding open a flash bolts out of the elevator. I'm in too much of my own personal panic to pay close attention to a neighbor's need to dart from the elevator, but it only takes one quick glance for me to recognize the runner. It's Colt. I can even smell him as he races past me.

"Hey!" I'm confused why he's here, but so relieved to see him. I know we're not together, but Colt is a nice enough person to help me when I am in serious trouble. "Colt! Help! Help me, please!"

He halts when he hears my voice. He spins on his heel and once his eyes connect with me, he takes two big strides and I am in his arms. He pulls me so close, I can feel his heart pounding. "Lenni, ohmygod, are you ok?"

He pulls back and looks at my face. His eyes flick all over my face and body.

"Yes, I'm fine, but Rich is in my apartment with some other guy and he is trying to force me to marry him. We have to get to Mae before he does, he sa-"

Colt doesn't let me finish. "He's in your apartment now?"

"Yes! Colt, listen!" I'm pleading with him. I have to get away from Rich and to Mae. We have to hire security for her round the clock, who the hell knows what Rich is capable of doing to her.

He takes his phone out of his pocket and hands it to me. "Call the police."

"Ok, but Colt, listen about Mae!" I'm shaking his arm, trying to get him to listen to me.

"I will, but for right now, call the police and tell them your stalker is in your apartment. Do not under any circumstances open your apartment door. Go." He picks up my right hand, places his phone in it, closes my fingers around it, and kisses me on the cheek.

"Colt!"

"Valentina, get out of here. Now." His voice is so chilly and commanding that I don't argue back when I see him run down the hall and enter my apartment. What the hell is he going to do in there? What if Rich kills him?

Before I let myself spiral, I have to get help here. I call 911 and they make me stay on the line until the police arrive, which only takes about three minutes. Apparently, Colt called in and told them to send emergency services to my apartment on his way over, but he didn't stay on the line as instructed. That turns out to be a great move because it had them coming in my direction before I even called.

Once the police officers arrive, they find Colt in my apartment with a tied up Rich and Keith. After questioning, they let Keith go. Rich told him some elaborate story about his fiancé being too sick to come to the courthouse to get the marriage license and needed his help. Keith helped, even though he shouldn't have and he will probably lose his job, but didn't necessarily do anything illegal since he was lured to my apartment believing me to be too ill to leave. He had no idea Rich was holding me against my will or intended to blackmail and threaten me into a marriage I don't want.

Rich did not get off so easily. He was arrested and should be charged with a litany of crimes. Some will include stalking, harassing, menacing, kidnapping, and breaking and entering. Colt was far too involved with the police proceedings and they asked him to leave the crime scene. I stayed behind for questioning and then went to the station to give my official statement. The entire process is exhausting. It is nearly midnight by the time I am able to leave the station and go back home.

I only have one thing on my mind, climbing into my bed and going to sleep. I am going to ignore how my apartment no longer feels like mine. I am going to ignore the fake flowers and petals that are still scattered about. I am going to ignore the feelings of violation and fear my apartment will surely evoke. I am going to focus on my bed and remember how the angels helped me when I asked them to. Rich might have been in my home, but there were angels in my home, too.

———

I walk out the door of the precinct and pull out my phone to call for a car.

"Hey, how are you?" My head snaps up when I hear Colt's voice. He is leaning against the wall, right outside the door.

"What are you doing here?"

"Waiting for you."

"But, but I've been in there for hours." I point over my shoulder toward the building.

"Yes, I know."

"Why are you waiting for me?"

He pushes off the wall and walks right into my personal space. My mind tells me to take a step back and move away from the man that tore me apart. My heart tells me to stay close to the man I still love.

"I'm sure you don't want to go back to your apartment, I was hoping you'd agree to coming back to mine." Colt slides his hands in his pockets, almost looking shy.

"It's fine. I'm too tired to care right now and I've mentally prepared myself to go back." I know he's trying to be nice to me, and it was incredibly thoughtful of him to think about what I would want after this ordeal and offer his home to me. It would be too painful, though. I don't want to go back to his place and smell his scent everywhere, and sleep in his bed, and walk on his frumpy brown rug, and drink out of his non-matching water glasses, and see his things surround me. It would feel too much like we're a couple again and having that just for one night is too much. It would hurt too much.

He lifts his hand to my face. He smooths my hair. I let him. "Valentina, I am sleeping in the same room as you tonight. I don't care where. Your apartment, my apartment, a fucking hotel room - I don't care. You pick."

I'm confused. What is he talking about? Sleeping with me? "What if I don't want you to sleep with me?"

He looks into my eyes. "Then, I guess I'll sleep in the hallway."

———

"Colt, the hallway? Why would you sleep in the hallway?" I am exhausted and I don't understand.

His hands land on his hips and he shifts his weight. "Don't you know what tonight has done to me? How it tormented me? I need to be with you tonight. If you won't let me sleep with you, I absolutely *have* to be near you."

My eyes go a little misty and I don't know if it's the fervor that Colt is speaking with or my tiredness. It's probably both, but his words have an impact on me. "Tormented? Colt, I haven't seen you in so long, how could you be tormented? Sleeping near me? What are you saying?" I ask him as I begin to panic. My hands start shaking all over again, this time for a different reason.

"Shh, Lenni, listen sweetheart. You need to rest. I need to be close to you. I need to make sure you're safe. Like I said before, I'll take whatever you'll give me. Your apartment, the hallway, even the elevator." Both of his hands begin gently rubbing the outside of my arms. He draws in a long breath. "But, I'm hoping you'll let me sleep much closer to you than the hallway. I thought for a moment I might lose you. I don't ever, *ever* want to feel like that again. Today has taught me so much and there are many things I need to tell you tomorrow. But first, I want to hold you while you fall asleep and watch over you. Then after you sleep however long you want to, we'll wake up and talk. Talk about today, talk about our past, and talk, hopefully, about our future."

As much as I hate to admit it, all of that sounds perfect. I don't want to be alone right now. I want him to be in my bed with me. I want to feel safe because he is near. I want to talk to Colt.

"Ok. My house," I whisper. I give him a little nod.

When a car pulls up to the curb then, Colt nods to it. "This is us."

He holds the back door open for me and I climb across the back seat and he gets in behind me. He takes off his coat and wraps it around me like a blanket.

"You can lie down, or put your head on my shoulder, whatever you want. If you fall asleep, I'll carry you inside."

I don't say a word, but I slump down a little and rest my head against the top of the backseat. I don't close my eyes because I don't want to fall asleep. I have to keep some boundaries up with Colt. I have no idea what he is going to say to me tomorrow and until I do, I have to keep some distance between us. Him carrying me up to my apartment cannot happen if I want to retain my sanity.

Once inside, neither of us looks at the living room and walk directly into my bedroom. I shut the door behind us, blocking out the other portion of the house. I grab a t-shirt from my drawer and change in the middle of the room. I can feel Colt watching me, but I couldn't care less. I refuse to go back in my closet so soon after I was locked in it. I make another mental note to put a key on the inside of the closet. Besides, me naked isn't anything Colt hasn't seen before.

He strips down to his underwear and we both climb into the bed. I'm too drained and tired to even brush my teeth. Once we're under the covers, Colt wraps his arms around my waist and pulls me against him. My back is flat against his front and I can feel his face in my hair. I hear him pulling air in through his nostrils to smell my hair. I feel a slight kiss against the back of my head and before I can find the will to tell Colt to stop doing things that will make me feel attached to him again, I'm asleep.

February 15th

I open my eyes and the sun is filling my room. Light everywhere. It has to be in the afternoon, noon at the earliest. How long have I slept? Ugh, I still feel tired.

"Hey, how are you feeling?" Colt's voice is soft behind me. I roll over and see Colt sitting up in the bed behind me. My body is sore from the day before and stiff from so much sleep.

"Morning." I push my body up to a sitting position and yawn. "Is there coffee?"

Colt lets a quiet laugh escape. "There can be."

I swing my legs to the side of the bed and Colt jumps off the bed and runs to my side. "Don't get up, I'll get it. Just stay here."

"I, uh, need to go to the bathroom." I don't know why I'm being shy about this. Colt knows I pee.

"Oh yeah, of course." Colt chuckles again. He holds my hand as I stand from the bed. He puts his arm around my waist, as if he is going to support my weight while I walk.

"What the hell are you doing?"

"Helping you."

"I can walk to the bathroom alone, I don't need any help. Are you going to wipe my ass, too?"

Colt scrubs a hand down his face. "God, I know. I'm sorry." He shakes his head. "Today is not yesterday."

"No, it's not," I agree.

"There will never be another yesterday again."

"Colt, how did you know to come here yesterday?" I ask. We are sitting on a window seat in my bedroom drinking our coffee. I can't stand to be in the living room any longer than I have to. I will have to sell this place immediately.

He releases a deep sigh. "Well, honestly, I knew I was watching the cameras like I used to and it felt wrong. At first, I needed to know if you were coming home with men. I struggled with this though because I knew it was an invasion of your privacy. After I saw you come back to work before Thanksgiving, though, I knew you weren't seeing anyone. You weren't even eating." His voice catches. He clears his throat. "Anyway, I deleted the app. I knew if it was on my phone, I would watch it. Watch you."

I don't even know how to begin processing the information he just told me. "Ok, but if you deleted the app, how did you know?"

"Yesterday, I was eating lunch and something came over me. I don't even remember doing it, but I downloaded the app again. All I remember is that I stared at the app on my screen forever, but decided not to watch the camera. I locked my phone and began eating again. Next thing I know, my phone is making a horrible sound. When I unlocked it, the camera app was red and said that a new camera had been activated. I couldn't stop myself. I opened the app and clicked on the new camera. And then, there you were. Waving at the camera, asking for help."

"So, you came here?"

He barked out a laugh of astonishment. "*Of course* I came. I took a cab as far as I could and called the police from the backseat. About five blocks away, I couldn't stand how slow he was driving so I hopped out and sprinted the rest of the way here. As soon as I got in your building, the elevator was sitting open and waiting. I had to get to you."

"Wow, that's quite a story." I'm still taking it all in.

"I have to tell you a few more things, too," Colt admits. He shoves a hand in his disheveled hair. "I've been miserable without you."

I'm not sure what to say or how to respond, so I just wait in silence. I know he will have more to say so I stay patient and let him continue.

"It's been over a year without you, today is a year since I last laid eyes on you and I have hated every single second. Like I told you when we broke up, I hated the way everyone was treating us at work. I hated feeling out of control and like I couldn't properly demonstrate what our love was like. I hated that I couldn't show everyone how amazing our relationship was and it was all because of the crossover between work and personal. You told me once, years ago, we couldn't be together because of this crossover and I didn't understand what you meant until we got caught. You knew all along it would turn out horribly." He shakes his head again and holds my left hand. "None of that could even come close to touching how much I hated not seeing you, not touching you, not kissing you, not being with you. I never stopped loving you, if anything, my love for you has just grown stronger. But the thought of possibly losing you yesterday really knocked some sense into me."

"Why didn't you contact me if you hated it all so much?"

He rubs his jaw and gives me a crooked smile. "Well, that was my plan. I thought if I quit, gave us some space, I'd get my mind right and you would forget how idiotic I was. Then I would give it a month or two and lay my heart on the line and beg for your forgiveness. Then I saw you with Milo at the diner. At first, I thought you were together so I left you alone. Then the idea of you being with someone else blossomed in my head and I couldn't get rid of it. I just kept thinking over and over again that you would meet someone and honestly, I was too big of a chicken shit to just come over here and tell you I still loved you. That is *exactly* what I should have done."

"Maybe." I take a sip of my coffee. "But you sent me lunches instead."

"Yeah, yeah I did. Seeing you so frail and thin after our breakup almost broke me. It made my skin crawl to see you like that. I needed you to be healthy and you were anything but healthy then. Like a total maniac, I basically forced you to eat. But then I was so glad I did, because it gave me a reason to eat lunch with you every day. To see you every day. I lived for those lunches. No other part of my life mattered except watching you eat for a few minutes. I'd think about those few minutes for the rest of the day."

"I enjoyed those lunches, too," I confess.

"You did?" He perks up a bit. His eyebrows jump and his eyes look a little brighter. "Valentina, you have to know that I have loved you all along. I don't think about anyone but you, all day every day. I want you back in my life, I *need* you back in my life." He takes the coffee mug out of my hand and sets them both to the side. He takes both my hands in his and scoots closer to me. "Please be generous with me, please tell me how much damage control I have to do to win you back. I will never stop trying, no matter how much work is ahead of me. I will do anything and everything to win your heart back."

I search his face and see nothing but genuine love. His eyes are pleading and his jaw is working in nervousness. I sigh and give him a weak smile.

"Colt, if I am being completely honest with you, my heart has always been yours." A smile starts to spread across his face. "Hold on. I'm not done." His smile falls and he nods. "I have loved you for the past year. But I've hated you a little, too. It felt like you gave up on us and you left me. It was so painful. I do want you back in my life, but I'm nowhere near ready to date you."

"I understand," Colt says quietly.

"I have some things I need to take care of first before giving you all of me again."

"Ok. Anything I can help with? I'll do anything."

"I have some very un-fun tasks ahead of me that I will happily accept help with. First, would be selling this apartment and finding me a new one. I also need to make sure Rich is prosecuted to the full extent of the law. I need to hire security for Mae round the clock. Oh, did I tell you Rich threatened to kill Mae if I didn't marry him?"

"What? No!"

"Oh yeah, he did. So if you want to help me with anything, I will welcome that help. It will not be enjoyable and there will be no sex. Once we get through the logistical stuff, we can maybe start going on some dates and having fun again. Then we can see where it all goes. Are you in?"

He kisses my forehead and looks at me with eyes that are a bit too wet. "I'm so fucking in."

Thirty-Four

February 13th

Well, Colt was phenomenal over the past year. He was thoughtful and helpful and I feel like I can count on him for anything.

The first two months were filled with the tasks I listed for him. We sold my apartment and I stayed in one of my other properties while looking for a new place. He helped me find the most perfect apartment that just happened to be right near his apartment. Shocking, I know.

After the apartments were settled, we moved on to Rich's trial. I immediately got a protection order against him, and Keith, just to be safe. But Colt called the prosecutor's office on a daily basis to see what was happening with the case. I'm convinced they were so annoyed with his calls that they got Rich's trial moved up. He was found guilty and sentenced to some prison time. Colt is insisting we live together by the time he gets out.

We've spent a lot of time with Mae and of course had to come clean about all the security needs and hired her a full-time security team. I had to come clean to my friends as well, no one was happy that I kept this secret for so long.

No one has tried anything against Mae, but it makes both Colt and I feel better to have professionals keeping an eye on her. We spend as much time with her as possible since she continues to weaken and age every day. She has also stopped working so much and I basically run the company alone now. It makes us both happy to have her rest and take time off. She never comes in before 10:00 am and never stays later than 3:00 pm on the days that she does come to the office.

Colt and I have been dating and I have let him in more and more over the past year. Even more so since summer. We spent some weekends alone at the Sag Harbor house and went away for a couple nights for his birthday. He helped me at the women's shelter and even got his new company to donate as well.

Colt used his knowledge of the beauty industry to gain a new marketing position at a popular women's magazine. I hate not seeing him at work, but we know we can never work together again.

The way he has been so consistent and absorbed with me over the past year, has shown me that I can trust him. I am finally going to tell him on my birthday tomorrow that we are done with the runaround and tell him for the first time since our breakup that I love him. He's said it to me every day since my thirty-third birthday, but I haven't felt safe enough to return the verbal sentiment until now. I know he'll be excited.

He has no idea what I have planned for tomorrow. I have rented the same cabin in Maine that I was supposed to go to last year along with Mae renting the same private jet. We are going to spend four days alone, disconnected from the world, and together in Maine and just like last year, I cannot wait. I am so eager to be alone with Colt.

I called his boss and asked for the surprise time off, and his boss readily agreed. He told me what an amazing employee Colt has been and his team is better because of Colt.

I told Colt to pack a bag to spend my birthday with me and instead of staying at my apartment like he expects, we're heading to the airport.

Now, all I have to do is wait.

February 14

———

"Lenni?" I hear Colt call out my name as the alarm begins beeping, asking for the password. I hear Colt enter the needed four digits and the alarm beeping ceases. "Lenni? Where are you? Happy Birthday!"

In my upgraded apartment, I have two living rooms. I am sitting in the only one I use, waiting for Colt. I have a packed bag, sitting at my feet, excited for Colt's arrival. I can hear his footsteps coming down the hallway.

"Are you in here?" Colt pokes his head in the living room. "Hey! There you are! Happy Birthday, beautiful!" Colt approaches me with open arms and a gift in his left hand. He lets his overnight bag fall to the ground as he walks toward me. His eye catches the bag at my feet. He pauses and points at the bag. "What's this?"

"Colt! I told you *not* to get me a present!" I squeal. There is truth in my anger, I did not and do not want him to get me anything for my birthday. I just want to enjoy our trip away to Maine.

"I didn't listen." His face turns a little hard. His brows come together in confusion and he shifts his weight as if he's nervous or anxious. "What's going on? Why do you have a bag packed?"

"Well, we're going away. Last birthday, I was supposed to go to a cabin in Maine, alone. I was, let's say, *disappointed* to have missed the opportunity."

He takes a couple steps in my direction. "You were? Why didn't you tell me? We could have gone sooner."

"We had a lot going on this year." He nods in agreement. "I am ecstatic to go now, though, with you. We're going for four days and we are disconnecting. Hopefully."

"Why do you say 'hopefully'?" Colt's eyes flick all over my face.

"Because, we're only going if you want to. I already talked to your boss and he enthusiastically agreed for you to have the time off and to keep my secret."

Colt walks up to me and wraps his arms around my waist. "Are you serious? 'If I want to'? I always want to be with you."

He leans down and kisses me. He parts my lips and puts his hand on the back of my head to pull me close and deepen the kiss. "Why did you do all of this? Why the surprise? If you wanted to go, you should have told me. I would have made it happen."

I lick my lips, getting some of Colt's taste on my tongue. "I wanted to do this for you."

"You did? Why?"

"Because, I love you." Colt's jaw goes slack and his eyes go wide. "I do. I love you, Colt."

Colt drops the gift he is holding behind my back. It makes a loud clunk as it bounces off the chair that I was sitting on before Colt's arrival. I only hope it's nothing breakable. Colt pulls me close, holding me tight against him. It feels like every part of his body is touching every part of mine. His knees are pushing against my legs, our thighs are flush against one another. Our torsos, chests, arms, and heads are all touching and rubbing.

When he pulls away he looks me in the eyes and I see relief and happiness all over his face. His eyes are soft and warm, he's smiling, and his jaw is relaxed. "Valentina, I love you so much."

We are going to be late for the jet.

February 15th

We were two and a half hours late for the jet. I tipped everyone generously for our tardiness and apologized as much as I could. I would care more if it weren't for Colt's elation. I have never seen him so happy and at peace before.

I didn't realize it until now, but he has been holding his breath for the past year. He has been waiting for me to say that it's over, or I actually don't trust him, or that we're just not working. I feel remorseful about this. It's clear I wasn't doing a good enough job communicating my feelings and their progression to him. I should have done better.

I can't change the past so I am just going to focus on the future. The future, our future, is going to be bright. In the next year, I am going to take over the company entirely so my grandmother can fully retire. She deserves that. I am also going to move things along with Colt. I hope he'll move in with me so we can see each other every day.

I hope to talk to him about it while we're here in Maine, but right now he is dozing next to me. We hiked all morning and then Colt had to go into town to buy a few things he didn't know he needed to pack. After he returned to the cabin, we lit the fireplace and took a shower together. Now we are lying together on all the blankets and pillows we could find on the floor of the cabin loft. It overlooks the enormous fireplace and we can feel its warmth even up here. I am watching Colt's bare chest rise and fall as he rests in post-coital bliss.

I reach up to my neck where I feel for my new necklace. Colt found a company that makes necklaces of zodiac signs. He had my parents' signs put on a necklace for me and I love it. It is the perfect birthday gift.

I stand and go to the kitchen and get a bottle of wine that arrived with our grocery delivery yesterday. I take some glasses and the bottle up to the loft and pour us each a glass and start sipping while I wait for Colt to wake up.

I'm about halfway through my glass and watching the fire when I feel Colt's hand on my back. I smile at the warmth his hand spreads through my body. I look over my shoulder at him and he is fucking gorgeous. His wide shoulders lead down to a thin waist and hips, his abs are glistening in the firelight, and best of all, his face is smiling at me.

"Valentina, I have never been this happy in my entire life. Thank you for this. Thank you for Maine. Thank you for loving me." His voice is tender and I love him even more in this moment. This is as good a time as any to talk about moving in together. It feels right.

"Colt, I've been thinking about something and I want to talk to you about it."

"Yeah?" His face is still peaceful.

"Yeah," I reply. Not sure where my nerves came from, but I am nervous about proposing this to him. I'm fairly certain he will want to live together, but I'm still nervous. "I, uh, was thinking maybe we could live together when we get back."

He props himself up on his elbow and looks at me. I hand him his glass of wine. He takes it and holds it at his chest, in between his hands. He stays silent and my anxiety spikes.

"I would love for you to move in with me. You helped me find that beautiful apartment after all. But if you don't like that idea, we can figure something else out."

I take a sip of wine to hide behind my glass for a few seconds. His silence is letting me know that he might not be on board with the moving in plan. Did I majorly misstep?

When I'm done with my sip, I look at Colt. He is staring at me with sort of a mischievous smile on his face. It's a little crooked and his lips are pressed together.

"I was thinking we should get married," he says.

I'm stunned. My eyes go wide and Colt nods at me. He sets his wine glass down and sits up. He takes my wine glass and sets it next to his. He kisses me lightly.

"I didn't have to buy anything in town today except for a ring."

"A ring? You bought a ring?"

"I have two rings, actually." He reaches for his discarded pants. They're on the floor next to us and he pulls a blue velvet box from the pocket. "I have a ring in New York that I've had for years. I had no idea we were going on this trip though, so I didn't bring it. After yesterday, I knew I couldn't wait until we returned home to propose to you. So I went and bought a second ring this morning. We can return whichever one you like the least, or hell, you can have them both." His eyes search my face. "Valentina, I have loved you for a decade. You're the best person I know. I know what it's like to live with your love and without it. I don't ever want to spend a minute on this planet without your love again. If you're willing to give me a chance, I will spend the rest of my life loving you and doing everything in my power to make you happy. Will you marry me?"

He flips open the box and inside is a beautiful diamond ring. I feel the tears on my cheeks before my mind registers that I'm crying. I fly to Colt and wrap my arms around his neck. My body is shaking with sobs. I hadn't even considered that Colt would propose, but now that it's happened I realize it's everything I've ever wanted. I didn't know I wanted this commitment, the happiness of knowing I have a partner in this life, but I do want it. The feeling of unconditional love is sensational. Colt promising to love me forever is something I will cherish for the rest of my life.

On the loft of the private cabin, naked, wrapped in blankets and love, I give Colt my answer. "Yes."

Thirty-Five

Colt couldn't get the ring on my finger fast enough in that cabin. He said it made it more official and loved seeing it on my finger. I'm not sure if men are usually excited about wearing a wedding ring, but Colt sure is. He picked it out at the same time as he bought my second ring and we flew back to Maine a month ago to buy it. He talks about the excitement of wearing his wedding ring on a daily basis. It's adorable.

We didn't leave the cabin for the twenty-four hours after the proposal. We decided to finally leave so we could hike to a spot with service. We made one phone call. We Facetimed Mae and showed her the ring. She was euphoric, to say the least.

Colt only returned to his apartment a handful of times once we got back to the city. Every time he went, it was only to pack things or move stuff out. We donated a lot of his furniture, but sold some and moved some into my apartment, *our* apartment.

As you can imagine, my four ladies were overjoyed to hear about our engagement. They loved the way Colt came back to me and supported me through the disaster of Rich.

We already did our wedding rehearsal this afternoon and we are now at Mae's retirement party. I gave a speech about what Mae means to me and how much we all have learned from her and her guidance. I cried, she cried, lots of people cried. I know my parents were with us through it all, too. They've been with Colt and myself a lot lately as we get ready for the wedding. Colt has even started talking to them and getting responses as well. It's incredible.

"I don't know how I'm going to do it without you," I say to Mae as the night is wrapping up. We're embracing and tipsy. I know you probably shouldn't drink a whole bunch on the night before your wedding, but hell, your grandmother and mentor only retires once.

"Oh you're going to be just fine." Mae squeezes my arm. "You've been doing it without me for months now."

This is partially true. She only comes into the office sporadically. She joined a group of women who play a game called Bunco. Annie joined the group too, of course. They play weekly and her new friends take up a lot of her time. They're going on a trip next week to Aruba. I'm so happy for her.

"It's time!" Robin yells from across the room, grabbing our attention. Most of the guests have left and the venue employees are starting to do the initial clean up.

Colt leans into me. "I don't want it to be time," he whispers in my ear so low only I can hear. I nudge him with my shoulder.

"It's only one night. We can do it." This will be the first night we've spent apart since we left for Maine a year ago.

"I don't want to be away from you for a minute, let alone a whole night."

"I know, but it's tradition."

"Fuck tradition."

I laugh. "I agree, but I'm going to go spend the night with my girls and you are going to go spend the night with your brothers and then it will make seeing each other tomorrow so much more anticipated and exciting."

"I guess that's true." I can feel him starting to give up his fight.

"Just think of it like this, get through tonight and then tomorrow you can wear your wedding ring."

"Ooo, I do like that."

"I know you do. Now go on. Go with your brothers, they're waiting by the door." I nod to the door and Colt looks.

Sure enough, Colt's brothers are standing there waiting with his coat in hand.

"Ugh, fine, but you better answer if I call you." He kisses my cheek and runs off to his family.

An hour later Robin, Ansley, Nisha, Amy, and Mae are all in matching silk pajamas in my apartment. We are having one more celebration champagne before bed.

"I can't believe you're retired," I say to Mae.

"I can't believe you're getting married," she returns.

"I can't believe Colt let you go for the night," Ansley chimes in.

"Me either," the rest of the girls say in unison.

"It was a close call," I agree with a laugh. "Thanks for staying tonight. I know it must be hard with the new babies, Amy. And being a newlywed and all, Ans."

"I wouldn't miss this for the world," Amy says.

"Jake is doing just fine without me."

"Since what's-his-face and I broke up, it is not difficult for me to be here in any way. But I am extremely excited to see who is at the wedding tomorrow!" Robin tells us.

"Robin, it's not going to be very big. Just family and a few friends."

"Still you never can tell."

February 14th

After hours of getting us all glammed up and lots of electrolytes, me and my girls are reading to go to the wedding. My apartment looks like a disaster, but thinking of everything, my wedding planner has already hired a cleaning crew to clean the place once we leave.

We hop in the stretch limo wearing our pajamas and robes and long coats over it all. Our dresses are waiting for us at the ceremony site. We pull up and get dressed. As we're getting ready, I catch Robin and Dale making out twice. I guess she was right. You never can tell. Before I know it, it's time to walk down the aisle to Colt.

We decided not to have formal attendants, but of course my girls have been with me all morning and Colt's brothers have been with him. None of them will stand with us, though, while Mae marries us. It will just be the two of us.

The girls give me hugs and kisses and walk around to the main entrance and go sit with their partners. Robin sits in the front row on my side, the third seat in. The first two seats will remain empty, for my parents. Colt's brothers and their families will sit in the front row with his parents on his side.

The doors open and Mae walks down the aisle first, alone. I can see her for just a moment before the door closes. She looks sensational in a silver gown. She's been doing water aerobics trying to get some muscle definition. After seeing her in the dress, I have to agree that it's been working.

The doors close and I move to stand behind them. My dress is simple and sleek. It is flat white. It is one shouldered and flares just a bit at the bottom. My hair is down, long and wavy. I decided to not wear a veil, because as Colt says, fuck tradition. I am wearing the same stud earrings that Mae wore to her wedding decades ago. I couldn't bring myself to let Colt return the ring he bought for me in New York years ago. It was so sweet that he wanted to marry me before our breakup and that he kept the ring for so long. I love that ring and it means something to me, just not quite as much as the Maine ring. We had a chain soldered to the ring, so it is now a gorgeous necklace that I am also wearing. I wear it every minute of every day to represent our past. The ring on my finger represents our future. I am also wearing a beautiful diamond bracelet that Mae gave me last week. My favorite wedding day flourish, though, is the butterfly clip I am wearing in my hair. I was walking on my lunch break last week, thinking about how much I wished my parents would be at my wedding, when I saw the clip in a shop window. I went inside and bought it, feeling more connected to my mother than ever.

The doors open and our guests stand. There are only about sixty people here. Just how Colt and I wanted it. The room is gorgeous. Colt is standing at the end of the aisle with Mae. They are in front of the giant, stone fireplace. I can hear it popping and cracking from here. There are white Christmas lights hanging everywhere. They are wrapped around the beams of the ceiling. The only flowers that are spattered about are white. We didn't want or need to do much decorating. We just allowed the beauty of the old distillery to shine through. Colt and I thought for a moment we would get married in Maine, where we originally promised to love one another forever but the logistics were difficult in such a secluded place. I suggested our favorite distillery one night and Colt fell in love with the idea. It's a perfect venue for the small ceremony and our photography team has ideas for our photos after the ceremony that they are extremely excited about in the old building. The distillery owners agreed to let us take photos in the basement and in the barrel room, which only adds to their excitement.

I walk down the aisle, alone, to Colt and as I approach, I have never seen him smile so large. I stop at my parents' seats and silently thank them for coming before finishing my walk to Colt. Once I'm there, I toss my flowers to Robin in the front row and turn to Colt.

"Hi," I say.

"Fuck, I missed you," Colt replies.

"I missed you, too."

"Happy birthday, Valentina. I truly hope this is the best birthday yet." He leans in and kisses my nose with the faintest touch of his lips. It sends a shiver down my entire body.

"I think it's safe to say, nothing could top this," I whisper in response.

He smiles at me and squeezes my hand before leaning in and giving me a real kiss on the cheek "Let's get this show on the road."

February 15th

250

"Morning, wife," Colt coaxes me out of sleep.

"Morning, husband," I mumble.

"Wanna see my wedding ring?" he asks and I laugh without opening my eyes.

"Always," I respond. I pop my eyes open to see his finger right in front of my face.

"Looks great, babe," I tell him.

"Let me see yours." I pull my hands out from under the covers and show him my finger, now not only holding the ring he bought in Maine, but also the wedding ring we bought together in Maine a month ago.

"Damn, it's beautiful. Just like you." He leans in and kisses my forehead.

"Thank you," I whisper. I stretch and sit up. "Are you ready for the honeymoon?"

"Hell yes, we're packed and ready. Let's get some coffee and head out."

I stand and walk to the bedroom door. "I can't wait to get into the sun."

"Me neither. Beaches, hiking, coffee farms, Costa Rica here we come!"

"It's going to be amazing," I agree.

"You know what, wife?" Colt starts making the coffee and then turns to me to finish his sentence. "I've been thinking how you said during the ceremony that nothing could top yesterday?"

"Yes. That's true, husband." I smile at him, knowing he's up to something. He leads me to the couch and we sit together, facing one another.

"Well, it got me thinking about future birthdays."

"Yes?"

"And what I could do or how we could ever celebrate to raise the bar even more."

"Colt, I already told you..."

"Wife, looking forward to the next year of your life, of our lives, I think we *can* top it." He pulls me tight into his arms and moves me so I am sitting on his lap.

"How could that ever be possible?" I ask with a furrowed brow.

———

"I think that next year, on your birthday, we should be able to say that you are pregnant."

My eyes go wide and I feel my jaw drop, just a little. "Pregnant?"

Colt gives me a moment to allow the idea to wash over me. When I think about my belly growing and Colt and I being parents, the idea starts to feel more like a warm blanket and less like a bucket of ice water.

"That could quite possibly be the only way to top yesterday," I admit.

"Let's plan that in the upcoming year, we will do everything we can to start a family." Colt leans in and meets my forehead with his. His eyes close and I can actually feel his desire for me, for our future lives, radiating off of him.

I pull my head away and wait for him to open his eyes. Once he is looking at me again, I give Colt a small smile and nod in agreement.

"Husband, that is the best intention I will ever set."

www.ingramcontent.com/pod-product-compliance
Lightning Source LLC
Chambersburg PA
CBHW060303310726

48976CB00007B/2197